A Fox in Paris

A timeless story for children.

Mary Nelson Carter
Perry Vayo

Based on
an unfinished work by
Mary Nelson Carter

MOUCEAUX
LES TERNES
PARC
Avenue de Neuilly
Avenue de Neuilly
Allée des Veuves
Hôtel des Invalides
Invalides
CHAMP DE

Paris

MONTMARTRE
POISSONNIERE
ENCLOS DE ST LAZARE
Jardin de Tivoli
Rue Joubert
Rue de Provence
PLACE VENDOME
ISLE DU PALAIS
8.
5.
7.
10.
12.
19.
21.
37.
42.

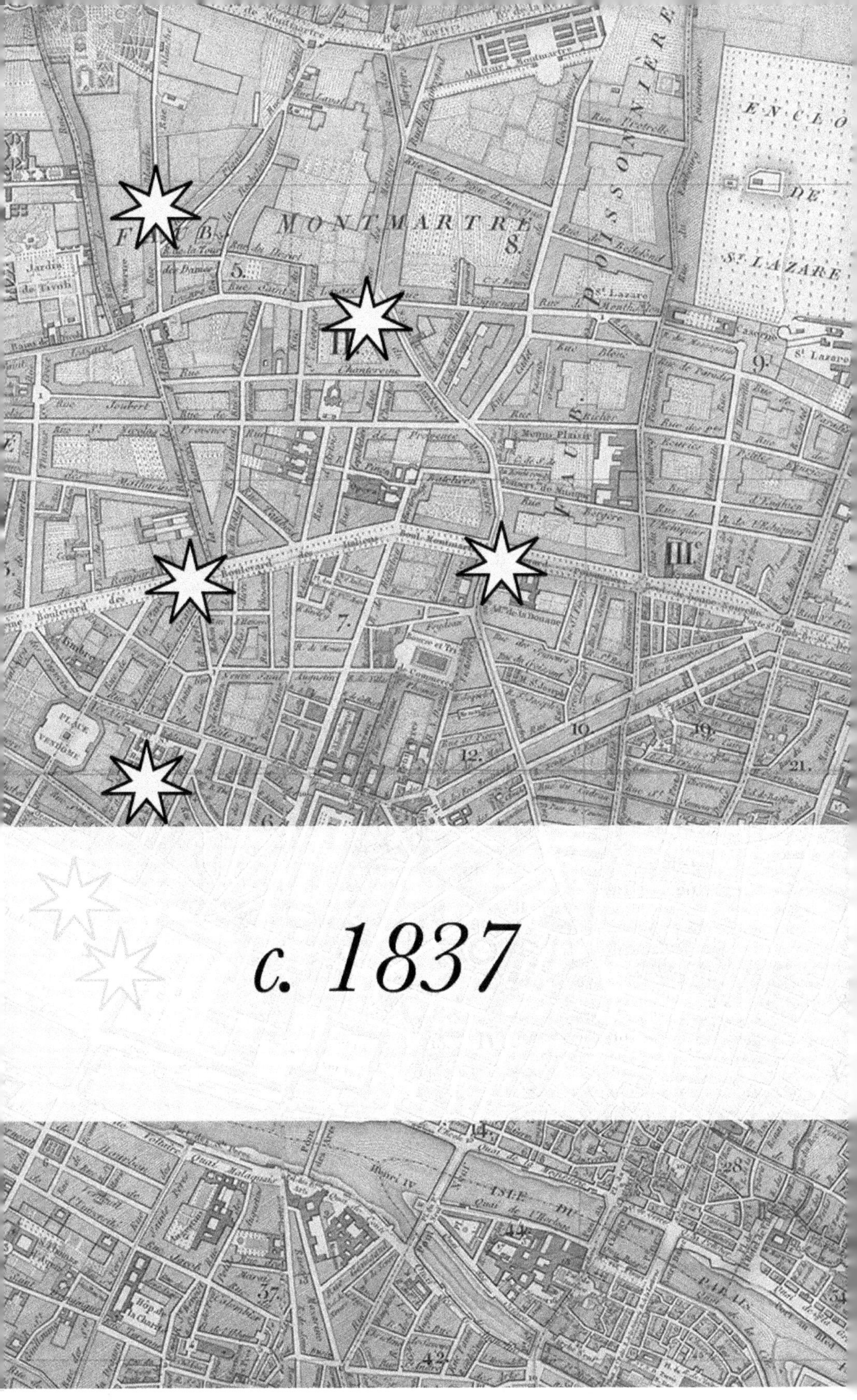

c. 1837

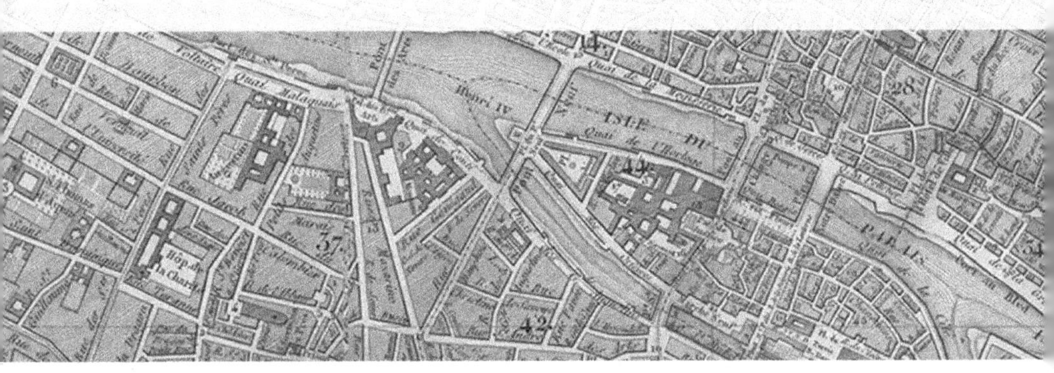

A FOX IN PARIS

ISBN:_978-0-9882680-0-5
Published: September, 2012
Publisher: Infonouveau™
Createspace Edition

Library of Congress Control Number: 2012948049

Find out more about Infonouveau™ and upcoming books online at http://www.infonouveau.com

Infonouveau
353 Oxford St.
Rochester, NY. 14607

info@infonouveau.com

Printed in the U.S.A.

DEDICATION

"A Fox in Paris" is dedicated to my great, great grandmother, Mary Nelson Carter. It was my honor to complete the tale she began so long ago, and to pass on her legacy of education and literacy. Being a teacher and a writer, she would have looked on this new medium, and this new kind of book, with wonder and approval. I have no doubt that she would have been just as eager to experience this book with her children, as her children would have been to explore the story with her.

Perry G. Vayo

Table of Contents

Chapter 1 Cousins 2
Chapter 2 The Tuileries. 12
Chapter 3 Castaway. 18
Chapter 4 The Old Soldier. 24
Chapter 5 The Masons 42
Chapter 6 The Sweep 54
Chapter 7 The Scullion 66
Chapter 8 The Teacher 76
Chapter 9 Small Fortunes 84
Chapter 10 The Strangers 96
Chapter 11 Mr. Raimond 118
Chapter 12 The Island....................................128
Chapter 13 The New Natives 136
Chapter 14 The Strangers in the Night..........144
Chapter 15 The Printshop..............................156
Chapter 16 Swept Away 170
Chapter 17 The Reunion................................178
Chapter 18 Wanted! 190
Chapter 19 Madame Marboeuf 200
Chapter 20 Fox's Plea 210
Chapter 21 Chance Encounter.......................222
Chapter 22 Confessions 230
Chapter 23 A New Family 246
Epilogue 255
Afterword: The Story of a Story.....................263
Explore Paris - 3D FUN 269
More from Infonouveau 273

Chapter 1

Cousins

Where's Lucien?
(Turn the page to see.)
After the service and internment were completed, the crowd of mourners melted away, hurrying to escape a drenching by the impending storm.

KINGDOM
Dunkerque
Lille
BELGIUM
Channel
Cherbourg
Rouen
PARIS
Nancy
Orléans
Nantes
Dijon
Here I am!
Limoges
Lyon
Grenoble
Valence
Bordeaux
Toulouse
Marseille
Perpignan
ANDORRA
200 km
100
200 mi

It was a sultry, simmering afternoon, and the city of Bordeaux was shrouded in the fast building darkness of an incoming summer storm. On the edge of the city, making its way up to an ancient cemetery, the gloomy clouds seemed to almost rest upon a sad funeral procession slowly winding along up the hills.

Stumbling along at the end of the well populated procession a fair, slight child, weeping bitterly, did his best to keep up with the dark train as it wound up toward the burial site. His ringlet curls and delicate appearance made him look to be a boy of no more than eight years, but, if asked, he would have proudly proclaimed, "My name is Lucien, and I am eleven years old."

At the head of the train, leading the mourners' labored ascent, was a fine, shiny black coffin, which was borne upon the shoulders of six strong men. It's polished handles and fittings seemed to glow in the retreating sun. Just behind the coffin and pall-bearers, in the place reserved for the chief mourners, walked a young man of about twenty years. He carried himself solemnly enough, but gave no real sign of his great loss. While others all about him were unmistakably sad and anguished, he remained unmoved and even a bit impatient with the proceedings. Amongst the other elegant mourners, all turned out in their best black funeral clothes, he looked as though he had committed considerable thought to his attire. No one would have supposed him to be the only son of the good-hearted old man who was being carried to his grave.

After the service and internment were completed, the crowd of mourners melted away, hurrying to escape a drenching by the impending storm. Only the child remained, standing alone beside the freshly covered grave. When he thought he was alone, he flung himself upon the damp mound of earth, giving vent to a wild burst of grief. In his fit, he had not noticed the sexton, who was standing near by. The old man, hearing his sorrowful cries, hurried to his side.

"Poor child," said the sexton, "was Monsieur Armand your father, my boy?" he asked, gently laying his toil-stained hand upon the child's fair head.

"Yes,...no," sobbed the boy, "I haven't any father or mother; they died when I was too little to remember them, but my dear uncle was both to me. He has raised me for as long as I can remember, and now, I'm all alone. Oh! What shall I do?" he wailed.

"But isn't Monsieur Gustave your cousin?"

"Yes, but he isn't a bit like his father. He has hardly spoken to me since Uncle died," said the child, grateful for a listener to his pent-up troubles. "The house is so lonely, too. Uncle always had me with him, and he made me so happy. Now it just seems dark and cold." The boy cried aloud, and the old man drew his coat sleeve across his own eyes.

"Well, my dear," he said, "you are learning the lesson of sorrow young; it is hard at any age, but you must try to be brave, and live as your uncle taught, no matter what comes. If you do that he will always be with you." A low rumble from above drew the sexton's attention skyward for a moment, "We mustn't stay here any longer, though, the lightning is getting closer, and the scent of the rain is in the air. Come, we must hurry out and lock the gates."

The child put his hand into that of the old sexton, and they walked silently out of the cemetery.

"Run home now, as fast as you can go, and try to cheer up," said the old man, as they parted.

The boy did just that, and he had scarcely reached home when the storm broke in full fury. As he burst through the door, there was a sudden blaze of lightning and crash of thunder. "Where is my cousin?" he asked breathlessly of the old servant who was fighting the blowing curtains to quickly close the windows.

"In his father's room; and he does not wish to be disturbed," answered the man as he hurried to shut out the driving rain.

"He'll not mind me, I know," replied Lucien, already halfway up the stairs.

Frightened by the summer tempest now raging outside, he was flying to his usual refuge, his uncle's room. To his knock upon the door, came a surly "Who's there? What do you want? Didn't I tell you people I was to be left alone?"

"It's only Lucien, Cousin. Please let me in. I'll not bother you. I'm so lonesome, and the lightning scares me."

"Run away Lucien, I'm busy, and don't wish to be interrupted...Don't make a baby of yourself," added Gustave as he heard the child's quick sobs at the rebuff.

The storm was at its blackest, and except for those moments when a new flash of lightning illumined the sky, the hall was completely dark. At such times, Lucien could see the trees bending before the wind, and the garden being laid low by the torrents of rain. He managed to stifle his sobs, but could not muster the courage to leave the doorway of that room, which was so full of warm memories for him, and now sheltered the only family he knew.

During the moments of darkness, between the storm's flashes, his eyes fastened upon a ray of light streaming from the keyhole, of the locked door - this was the first time he could remember this door being bolted against him. Longing for comfort and companionship, Lucien thought it no harm to peep through, just to catch a glimpse of the familiar room he loved. He was surprised, when he looked in, to see a bright blaze upon the hearth this hot summer day, and more so, to see that his cousin was feeding it with papers from his uncle's desk. This troubled him. That desk was the one thing in the room which his uncle had allowed no one but himself to touch, and it gave Lucien a strange feeling to see Gustave tossing its contents into the fireplace. He watched Gustave for a moment, as he built up his fire, then, Lucien caught sight of his uncle's easy chair by the hearth, and before he knew it, his sobs and tears broke afresh. Gustave heard him, and immediately rushed to the door and flung it open. He glared down at Lucien and spit, "If you don't go way when I tell you, I'll soon know the reason." Lucien was completely caught off guard by his cousin's harsh tone, and could do no better than to flee downstairs to the servants for companionship. They were silent and subdued but he laid it to grief for the loss of a grand master.

Later on, at supper, Lucien found himself alone at the table. The old butler said that the young master had ordered his own supper to be served upstairs, and he was busy arranging it on a tray.

"Don't you think he'd let me have mine up there with him?" asked Lucien wistfully.

"No," replied the servant tiredly, "He said he didn't want you, that is, he didn't want to see anyone at all."

With that, Lucien ate his supper in lonely silence, suddenly aware of how large and cold the empty dining table was. It had never seemed so before, but now it seems that even the house was in mourning at the loss of its former owner. He was glad to creep away to bed as soon as he could finish his food.

Lucien was up early, and when he had dressed, he hung out of the window looking at the flowers in the garden lifting their bright heads to the sky after the rain. The rising sun filled the old garden with such splendor that the boy forgot, for a time, his sorrow by watching what to his childish eyes seemed a fairyland of fiery jewels. The sweet scented air fanning his face seemed alive with insect hum and bird song. It was like a fresh, new world to the child, washed sparkling clean by the passing storm. He forgot, for the time being, the deep sadness that hung over the house and himself.

Reminded by the striking of the big clock in the hallway that it was breakfast time, he hurried downstairs to find that his cousin had finished his morning meal. He sat by a window reading a paper and took no notice of Lucien's "Good morning."

"Why didn't you wait for me, Gustave, or call me?" asked the child. "I've been dressed ever so long."

"I can't be waiting for children, and I'm not going to be bothered with them either," replied his cousin curtly.

Lucien rang the table bell.

"What's that for?" demanded Gustave.

"My breakfast; there's nothing here."

To the servant who answered the bell, Gustave commanded, "Take this child to the kitchen and give him his breakfast. From now on, he is to eat with the servants."

"Who? Me?" cried the astonished boy. "You are surely joking, Cousin."

Gustave turned sharply to the servant saying, "The sooner you people learn that I'm master of this house, the better. Now, take this child to the kitchen and give him his breakfast."

"What have I done, Cousin, to be treated so?" exclaimed Lucien, running toward Gustave with his heart beating to suffocation.

"Don't cousin me," replied Gustave. "It wasn't my doings bringing a pauper like you here, and making him think he's somebody."

"What would my dear uncle think to hear you, Gustave? You must be joking; you couldn't say such dreadful things in earnest," replied the child.

"I guess you'll find out before you are much older, that I mean what I say," snarled Gustave. "And stop that cant about your 'dear uncle.' I'm sick of it. My father could do what he liked when he was alive, but I'm master here now, and I want you gone. The sooner the better."

The servant had slipped away into the butler's pantry, leaving the door ajar, and he and his fellow servants were now listening with great concern to the words of the new master of the house.

"Leave the house?" cried Lucien, wide-eyed with fright. "Where could I go? Who is there but you to take care of me?"

"You'll have to find somebody, that's all," answered his cousin brutally.

"Why, Gustave, I should starve to death all alone in the world. What would people say if you turned me out to die?" The child was crying. "Why the very street boys would throw stones at you," he sobbed.

The reaction of the community to Gustave turning out his own young cousin had not occurred to him, and it gave him pause; "Lucien" he said, "Forgive me. I am not myself. I didn't mean what I said." He paused a moment, then added, "You know, I'm going to Paris for a pleasure trip in a few days, and I'll take you with me."

Lucien, smiling through his tears, tried to embrace his cousin. Pushing him off roughly, Gustave bade him ring again for his breakfast. "I'm not hungry now," replied the child, "my heart feels so big, it chokes me." "Suit yourself," was the short answer as his cousin stood, dropped the paper on his chair, and left the room.

Chapter 2
The Tuileries

Where's Lucien?
(Turn the page to see.)
"Is the whole city of Paris so beautiful as this?" cried the boy, looking around at the fine buildings they were passing.

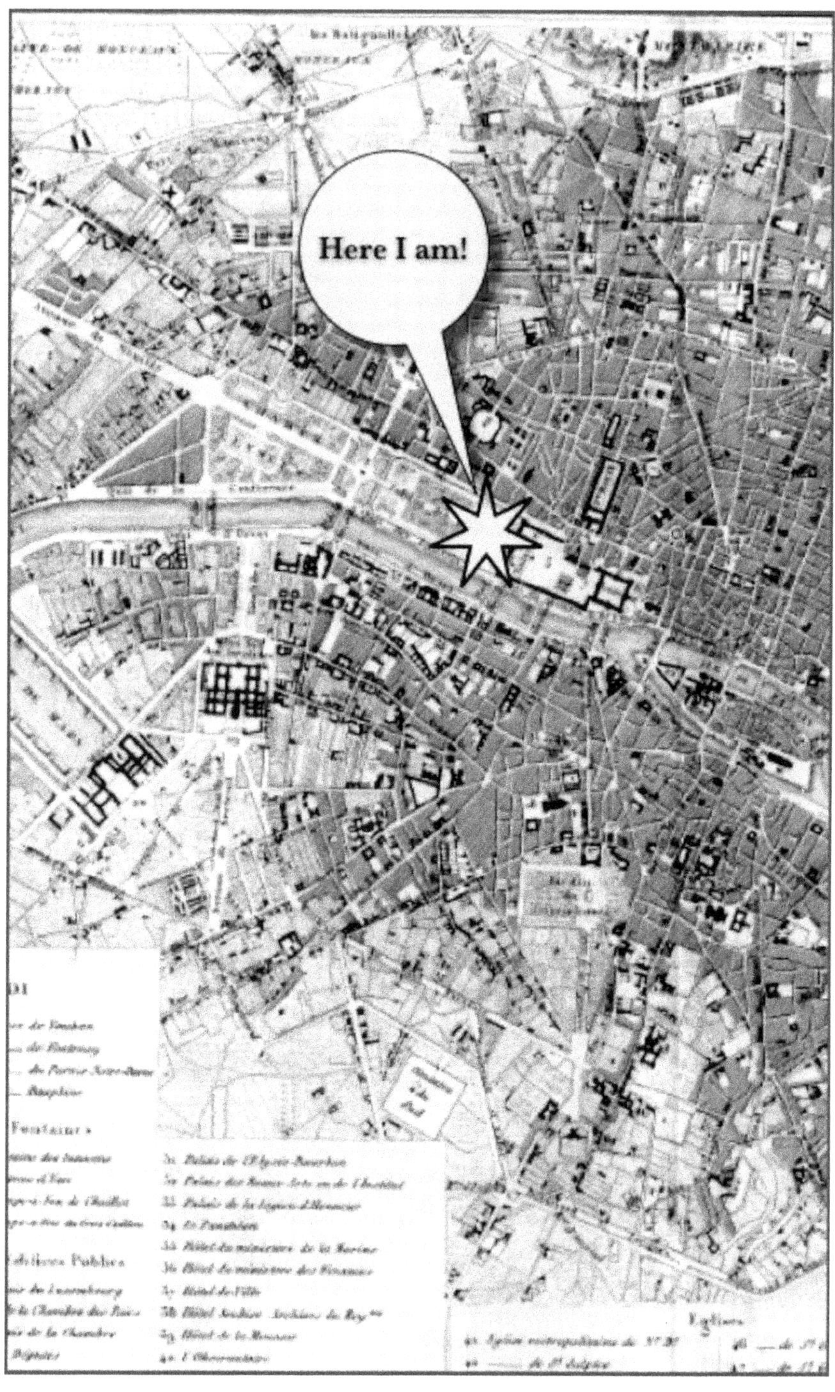
Here I am!

Like a lace curtain, lifted by the breeze, the mist was rising from the Seine at the first touch of the sun; as with cracking whip, and hooting horn, the Bordeaux stage came lumbering into Paris on the first day of August 1836. Two weary travelers clambered out stretching, their stiff limbs as they did so. They were Gustave Armand and his young cousin Lucien Lehun.

"Wait for me here a moment," said Gustave, "I have to run into the ticket office." He rushed through the station doors leaving Lucien standing along outside.

Inside, Gustave was hastily trying to secure a place aboard the return coach. He was just paying for it when Lucien appeared at this side, saying, "Are we going right home again, Cousin? Do let's get rested first."

"Didn't I tell you to wait for me outside?" Gustave snapped. "Why can't you do as you are told?"

"I'm so tired, Gustave, I thought perhaps I could rest in here till you were ready to go."

"I'm ready now," returned Gustave pocketing the change handed to him by the ticket clerk. "Come along. I'm going to the Tuileries to set my watch by the clock there."

"Why that's just what Uncle told me he always did first thing when he got to Paris," said Lucien brightening. "Dear Uncle! I wish he were here now."

"Oh, be still, can't you? You're enough to drive a man crazy. I'm sick of your whining," said his cousin sharply.

The child did not reply. He had to listen to a great deal of such talk and was trying hard not to mind it.

Once outside the station, Gustave had Lucien by the hand, and was dragging him rapidly along the street, but Lucien, although troubled by his cousin's manner, and the strangeness of everything, was much diverted by the novelty of his surroundings. He was constantly exclaiming at the beauty of the shops and wanting to stop to look in their big windows, but Gustave strode on taking no notice.

"Is the whole city of Paris so beautiful as this?" cried the boy, looking around at the fine buildings they were passing. His cousin did not answer. When they reached the Tuileries, he seated the boy upon a bench under a tree, and gave him a roll and some pears, which he took from his pocket.

A wan smile flitted across the child's face as he bit into one of the pears, "I believe I am more tired and sleepy than I am hungry," he said.

"Then stretch out on the bench and go to sleep. It is cool and shady here and you can have your lunch later."

"But what will you do, Gustave?"

"Oh, I've got an important letter to write. I will do that while you sleep. What book is that your have there, Lucien?"

"My *Robinson Crusoe*, the last present my dear uncle..." Noticing Gustave's dour expression, Lucien continues, "...uncle Armand gave me. I brought it along to read on the way, but there was too much to look at. Do you want to read it, Gustave? It is about someone who was cast away, alone on a desert island. I believe he was older than I am, but he was all alone. It must be awful to be all alone," said the child, trying to hide with a laugh the shapeless dread he felt while talking in this vein to his cousin. "You'll not leave me alone, if I go to sleep, will you Gustave," he asked with as unconcerned an air as he could assume.

"What nonsense, how you do go off?" returned his cousin impatiently. "Give me your book to write on, and go to sleep. I'm tired of your foolishness," he added, as he spread a sheet of writing paper upon the book now perched on his knee.

Worn out by the long journey, the child fell asleep while Gustave was speaking. His last waking thought was that he wished his cousin would sit nearer to him, he felt a sense of protection from Gustave's presence in this strange place as he watched him arrange his writing materials. Then he, and the passing strangers, and the thick trees overhead blended into shadowy haze, and the child's joys and sorrows were forgotten in a dreamless sleep.

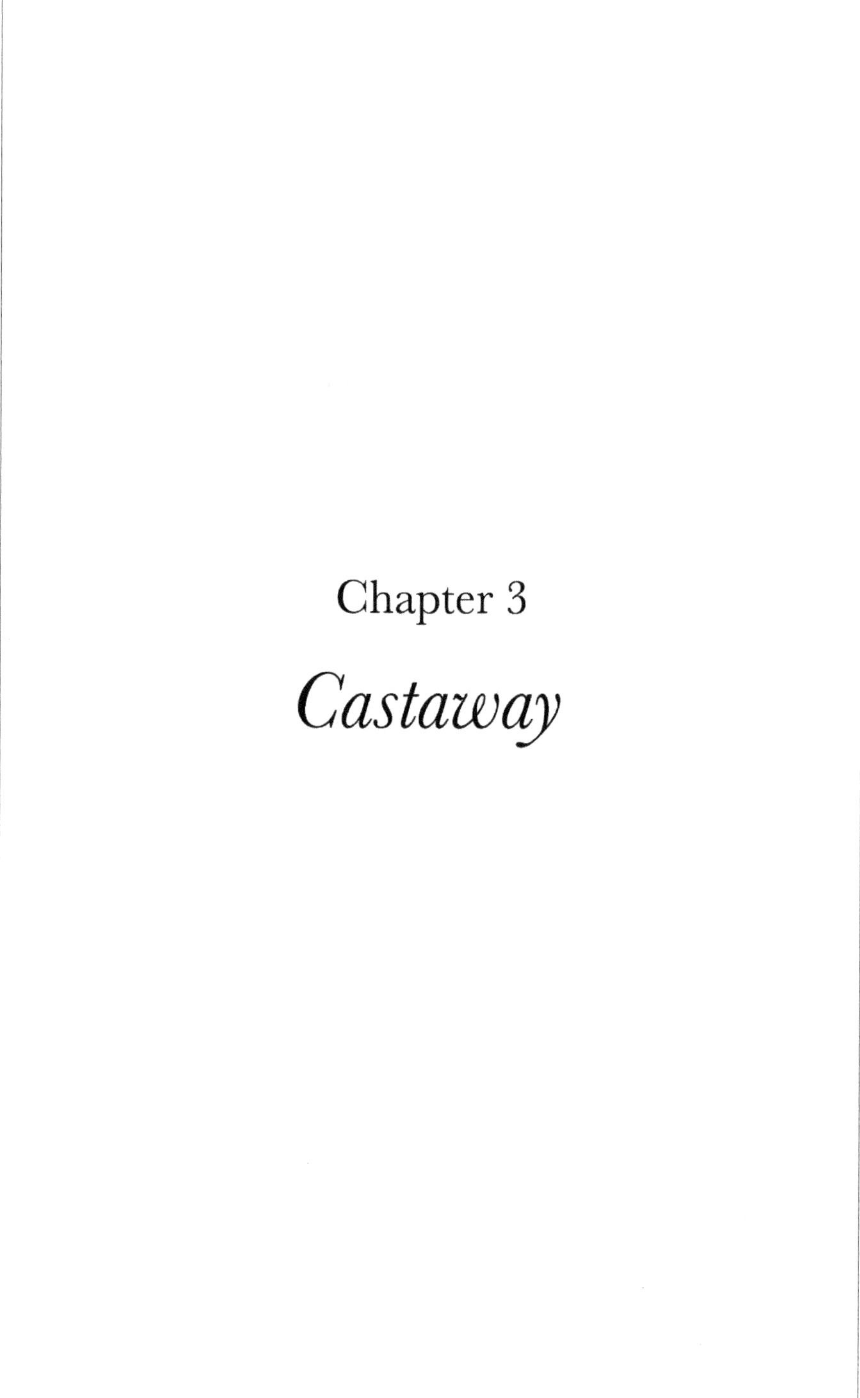

Chapter 3

Castaway

Where's Lucien?
(Turn the page to see.)
"You've been asleep a long time, little one," said a big man in uniform approaching him. "What are you doing here alone?"

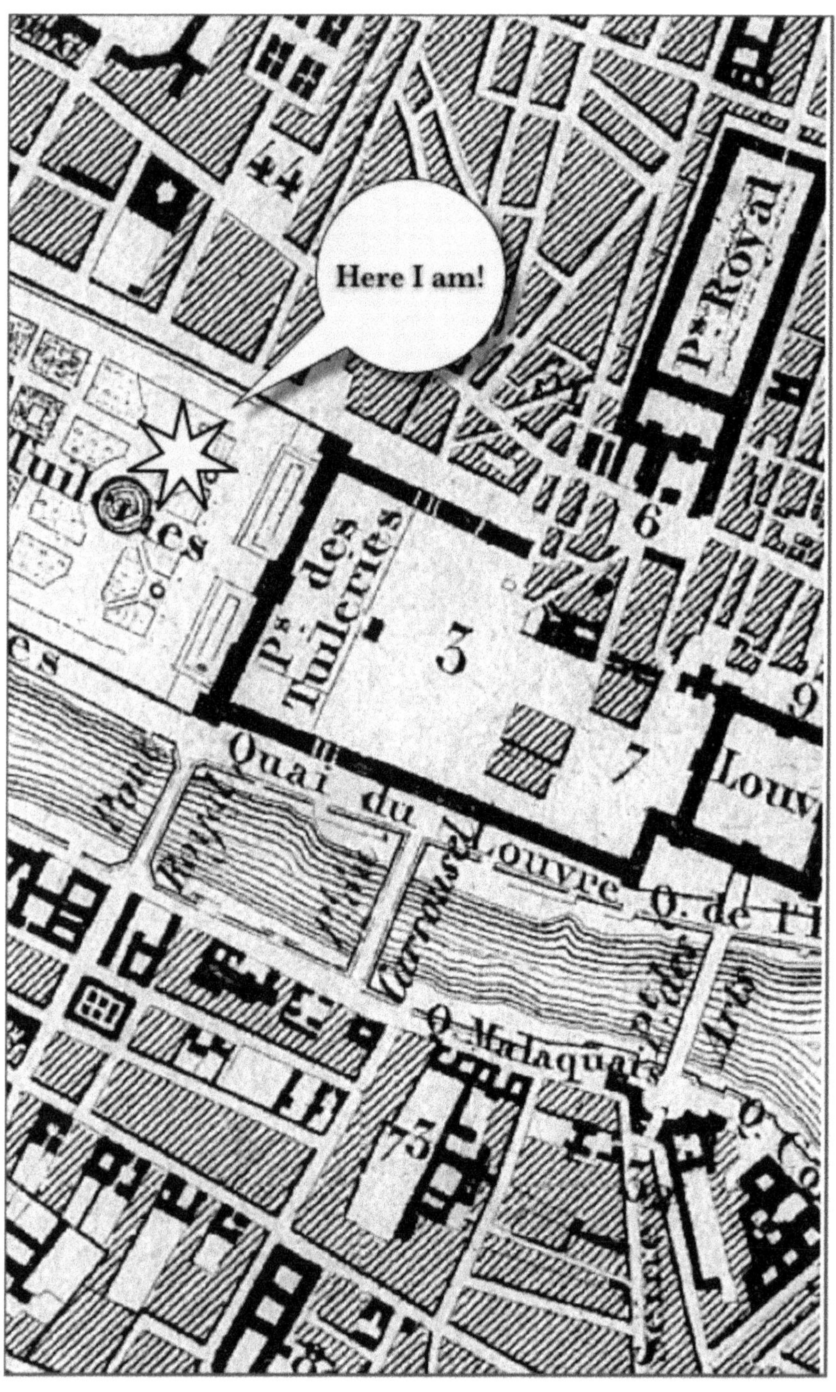
Here I am!
P.s Royal
P.s des Tuileries
3
6
7
9
Quai du Louvre
Q. Malaquais

From that comfortable place, halfway between asleep and awake, Lucien listened drowsily to the big clock striking seven. Slowly, the soreness of his muscles made him conscious of the hard bed he was lying upon. Lazily, he stretched himself and opened his eyes, blinking them at the setting sun. "Where am I?" he mumbled, sitting up, "Oh, yes, I remember now; I'm in Paris. I've had such a good long sleep, you must be tired waiting for me, Gustave."

There was no reply, and Lucien, rising on his elbow, looked about him. He saw nothing of his cousin. "Where could he be?" he asked himself carelessly. "I suppose he's hiding away just to frighten me." Interested in his surroundings, he was not anxious until the half hour struck. "I must have slept almost twelve hours," he thought to himself, counting upon his fingers. "The guard was just opening the gates when we came into the garden this morning. No wonder Gustave got tired of waiting for me. I wish he'd come back. He must be getting his dinner somewhere. He is so different from dear Uncle," the child went on, the ready tears springing to his blue eyes, "he would have remembered how hungry a little boy gets, and woke me to dine with him. My! but I'm hungry," he added with a yawn.

"You've been asleep a long time, little one," said a big man in uniform approaching him. "What are you doing here alone?"

"Waiting for my cousin," answered the child promptly, glad to have someone to speak to.

"Where is he?" inquired the man.

"I don't know," responded Lucien looking around the Tuileries garden again with a puzzled air.

"Are you sure he is coming back?"

"Of course. Why, I'd be all alone in Paris if he didn't."

"Does he live in the city?"

"No, but he and my uncle spent two whole months here last year."

"And you want to wait here for him?" asked the stranger.

"I must; what else can I do?'

"Suppose your cousin does not appear before it is time to close the gates? Even if he has spent two months in Paris, it is an easy city to lose one's way in. He might get lost."

"Then, Sir, I must sleep here, I suppose," said Lucien in a troubled voice.

"I'm afraid you can't do that. Everybody has to leave when the drum beats."

"Suppose my cousin doesn't get back in time?" said Lucien.

"That will be hard on you, I admit, but I'm one of the guards, and we have to see that everyone is out when we close the gates. I'm sure your cousin knows the rules and will be here in time," said the guard giving chase to a big dog.

Lucien tried to get up an interest in the boisterous crowd now thronging the Tuileries, but he was saying to himself, "What could I do here alone? And I'm so hungry now that I'm almost starved. I shouldn't mind waiting so long if it weren't for that." He took up his book idly, and as he did so, a letter dropped out of it. He was much surprised, upon picking it up, to find it addressed to himself. Hastily opening it he read it aloud:

> "*I cannot afford to support you. At any rate, you have no claim upon me. In fact, you already owe me for your board and education, and all my father spent upon you. I don't reproach you for that, but from this time, you must take care of yourself.*
>
> *Paris is not a desert island, but a big city full of opportunities. A boy who can read and write as well as you can will always find a way to get on.*
>
> *You have had more than your share of my father's money spent upon you, and his house can never again be your home, so you need not try to come back. I am master there now.*
>
> *I shall be far away when you read this, so there's no use trying to find me.*
>
> *From this time, I am as dead to you as is my father, so don't try to write to me, or to hear of me. I want nothing whatsoever to do with you.*
>
> *I need not sign my name. You know well enough who wrote this.*
>
> *And so, good bye forever.*"

When he had finished reading the letter, Lucien sat for a few moments, stunned. Then he reread it in the waning light to assure himself there was no mistake. Alas! There could be none. The only relative he had in the world had cruelly deserted him here.

"Oh, it can't be true!" cried the poor boy bursting into tears. "Even Gustave couldn't be so cruel; he is only trying to frighten me." Yet in his heart he feared the worst. Still he dared not move from his place, lest his cousin reappear and miss him.

His gnawing hunger was forgotten, as he said over and over, "Alone! Alone! Oh, what shall I do? Where shall I go, if it is true?"

The turbulent sea of people surged past him, but no one took any notice of the beautiful boy, whose tearful eyes searched in vain for a familiar face. When the pangs of hunger again seized him, he said aloud, "Surely God will punish my cousin," and then softly, like a prayer, "May dear God take pity upon poor me!" and he sat back on the bench, staring into the crowd, not knowing what else to do.

Lost in his misery, he didn't immediately notice the feel of something rubbing his leg. With a start, he snapped back into the present and looked down at his feet. There, a little dog, badly wounded and cowering in fright, sought refuge between his feet. "Get out!" Lucien snapped reflexively, giving the dog an angry push, then quickly checking himself. "I just asked God to pity me, and yet I show no pity for a poor, wounded little dog." Stooping down, he gently lifted the trembling dog up onto the seat beside him.

"So that is your dog, is it, little one?" inquired an old gentleman, who had been watching them. "You'd better not let him run loose again, if you don't want him killed. The guards were after him with their bayonets. He's a brave little dog to outwit them, but I'm afraid he is badly hurt."

"He isn't my dog, Sir, I never saw him before now. Couldn't you take him home with you, and keep him till he gets well? I wish you would. He's a dear little dog. You've got a home to take him to," said Lucien sadly.

"Dear me!" said the old gentleman in mocking tones, "of course I've got a home, everybody has, but I hate dogs. If you want to get rid of him, you have only to let him run at large in the gardens. The guards will soon finish him. My you're a queer boy!" said the old gentleman, walking on with the crowd, "Take a dog like that home with me indeed!"

"Selfish old man!" said Lucien, caressing the dog, who whined and licked his hands. "Poor doggie, let me see where you are hurt. Oh, your poor little foot is all cut by the guard's horrid old bayonet, and your nose is hurt, too. Let's wash off the blood," said the boy, carrying the dog to the fountain near by, and tenderly bathing his wounds. Taking a fine handkerchief from his pocket, he tore a strip from it, and used it to bandage the wounded paw. The other piece Lucien tied tightly to the dog's collar, that he might insure his not falling into the hands of the guards again.

As the pain in his foot eased under Lucien's kind treatment, the dog's affectionate gratitude moved the heart of the lonely boy. Seated upon the bench, looking into one another's faces, they made a pretty picture. A kindly pat or a gentle word from Lucien made the dog spring up quivering with pleasure, only to sit down again whining with pain.

"You'd better stop jumping up and down, doggie, if it hurts your poor foot," Lucien said to him, at which the dog cocked his head on one side, and wagged his tail. "You understand, don't you, old fellow?" said the child patting him gently. "I wish I knew where you lived. It is too bad for a nice dog like you to be lost." Lucien choked back a sob, and the dog licked his caressing hand.

A fine black Spaniel with long, silky ears. his paws and tail tipped with tan, and a white spot on his breast, is, as the boy noted, a very handsome dog; too handsome to be lost; especially as he seemed to have such a good disposition, and to be so intelligent. Lucien felt sure that he must belong to some very fine people, and he thought sadly that they must even now be bemoaning his loss, while there was no one to give a thought to his own disappearance. Being so handsomely turned out, and owing to his delicate health, the boy looked so much younger than he was, that had the passers by even noticed him, they would have supposed him to be the child of rich parents, left alone for a moment by his attendant.

The sudden roll of a signal drum close behind them made Lucien and the dog jump, calling forth boisterous laughter from the strollers nearby. Then, there was a turn of the tide, and all feet were set toward the gates. Taking the dog in his arms, Lucien followed slowly toward the Castiglione entrance. Still hoping that his cousin might come back for him, he looked wistfully into passing faces. All were strange to him.

"Well, I'm better off than Robinson Crusoe," he said, trying to keep up his courage. "He had only a desert island, and was all alone, but there's everything here, and lots of people for company."

Out on the street, passing the brilliantly lit shops on Rue de la Paix, he exclaimed, "Robinson Crusoe would never have written such a long story about his troubles if his island had been such a beautiful place as this." All the same, hunger had him in such a grip that he couldn't get any real enjoyment out of his novel environment, and he began looking about for a place to dine.

Accustomed to a sheltered life and living in a beautiful house, where all things moved on oiled wheels, he was utterly ignorant of the ways of the world, and the uses of money. Nothing but childish timidity kept him from seating himself at one of the tables in front of a large restaurant and asking to be served. At last he entered, where he hoped someone would hasten to invite him to dine, for the dinner smells in the air were becoming insufferable. The wife of the concierge noticed him quickly; "What do you want here, little boy?" she asked sharply.

"Nothing, my good woman," replied the child, still advancing.

"Then what brings you in here?" she demanded so fiercely that he sprang backward, and the dog gave an affrighted howl.

Recovering himself, Lucien said earnestly, "I thought if you saw me, you'd ask me in."

The women eyed him as though he spoke a foreign tongue.

"I'm so tired and hungry," said the child simply.

"There's no place for you here," returned the woman roughly. "Clear out, you're only in the way."

As the boy, eyes brimming with tears, stood looking at her without offering to move, she seized him by the shoulders and rudely thrust him back into the street.

"I didn't know there could be such a wicked woman," he said, resting his head for a moment upon that of the spaniel. They walked on listlessly till he came to a baker's shop. "Surely they will give me something there. I'm so hungry, I could eat dry bread," he said to himself, and went in. The old woman's treatment of him had frightened him, and he said timidly to a young girl sitting behind the counter,

"Would you be good enough to give me a piece of bread?"

"With pleasure," responded the girl, jumping up with such youthful enthusiasm that her knitting was sent flying, and she had to rescue it from the black kitten lying in wait. She and Lucien looked at one another and laughed, and the boy felt almost happy again, being in touch with someone young and cheerful. When, much to the spaniels' disgust, the kitten was shut out in disgrace, the girl said with a friendly smile, as she held the knife over the loaf, "How much do you want?"

"How much?" returned the boy laughing, "Oh, as much as you'll give me. I'm dreadfully hungry."

"It make no difference to me," replied the girl. "I thought you were getting it for your dog though," she added with a significant glance at Lucien's fine clothes. "Shall I cut you two or four cents worth?"

"You don't expect me to pay for it do you?" cried the boy.

"Did you think I meant to give it to you?" asked the girl laughing.

"Amanda," shot a voice from the back of the shop, "what do you mean by joking with the young gentleman instead of waiting upon him? Cut two cents worth of bread for him, and if he thinks that isn't enough, cut another piece. Be quick about it."

The girl handed Lucien a slice of bread, saying, "There's two cents worth," at the same time holding out her other hand for the money. After feeling in all his pockets, the child, very red in the face, produced one penny. "That's all I have," he said, looking so eagerly at the bread that the girl, giving a nervous glance over at the woman, thrust it into his hand and dropped the penny into the drawer.

Thanking her gratefully, Lucien hurried out, and sitting down upon a step began to devour the bread. The spaniel sat by, watching him with eagerness; licking his chops and wagging his tail every time the child took a bite. Presently, he barked.

"Poor fellow!" exclaimed Lucien, patting him. "I forgot all about you. Are you hungry, too? This isn't enough for one, let alone two, but never mind, I'll go shares." And now, for every piece he himself ate, he gave one to the dog, who seemed to have forgotten his wounded foot, for with every mouthful, he was ready to show off some new trick. He sat up and begged, and gave his paw, or spoke when Lucien told him to, and was altogether so cheerful and entertaining that the child's spirits rose in sympathy.

"Good doggie!" said he, "What a great many tricks you know. I wonder who taught you. It's plain you've got a master; I wish we could find him; perhaps he'd be good to me, too." The dog looked wise, but he didn't offer to show him the way.

"I didn't know I was so tired," said Lucien. "I wonder if dogs get so tired as folks. They get pretty hungry, I'm finding out" he said, tossing the last morsel to the spaniel who eagerly snatched it out of the air.

"That's all, old fellow. I wish we had a whole loaf; I didn't know dry bread was so good, but oh, dear! I'm hungrier than ever."

To divert his mind from his unsatisfied hunger, he went on playing with the dog, and trying to teach him new tricks. "I wish I knew your name," he said, but the dog's only reply was an intent look out of his soft eyes. Lucien tried calling him by every dog's name he could remember, but the spaniel answered to none. Then, without warning, he bounded away toward a passing stranger, who had at that moment whistled and called "Fox." Another dog answered the call also, and the spaniel returned with a disappointed air to Lucien.

"So that is your name, is it?" cried the boy, delighted to have discovered it so quickly. "Here Fox, Fox," he called trying it on. The dog gave such ready response that there could be no doubt as to his claim to the name. Lucien kept talking to him for the mere pleasure of using it. "He likes it as much as I do," he said to himself. "I wonder if he'll understand if I tell him I'm Lucien Lehun?" Fox acted as though he did anyway and the child said with evident satisfaction, "Now we know one another's names, we're real friends, like Crusoe and his man Friday. Well, Fox, I'm so thirsty, I wish we could find a drink," he added, looking around him. Fox sprang up, wagging his tail, and started for the corner, looking back for Lucien to follow.

"I do believe he understood," said Lucien racing after him. The dog trotted gingerly on ahead till he came to a fountain, where he began eagerly to lap at the brim of the overflowing basin.

"Well done, Fox. I got bread for you, and you find water for me," cried Lucien, seizing the chained cup and dipping it into the upper basin. "Let's rest here awhile, I'm awfully tired, aren't you?" Fox didn't say, but he wagged his tail and seated himself upon the ground close to the child.

Without their knowing it, they had been watched and followed by a man, who now came up to Lucien, saying, "What are you doing here, little man?"

"Playing with my dog, Sir," answered the boy, looking up fearlessly into his face.

"I thought perhaps you were lost, but I see by your dress that I must be mistaken. Boys like you always have someone to take care of them."

"And suppose I were lost, what then?" asked Lucien, trying to speak with indifference.

"I should try to find out where you lived and take you home."

"You are very good," replied the child rising. "Do you take care of all the lost children?"

"Yes, all I find; I'm a policeman."

"And what do you do with those who have no homes?"

"Oh, those are vagrants. I take them to prison."

"But perhaps they are not all vagrants. Sometimes good children are deserted by their bad relatives."

The man laughed. "Their relatives must be a bad lot then," he said.

"But suppose it happened so?" asked Lucien with a tremor in his voice.

"I should have to take the children to prison if they had no home, for it is against the law to let them sleep in the streets. Prison isn't such a bad place. Once there, we try to find the children's relatives, and if we can't do that, we put them in a home, where they are taught a trade."

"Do you mean a school?"

"Yes and no. The children can't go and come as they like, and no dogs are allowed there," added the man with a light laugh, as his eye chanced to land upon Fox, rolling about to scratch his back.

"So sleeping in the streets is forbidden? How strange," said Lucien thoughtfully. "Come Fox, we must be going. Good night, Sir," and the boy and the dog hurried away.

The policeman scratched his head. "I'm blest if I know what to make of that youngster," said he. "I don't believe I ought to have let him go. It's too late to catch him now though," said the officer, turning about to continue walking his beat.

A Fox In Paris

Chapter 4
The Old Soldier

Where's Lucien?
(Turn the page to see.)
"We found one another on the battlefield of Austerlitz, where we both lay wounded. We were together ever since."

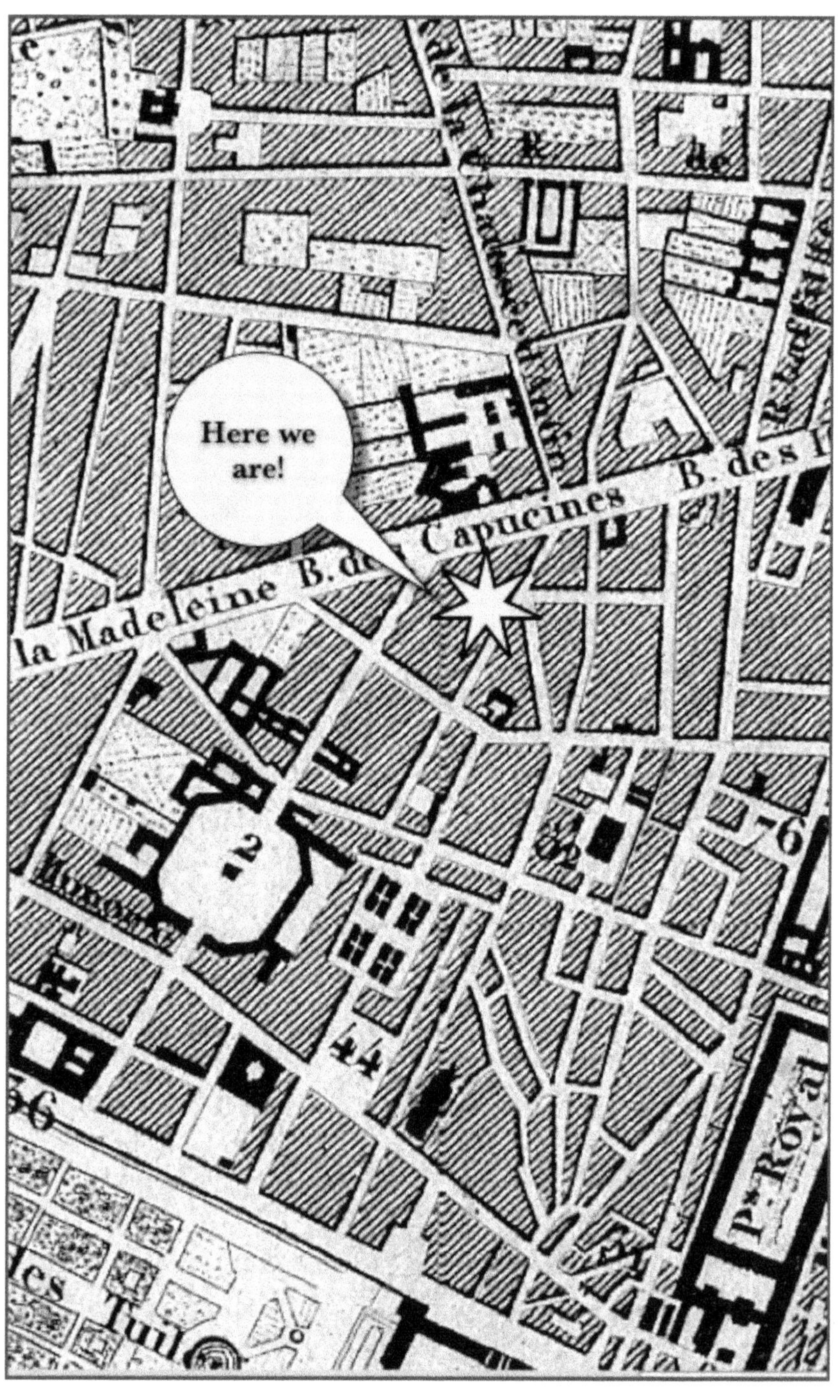
Here we are!
la Madeleine
Capucines

An hour later, afraid of being arrested as a vagrant if he stopped to rest, Lucien was still walking wearily up and down the now dark and deserted streets. When he could, Fox limped along at his side, the rest of the time Lucien picked him up and carried him. "It's about all I can do to carry myself along, Fox," he had said to the dog the last time he set him down. Fox appeared to understand, and in spite of his lame foot, made no complaint.

"There must be some place in this great city for lost children to sleep besides a prison," said Lucien, talking to the dog. "I'd knock at the doors of some of the houses, but I'm afraid I'd meet another cross old woman. If we could only find an empty house, we'd be all right."

They wandered on into the night, not noticing as the streets became ever darker and more empty. Lucien had just bent down to pick up the dog again, who was now limping terribly, when he noticed an open gate in front of a house across the street they were walking on. He stood up and eyed the big house beyond it, and after a minute his eyes brightened.

"Here's the very place for us, Fox," said the boy, with renewed energy, as he hurried across the vacant street, and paused at the open gate. It was in fact, really no gate at all, but, it would be soon. Presently, it was scaffolding and stones and lumber. They were standing in front of a row of several large unfinished houses, the doors and windows not yet in place, and the gates not yet installed. Passing under the scaffolding to enter the unfinished front door opening of the nearest house, Lucien froze when a hard voice croaked out of the darkness beyond. "Who goes there?"

"There's somebody after us even here," said the frightened child bursting into tears. "Oh, God, what shall I do?" and falling upon his knees, he prayed for guidance and protection, speaking as to an earthly parent, as he had been taught by his good uncle.

"Who goes there?" barked the voice again, more roughly than before. Fox growled, as a dull thumping sound emanated from the black opening and came toward them. Hearing the strange noise, Lucien rose quickly to his feet, snatching up the dog as he did so. He wanted to be ready to run for his life, and knew that Fox would not be able to. Just as fear was about to send him flying down the street with the dog, an old man with a wooden leg, and carrying a lantern, appeared in the doorway.

"So it's you, you wicked boy, making all the noise is it?" he said angrily.

"I didn't think I made any noise, sir."

"Well, if you didn't, then your dog did. What business has he growling around here, I'd like to know. A body can't get even an hours sleep here on Louis Le Grand Street."

"You're lucky that you can sleep at all, Sir," responded Lucien sadly.

"Sleep indeed!" retorted the old man. "You see how much sleep I get. When my poor dog Austerlitz was alive, he watched while I slept, but now I must do all the watching myself."

"Where is he now?" asked Lucien.

"Dead, poor old soul. I forgot to muzzle him one day when he went out, and he ate a poisoned meat ball meant for the rats, though I had often warned him not to eat anything he found in the street. But...dogs are greedy. He died in my arms, poor fellow. He was my only friend," said the old man sadly at the memory of his dog.

"Had you had him long?" Lucien asked sympathetically.

"Yes. We found one another on the battlefield of Austerlitz, where we both lay wounded. I bound up his wounds and he tried his best to clean mine. We were together ever since."

"He sounds as though he was a very good dog," said the boy, much interested and suddenly unafraid of the old man.

"None better," answered the old man. "That's a brave looking dog you've got there; wounded and still standing up for you. What will you take for him? Though, to tell the truth, my purse is empty, so it would suit me better to have you give him to me."

"This isn't my dog, Sir, so I can't either sell him or give him away, but if you will let us sleep here, he'll keep watch for you."

"All right, that sounds like a square deal. You speak like a decent boy, and I know a brave dog when I see one, so come in. You'll find everything new and fine, though maybe a little in the rough. When I was a soldier, I didn't always have things so comfortable. Have you had your supper?"

"No, Sir, I have eaten nothing but a piece of bread since morning," replied the boy, ashamed of his forlorn estate.

"Poor child!" exclaimed the old man hanging his lantern on a peg. "Let's see what I can find for you. Yes, here's some bread and meat. I haven't any wine to go with it, for I have a way of drinking it all when I get any, but you'll find water in that pitcher."

Thanking him, Lucien hurriedly began to eat, sharing with Fox, who sat up beside him begging. The old man chuckled with pleasure over the child's evident relish of the simple food, and the dog's cunning devices to attract attention.

Suddenly, Lucien looked at him and stopped eating. "Must I save part for tomorrow?" he asked seriously. Fox dropped upon his fore feet and hung his head at the tone.

"Heavens no, child; eat away, both of you. Life is too uncertain to be bothering about tomorrows. My father was a soldier, and I came near being born on a battlefield. I've spent most of my life where bullets and cannon balls were flying. I'll just say, I've helped many brave men past their worries about tomorrow. This leg," added the old soldier giving his wooden leg a resounding blow with his cane, "entitles me to a place in Les Invalides, so God has provided for me. So eat your fill; there'll be plenty more when we need it."

The old man's optimistic philosophy fit well with the mood of the tired child, who looked up into the man's weathered face with a grateful smile, too busy eating to use his mouth to repeat what his eyes had already said. The old soldier, as he talked, had been regarding Lucien with curiosity by the dim light of the smoky lantern on the wall. "But here I am running on about myself," said he, "and forgetting to ask how a well-dressed young gentleman like you happens to be wandering about the streets at night, and so hungry."

Lucien's face flushed, and the mouthful he was swallowing was close to choking him, as he answered, "I can't explain it, Sir. It is too sad a story to tell anyone."

"You don't look as if you had done anything wrong," returned the old man.

"I haven't. It was my cousin. His father was the best man that ever lived, and for his sake, I mustn't tell about my cousin's wickedness."

"Well, never mind. You can sleep on that clean straw over there. If you're as tired as you were hungry, you'd better get to bed," said the old soldier, stumping away to a sort of tent, made by suspending an old awning across one corner of the big unfinished room. As he ducked under he looked back and added, " Good night, and good sleep to you."

Chapter 5
The Masons

"What does this mean? A pretty time of day to be starting in to work! The plastering on that wall ought to have been nearly finished by this time!"

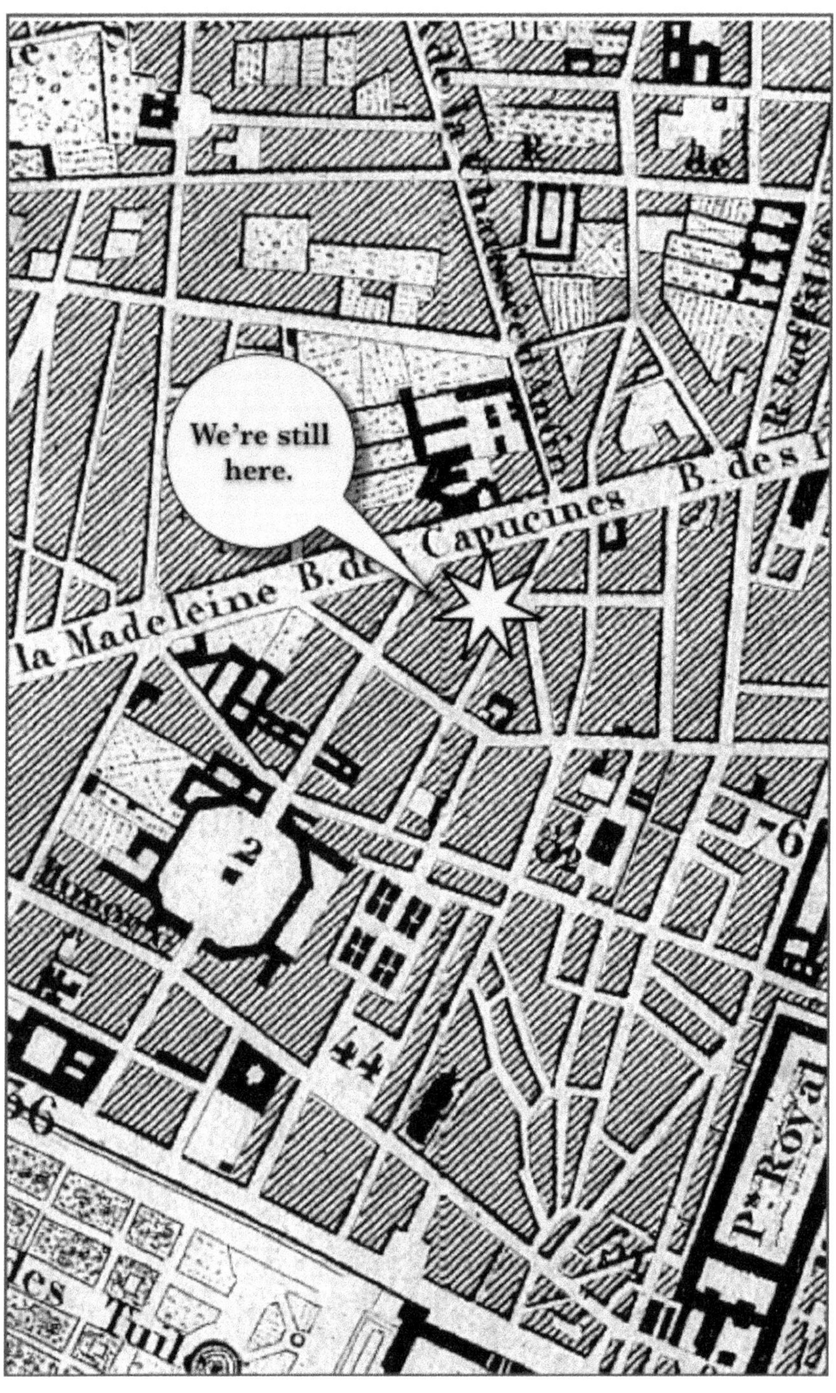
We're still here.
la Madeleine B. de
Capucines
B. des
Tuil

Early the next morning Lucien was awakened by Fox, who caught between fright and bravado, was barking himself hoarse at a crowd of burly masons entering the house.

"Voilà! Father La Tuile," cried one of them, "who's this you have here? It seems they don't want us to finish the house," added the man with a loud laugh, in which the others joined. The old soldier raised a corner of the ragged curtain and looked toward Lucien, who was still half-buried in the straw, and trying his best to quiet Fox.

"They're friends of mine, what have you got to say against them?" retorted Father La Tuile, turning sharply upon the young man who had spoken.

"Nothing," replied the mason carelessly, "but now I look at that little chap, I should think you aught to have taken him home, instead of letting him sleep in such a place as this. He has been used to better things. His family must be raising the whole city about him by this time."

"I haven't any family," Lucien interjected, as he stood and began brushing the straw from his hair and clothing. The gang gathered about him, eager to learn more. Their curious gaze made his cheeks burn.

"What no father or mother?" asked one.

"No, I had only a dear Uncle, and he is dead," answered the boy simply, his eyes filling with tears.

"No parents! No home!" cried the workmen in chorus. "Where did your uncle live? What was his business? Was he rich? Didn't he leave you anything?"

These questions, fired rapidly at him by one and another of the men filled Lucien with bewilderment. His only reply was to look into these strange staring faces with the tears coursing down his cheeks.

"Attention, comrades!" exclaimed the old soldier, pounding on the floor with his cane. "Give the boy a chance to breath!"

The men laughed loudly.

"Go ahead, youngster, tell us all about yourself," said one.

"I won't tell you my uncle's name, nor where he lived, but my name is Lucien Lehun. I never saw Paris till yesterday morning, and before I had been here an hour, my only relative deserted me. That is all there is to tell," said the little boy.

To the men's eager questions as to the name of this heartless kinsman, he replied, "I won't tell you. Nobody ever had a better father than he had, and it would be wrong of me to betray his son's name."

"You're a queer little chap!" exclaimed one of the masons, looking with respect at the child.

"See here," cried another, "just tell us fellows where to find that cousin of yours and we'll pay him up for you. Heavens! I'd like to smash his ugly mug for him myself."

"I'd like to duck him in the river and hold him there till he roared for mercy!" said another, rolling up his sleeves, as if making ready.

Lucien couldn't help wondering what chance of escape there would be for his cousin if these men's brawny arms had him in the clutch.

"No," he said firmly, "for his father's sake, I will not betray him."

"Pohaw!" said one of the men tauntingly, "You're just a naughty runaway boy; that's what you are."

"Why should I run away?" retorted the child, with sparkling eyes.

"Because you're afraid of being punished for something you've done."

"I wish I were," returned Lucien drooping. "That would mean that I still had a home to go to, and I shouldn't mind a whipping, if I only had."

"Then why don't you tell us the whole truth?"

At this, Lucien stepped forth as if to confront an enemy, and looking at the men straight away declared resolutely, "If one of you had a brother or a cousin who did something very bad, should you go about telling of it?"

"Perhaps not, but we'd make him suffer for it," answered one of the workers.

"Yes, because you're grown men. I'm only a little boy; he knows he has nothing to fear from me."

Puzzled and interested, the men continued to hang about Lucien, plying him with questions. "Where are you going to get a breakfast?" asked one.

"I don't know," replied the child, suddenly realizing that he was very hungry again. The ready tears came to his eyes.

"Never mind, little gentleman," said the man hastily, "we've got enough for ourselves and you, too."

"That's so," said another mason heartily, "he's sure of his breakfast, but what about dinner and supper?"

"Can't we go shares with him then, as well as now?" answered a comrade.

"Yes, today, and perhaps tomorrow, but we can't keep it up. What a pity he isn't old enough for an apprentice."

"Or, a soldier," added Father La Tuile.

"Well, we must try to find him something to do," one of the workmen said.

At the sound of a carriage rattling up to the door at this moment, the men seized their tools, and were busily at work when a gentleman stepped briskly into the house. He was the builder. Not in the least deceived by the sudden industry of the masons, whose grouping about the boy he had observed through the sashless windows as he drove up, he exclaimed brusquely, "What does this mean? A pretty time of day to be starting in to work! The plastering on that wall ought to have been nearly finished by this time!"

"We were listening to that child's story, Sir," said the boss, stepping forward, "but we'll soon catch up."

"What story?" asked the builder, looking so sharply at Lucien that the boy hung his head.

In a few words, the old soldier, who was standing beside the child told what he knew of him, while the men went back to their work.

"A pack of lies, the whole of it!" said the builder harshly. "The boy is a runaway. A fool could see it." Turning to Lucien, he demanded, "What's your name, boy?"

"Lucien Lehun, Sir," answered the child frankly.

"And you say you're an orphan?"

Lucien could not keep back his tears, and he bent his head without speaking.

"What can you do?"

"Nothing, Sir," Lucien sobbed.

"A pretty way to bring up a child!"

"Excuse me, Sir," returned Lucien quickly. "I thought you meant what kind of hard work could I do. I always had a tutor, and he taught me Latin, Geography, Arithmetic and a lot more things. I also went to dancing school, and I can play on the violin and sing."

The builder who was listening with evident impatience now broke in with, "Your uncle was rich then?"

"I don't know, Sir. He was good to the poor, and there was always enough of everything for us."

"And you say he's dead now?"

Lucien's only reply was to look at him with brimming eyes. The builder returned his gaze, and then asked in his abrupt way, "How old are you?"

"Eleven and a half, Sir."

"Humph! Pretty young. Can you ride horseback?"

"Yes indeed," replied the boy with animation. "I've got the dearest pony, and I can ride him bare-backed as well as with a saddle. I always went out with my uncle, and he said I was a born horseman. Why my pony stands right up on his hind legs, and sometimes he kicks up, but he can't throw me," added Lucien proudly.

"Very good," said the builder dryly. "That will help you to earn your own living. I suppose you want to do that."

"Yes indeed, I do, Sir".

"You are rather young, but I'm in need of a groom for one of my daughters. I suppose you might do," the builder said patronizingly.

"Thank you Sir, but I'm afraid I wouldn't," answered the child so fearlessly that the workmen exchanged frightened glances, and held their trowels suspended waiting to hear what came next. Even Father la Tuile coughed and shifted his cane to the other hand.

"And why not pray?" demanded the offended builder.

"Because I know my uncle would not want me to be your servant, Sir".

"No? He'd rather have you a good-for-nothing beggar," retorted the other angrily. "Well, I'll have none of your stripe around here, so, out with you, as fast as your legs can carry you. If I catch you in here again, I'll have you arrested."

"Oh, Sir, you couldn't be so cruel as that. It isn't that I don't want to work. If you will let me help these men, you'll see how hard I'll try."

"You little simpleton!" answered the irate builder. "It is a great deal easier to be a servant to my house, than a tradesman. If you lived with me, you would have very little to do but to ride after my daughter when she went out."

"Then I'd get lazy and not want to work," returned the boy with a passing smile. "And you would expect me to live in your kitchen with your other servants. We had good faithful servants at home, and I loved them all, but Uncle would not let me go into the kitchen very often, and he always corrected me if I talked like the servants. He would say that a gentleman's son must always remember 'Noblesse oblige' and live to a higher standard," said Lucien with conviction, "No Sir, I can not be your servant without dishonoring my uncle, but I thank you for the offer!"

"Very well, young man," said the builder shaking his cane at the boy, "I'm done with you, and I want you to get out of here, and not let me see you again. It would serve you right if you had to come to my kitchen door to beg for bread."

"Don't strike me, Sir," Lucien said with gentle dignity, "I'm not your servant," and picking up Fox, he walked from the house.

The two of them made their way slowly along the street, the limping dog keeping pace beside him, until arrested by a sound behind him. "Hist!" said a voice, and looking back, he saw the old soldier stumping after him. He ran back to meet him. "Here," said the old man, "the masons have sent you part of their breakfast. You're a brave boy, and you spoke like a little gentleman. If you can't find better quarters, come back tonight."

"No, no," cried Lucien, shaking his head. "That man said he'd have me arrested if I did."

"Oh he's just a big wind," replied Father La Tuile with a knowing smile. "He's too busy having a good time to bother us at night. You needn't mind him."

Thanking the old man and bidding him thank the masons heartily for their kindness, he shook hands and went his way.

The old soldier hobbled back to his post with glistening eyes.

A Fox In Paris

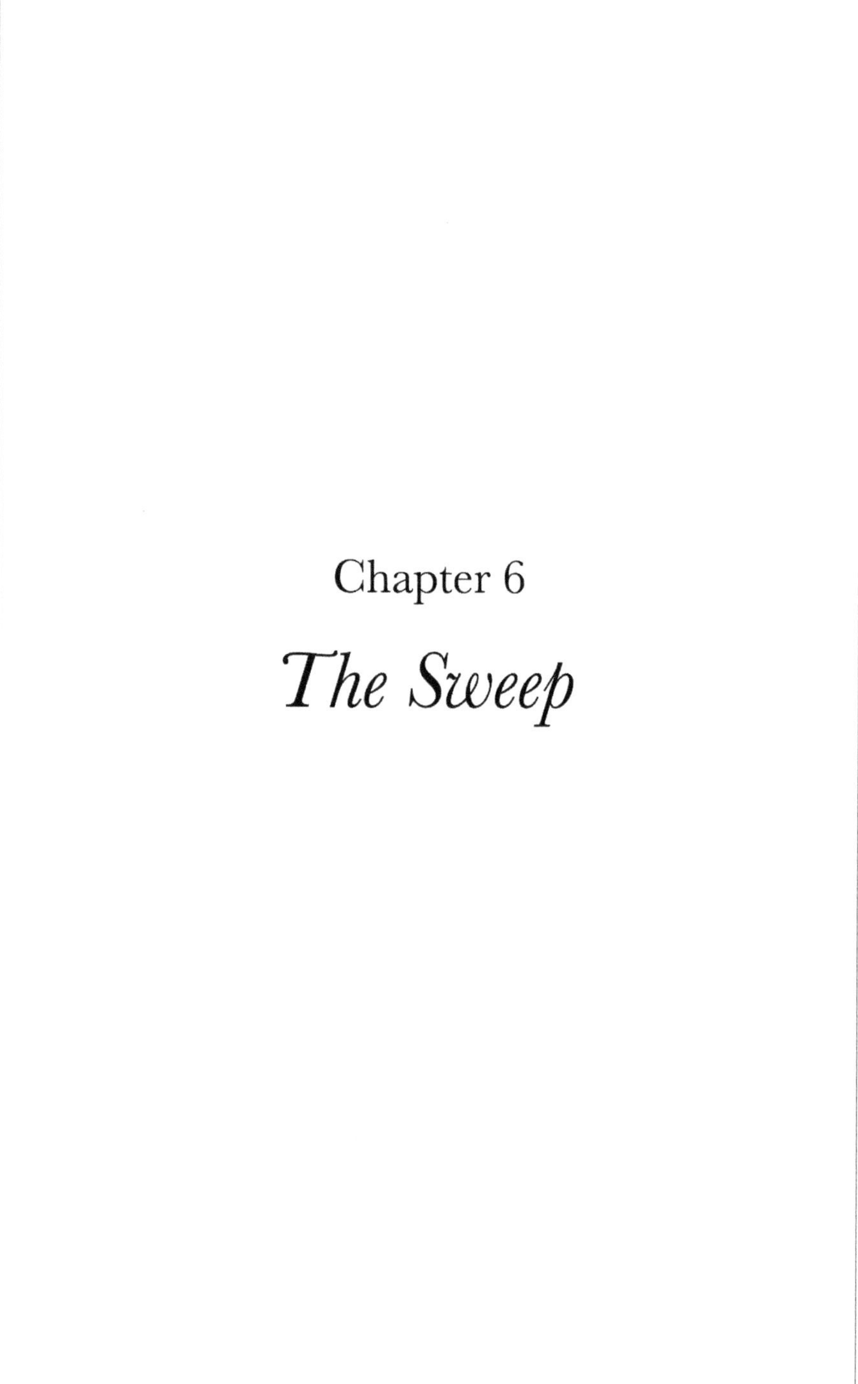

Chapter 6

The Sweep

Where's Lucien?
(Turn the page to see.)
"You couldn't be a sweep," replied the boy, "you'd spoil those fine clothes. I guess your mother and father would have something to say about that."

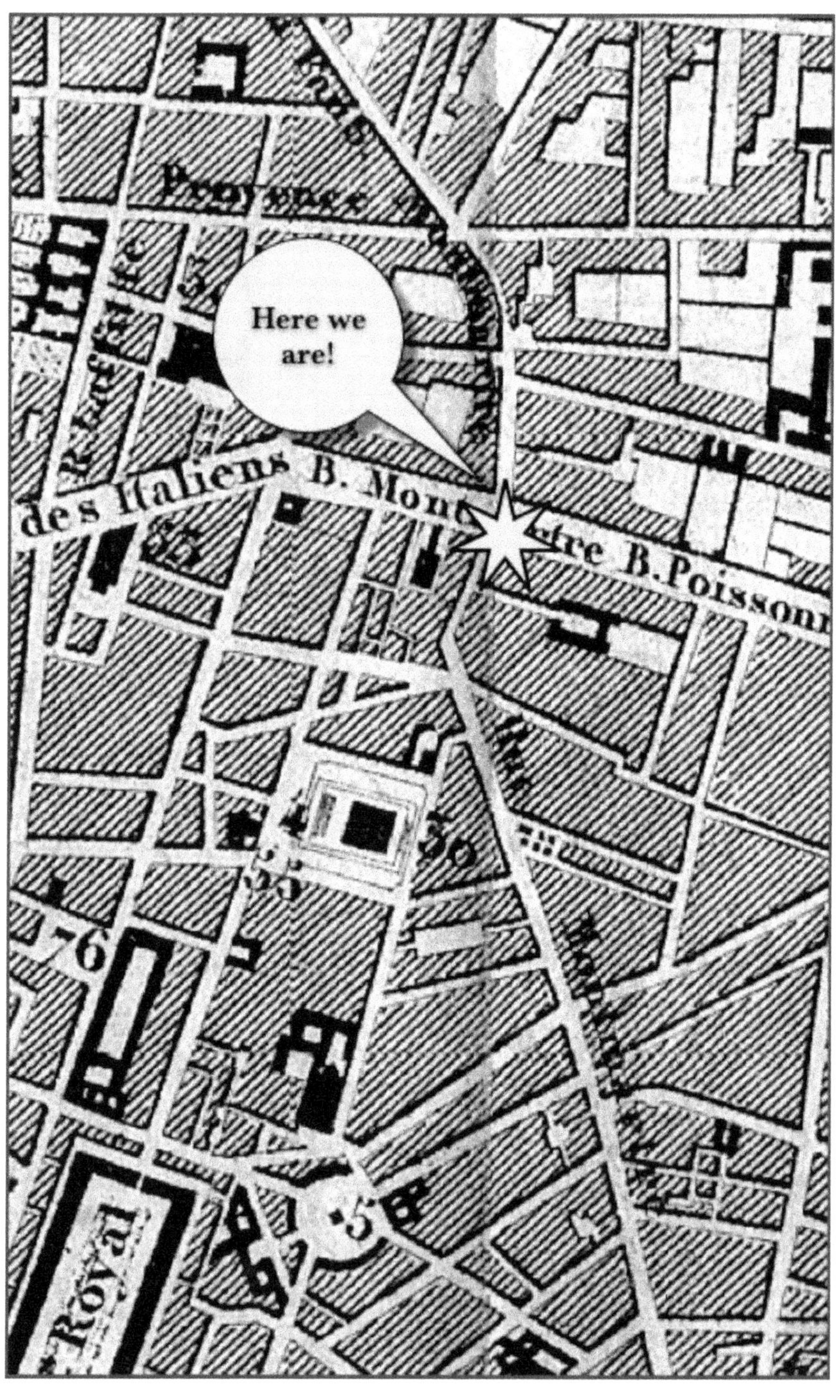
Here we are!
Provence
des Italiens B. Mont
tre B.Poissonn
76
30
Royal

Continuing listlessly along the street, Lucien listened to the halting steps of the old soldier fading behind him. When he could no longer make them out from the background din, he felt alone again. It seemed to him as if he were being deserted once more in the great city. He quickly gathered the dog protectively in his arms and cried. Fox licked his hands and whined in sympathy, and the child suddenly remembered that they were both fasting.

"Never mind, Fox," he said. "We shall feel better after we have eaten something."

He sought a quiet corner and sat down to eat his breakfast, sharing the food, bite for bite, with the dog. His spirits rose as he ate, and he found great diversion in the dog's ready display of his talents. When he stood on his head, Lucien fairly doubled up with laughter, and the little dog laughed, too, just as plain as any dog can.

After awhile, they started out along the Boulevards once more, the child eagerly admiring the beautiful shop windows. He had left his book in the new house, but he had it in mind all the time.

"Now the first thing Robinson Crusoe did," he said to himself, "was to explore his island. That's what you and I are doing now," he said to Fox, who wagged his tail and barked. He liked being talked to.

"Crusoe was afraid of cannibals," the child went on, adding; "Do you think the people here don't look as though they might eat us, Fox?"

"Certainly no," responded Fox's wagging tail and cocked ears.

"We needn't be afraid of starving here either," added Lucien, "just look at all the fine pastry shops."

They paused to look in the window of one of the shops, having completely forgotten their experience of the day before. After a moment spent gazing at the delights inside, Fox sat up and gave a short bark.

"You're a first rate man-Friday," said the boy laughingly patting him. "I wish I could get you that nice little meat pie in the corner of the window."

"So do I," barked Fox so plainly that the boy's merry laugh rang out upon the morning air. A man standing at a shop door near by was watching him, and as Lucien moved on, accosted him. "Walk in, young gentleman," he said "and let me take your measure. We can make you any kind of a garment, and our prices are always satisfactory."

Pleased to be so politely spoken to, the child thanked the man, saying that his clothes were quite new, but that he might perhaps need something later, and as the shopkeeper had been so polite he'd be sure to come back to him for it. This, in its turn, pleased the shopkeeper, who paid the little boy many parting compliments.

Further on, a man selling canes asked Lucien to buy his wares. He, too, was very polite, though the boy did not buy anything. Being treated so civilly was balm to the child's spirit, but he was getting very tired, and looked about for a quiet place to rest. The entrance courts of the large houses attracted him, but he passed a good many before he took courage to enter one.

Finally, one big house caught his eye. It had a beautiful court. There was a broad marble step, like a low seat, running around three sides of it, cushioned with crimson velvet carpet. In the center of the court the spray from a fountain fell with a musical tinkle into a marble basin, in which birds were dipping and fluttering, scattering jewels as they shook off the water. Beautiful plants and soft turf surrounded the basin, and as Lucien gazed in, the desire to enter and rest awhile became irresistible. He walked in and threw himself at full length upon the soft carpet, giving a sigh of satisfaction as he did so. In another moment he would have been asleep had not the concierge's door flown open, and a sharp-faced woman confronted him. He sat up affrighted, suddenly recalling his adventures with the other woman the previous day.

"What are you doing here, I should like to know?" this woman demanded.

Lucien did not look like a vagrant and she hesitated at first to treat him as such. Fox growled. "Be quiet, Sir," said the boy putting his arm around him. "I came in to rest awhile, the sun is so hot on the street," he replied to the woman.

"Why don't you go home then?" she asked.

"I haven't any home."

"Oh!" said the woman, enlightened, "fine feathers don't make fine birds, it seems."

Lucien smiled, thinking she was talking about the bathing birds. The concierge undeceived him.

"Well, young man, you can't stay here. It's my orders to keep away loafers, so take your dog and trot."

The boy arose without a word, and with Fox in his arms, passed under the archway into the street. Poor child! He was learning hard lessons.

Presently he stopped before the same pastry shop, his mouth watering at sight of the good things in the window. Fox squirmed in his arms and whined when he saw them. The sleek proprietor, who evidently fared well upon his own stock in trade, came to the door and asked Lucien obsequiously what he could do for him. With flushing face, the child said he was hungry. "Come in, come in, and help yourself, young gentleman," replied the man, waving his hand toward the array of good things inside.

"But I haven't any money, Sir," returned the child, fast learning wisdom.

"That's another matter," said the man coldly.

They were already in the shop, Lucien having entered when invited to do so.

"I've been deserted in this big city, Sir," he was saying to the man, "and I'm tired and hungry."

"That's nothing to me," was the curt reply. "Here take that, and be off," tossing a penny across the counter. It fell upon the floor, where the child let it lie.

"I'm not a beggar. I didn't ask for your money," he cried indignantly, as he rushed out into the street.

Across the way was a row of empty chairs. He went across and seated himself upon one. Instantly a woman's hand was held out to him.

"What do you want?" he asked in surprise.

"You're for having some fun, I suppose. I want two cents for the use of that chair," the woman replied.

"What? You don't mean that I can't sit down on an empty chair without paying?"

"Of course you can't; two cents if you please."

"I haven't a cent to my name," answered the boy.

"Then sit on the ground," said the woman giving the chair such a jerk that the child was glad to jump out of it.

"If you can't afford a chair, come and sit here," said a youthful voice with a provincial accent.

Turning about, Lucien saw, sitting upon the steps of a restaurant, a grimy boy holding a monkey on his knee. He went toward him. "You seem to be down on your luck; what's the matter?" said the boy.

"Matter enough," replied Lucien petulantly. "I wish I were on a desert island."

The other boy showed his fine teeth in a broad grin.

"Nice pickle a young one like you'd be in on a desert island," he said, "you'd starve to death. And where would you sleep? Tell me that, will you?"

"It looks as though I'd starve to death here," returned Lucien ruefully, "and it's as bad about sleeping. Did you ever read Robinson Crusoe?"

"Can't read. Who is he?"

"Oh, there's a whole book about him," and Lucien went on giving the boy an outline of the story.

"Fiddlesticks!" interrupted the gamin, "that ain't a true story. How could he do all those things alone on a desert island?"

"For my part," replied Lucien, "I'd rather be alone on an island than in this cruel city full of people."

"You talk like a dunce!" exclaimed the other.

"Dunce indeed!" retorted Lucien. "I don't think you're very polite."

The other boy grinned, and gave Fox a fillip for sniffing at the monkey.

"If I were on a desert island," continued Lucien, I could go where I liked, and find a nice place to rest when I was tired. Crusoe had everything he needed on his island, and nobody bothered him."

"I guess you're right there," said the smutty-faced boy with a loud guffaw. "Everybody to his taste. I'll take Paris every time, I will."

"Why?" inquired Lucien, who knew only the seamy side of the city.

"Because a feller can get work and earn money here."

"Work? Do you work? I don't believe you're any older than I am".

"I'm twelve," answered the boy. "How do you suppose I live if I don't work?" he asked grinning again.

"I don't know. What do you do?" Lucien asked.

"Sweep chimneys, when I can get it to do, and exhibit this monkey between times. I make a lot out of him."

"Why couldn't I work, too?" said Lucien gravely.

"I've no objection," laughed the sweep.

"But what could I do?" asked Lucien of this youth of superior worldly wisdom.

"You couldn't be a sweep," replied the boy, looking the other over with a critical eye, "you'd spoil those fine clothes. I guess your mother and father would have something to say about that."

"I'm an orphan," said Lucien softly.

"Haven't you got any home?" inquired the sweep, staring at him.

"No, have you?"

"Yes. My home is in the country."

"So was mine, but my cousin brought me here and deserted me. Why did you leave your home in the country? Did somebody desert you, too?"

"No indeed," returned the sweep laughing. "My folks are poor and we all have to work for our living. I came to Paris with my big brother. He's a floor polisher. He makes lots of money."

"Does he give you any?"

"Not much! He sends it home. I earn my own money."

"Perhaps I could, too, if I had a monkey like that."

"You've got a nice dog, haven't you? Dogs like that know a lot. If you'd teach him tricks, he'd help you to make a living. Teach him to beg, first thing. Here, this way," said the boy making Fox sit up and hold his old cap in his mouth. The boys laughed together. The sweep tossed a copper into the cap.

"You didn't mean him to beg for money, did you"" cried Lucien distressed.

"Certain!" replied the other promptly. "How do you expect to make a living without money? You're a green one, you are. Look here, do you see this fine restaurant? Lots of rich folks come here to dine. Now you give your dog your cap to hold and send him among them, and make him sit up and beg. You'll get rich, you will," said the sweep, warming to the subject. "I shouldn't be telling you about this place, but they won't let my monkey in any more since he bit a waiter who was teasing him."

"That's too bad," said Lucien sympathetically.

"Oh, I know lots of other places. Now you just work this one. You're such a fancy looking chap, they'll all give you something. There's nothing to be afraid of; nobody's going to eat you," he added, seeing the strained look on Lucien's face.

Before the latter could collect himself to speak, the sweep sprang up, giving the monkey a toss upon his shoulder.

"Hullo yourself!" he shouted to the call of a big boy down the street. "That's my brother, he wants me. Good bye, I wish you luck," he said to Lucien as he ran off to join the older boy. They disappeared in the crowd, and Lucien was alone again.

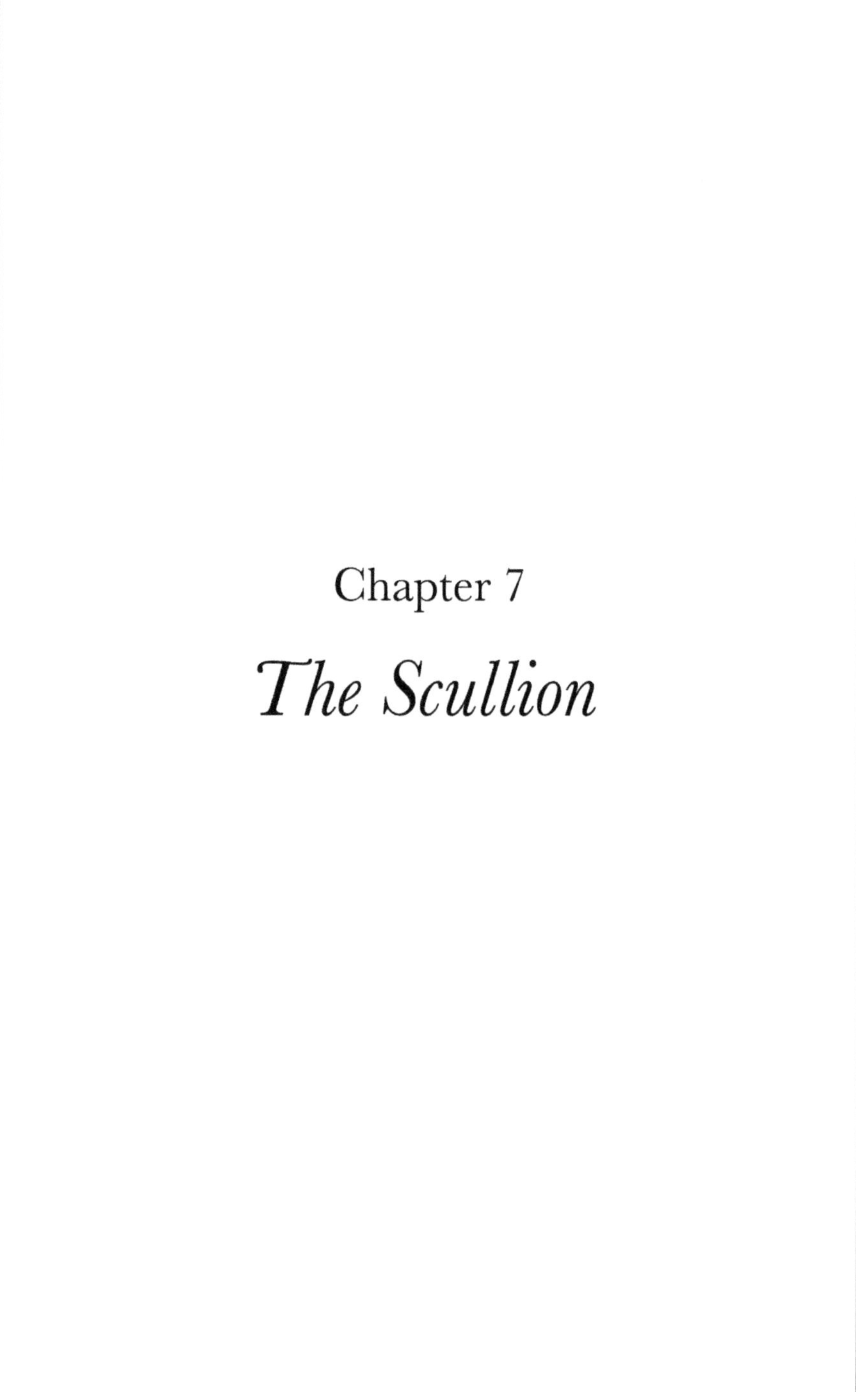

Chapter 7

The Scullion

He was now dodging about under the tables quite unperceived, devouring greedily every morsel the cooks let fall.

We're still here!
Provence
des Italiens B. Mont
tre B.Poissonn
Royal
39
76

Glad of a resting place, Lucien drew into the corner of the step, holding Fox, who seemed quite as tired as he was himself.

They both fell asleep, and it was late in the afternoon when the boy was aroused by a rude shake. One of the waiters from the restaurant had discovered him. "Wake up, child," said he, "What are you doing here?"

"Nothing," answered Lucien drowsily.

"Clear out then."

"What harm can I do sitting here?" the child asked wearily.

"Come, clear out," repeated the man roughly. "You can't stay here under foot at dinner time. Be off."

Lucien stood up, feeling weak and stiff. He and Fox looked at one another as much as to say, "Where shall we go now?" They had gone only a few steps when they passed an open door to a dark passageway. Warm air could be felt blowing gently from the passage, and without warning Fox darted through it and disappeared. Not daring to follow him into the black tunnel, Lucien stood calling him in despair.

In the meantime, the dog's keen snout had led him straight to the restaurant's kitchen, to which this passageway was the entrance. He was now dodging about under the tables quite unperceived, devouring greedily every morsel the cooks let fall. As he grew bolder, he ran in and out among them, lapping from their very boots the gravy they slopped over in their hasty serving.

Presently, a busy little scullion caught sight of him. "Hullo! Whose dog are you?" said he. Fox ran up to him eagerly.

"Poor doggie! Are you hungry?" said the boy patting him.

"Here," said one of the cooks to the scullion, "throw out this piece of chicken and wash this dish. Be quick about it."

Fox began prancing, and sniffing at the dish, which contained a nice, juicy chicken leg. "Do you want it so bad?" asked the boy kindly. "Take it then." With that the boy tossed the tasty piece to the dog. Fox catching it deftly, rushed from the room with it in his mouth.

"Greased lightning, he is!" said the gaping scullion, whose memory required a sharp jog from the cook to remind him to wash the dish.

Fox was already beside Lucien, whom he found crouching outside bemoaning his loss. He dropped the chicken into the boy's outstretched hand, and sat up bright-eyed looking at him. "Eat it, I got it on purpose for you," he seemed to say, but the child was so thankful to have him back again that he had not looked at the chicken.

"Oh! Fox, you haven't been stealing, have you?" he cried, when he saw what it was. Fox barked, and looked at him so reproachfully that Lucien ought to have understood him, but he didn't. Dogs find children very stupid sometimes.

"Why, Fox..." said the boy, as he examined the chicken, "I don't believe any of the people in the restaurant have got a better bit of chicken than this on their plates. I wish I knew where you got it. Perhaps somebody gave it to you," he added more cheerfully. "I might as well eat it, I suppose; I'm so hungry," and he bit into it with relish.

Fox jumped about him with evident pleasure, but refused to touch any of the chicken when Lucien offered to share it with him.

"You seem to have dined," said the child laughing. "I hope your dinner was as good as this! This chicken is fine but I wish I had some bread too."

Hardly were the words uttered before the dog darted through the door and disappeared down the dark passageway. This time Lucien was not so fearful of losing him, and he was not surprised when Fox reappeared with a roll in his mouth.

"Oh, you dear little Fox!" cried the boy, hugging him. "It's just like a story book. I'm Robinson Crusoe and you're my man-Friday, after all. What should I do without you?"

Fox was sure he didn't know, but he didn't say so. He caught the chicken bone, and after he had gnawed it clean, made Lucien laugh by the way he tossed and worried it. It doesn't take much to please children and dogs sometimes: in this case relief from hunger did the trick.

"I wish I had a drink!" Lucien exclaimed presently. "They say fish swim twice, but that's nothing to what chicken and dry bread do," he said laughing and supposing himself to be talking to Fox, but as he looked for him, he found him gone again.

"I declare, he must have understood me when I said I was thirsty. Why, yes, it was he who found the way to the fountain last night," said Lucien, watching with interest for the dog's reappearance.

This time he did not come back alone. When the child heard heavy footsteps coming through the passageway, and Fox keeping time to them in happy little barks, Lucien's first thought was that the person from whom the dog had probably pilfered the food was coming out to see who had eaten it. He was so frightened at first that he could not lift his eyes. When he finally did so, he discovered, to his relief, that the dog's companion was the moonfaced scullion who carried a bowl of water. "Well what do you want me to do with this here?" he said to Fox when they reached the door. The dog began dancing around Lucien. The boy had not seen him before.

"Oh, ho! Young master, so it was for you this dog wanted victuals and drink, was it? How funny!" he cried, laughing so hard that Lucien would have had no drink if he had not taken the bowl out of the boy's unsteady hands.

"I hope you don't mind my dog sharing his dinner with me," said Lucien in a shaky voice. He was not yet over his fright and the bowl he was eagerly raising to his lips showed his own hands to be unsteady.

"No, no," replied the older boy, "but it's too good to keep to yourself. He's a cute one, he is; I wish he was mine. I'd exhibit him, I would," he said fondling Fox, who evidently regarded him as a friend. "I must go and tell the others," he added, hurrying into the kitchen with the empty bowl.

He was back in a moment with a white-aproned crowd at his heels. Then began a rain of questions upon Lucien. He answered them as best he might, and in his turn, asked if they were angry.

"No, no," replied one of the men kindly, "but what is a little gentleman like you doing here, and so hungry?"

Lucien repeated his story. In the midst of their excited comments, a bell struck, and the men hurried back to their work. The young scullion lingered a moment longer than the rest to speak to Lucien.

"Wait here till I come back," said the scullion, who then turned and disappeared into the inky tunnel.

"Dear little Fox," said Lucien, caressing the dog; "it is all your doing. If I hadn't taken care of you when you were hurt, I shouldn't have had a place to sleep in last night, nor any dinner today. I love you, dear old doggie, and I mean to never to part from you."

Fox was rolling about at the boy's feet, giving grunts of satisfaction, as if he understood this all perfectly well.

"If I only knew how to find work, Fox, we'd be all right, but I don't. Robinson Crusoe didn't need any money; that's the best part of a desert island, but you certainly do here. Oh, dear, I wish I wasn't always thinking that perhaps my cousin was joking after all, and expecting him to come and take me home. You'd love the dear old house and garden, Fox, and my pony," said Lucien beginning to cry, but hearing steps in the passageway, he hastily dried his tears.

The heavy footsteps stopped as the young scullion appeared with an old covered basket in his hands.

"Are you very fond of your dog?" he asked abruptly.

"Fond of my dog?" repeated Lucien slowly. "I should say so! Why he's all I've got in the world."

"Then you'd better get away from here as quick as you can. The head cook has taken such a shine to that dog that he's coming out here, the minute he's free, to get him."

"What to steal him?" cried Lucien.

"He wouldn't call it stealing, but he'd have your dog, all the same. Might makes right too often in this world. It's easy to see that you're pretty green, but never mind," said the boy noticing the distressed look in Lucien's eyes. "Here, take this basket and run. There's enough in it to keep you from starving tomorrow."

"Thank you, and God bless you," said Lucien, taking the boy's rough red hand in his for a friendly shake. Then, seizing Fox and the basket, he hurried around the corner, where they disappeared among the throng of evening loungers.

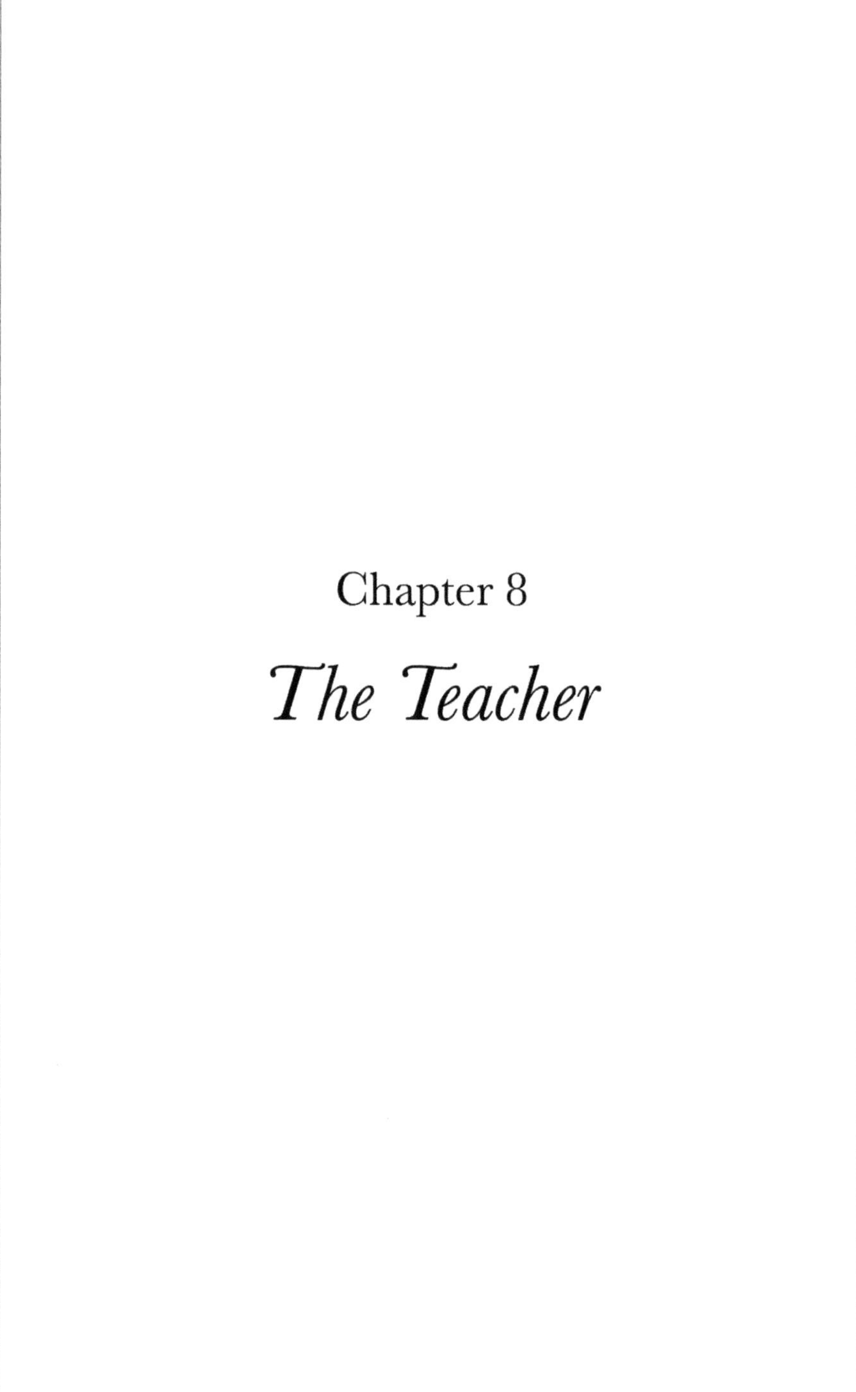

Chapter 8
The Teacher

Where's Lucien?
(Turn the page to see.)

JUNE 24, 1814.

to liberty all persons, who from attachment to their ancient and legitimate Sovereign, have been imprisoned until this moment.

You will be so obliging, Monsieur le Baron, as to cause this letter to be inserted in all the newspapers.

(Signed) The Count of NESSELRODE.

His Excellency the Governor of Paris, informed that several communes have desired Russian Officers wounded, to permit them to afford them the attentions and care which humanity demands, accepts with gratitude these benevolent dispositions. His Excellency authorizes, in consequence, M. Viguel, the Director of the Russian Hospitals, to give a favorable reception to requests of this kind. M. Viguel lives in the street of the Capucines, No. 16.

The wounded Officers who shall be attended in the communes must be careful to prevent every kind of disorder, and to sup-

(Signed) SACKEN.

Chatillon on the Seine, 16th March.

When they had returned to their work the old soldier produced a file of old newspapers. "Now I'm ready to hear about my battles, little one," he said.

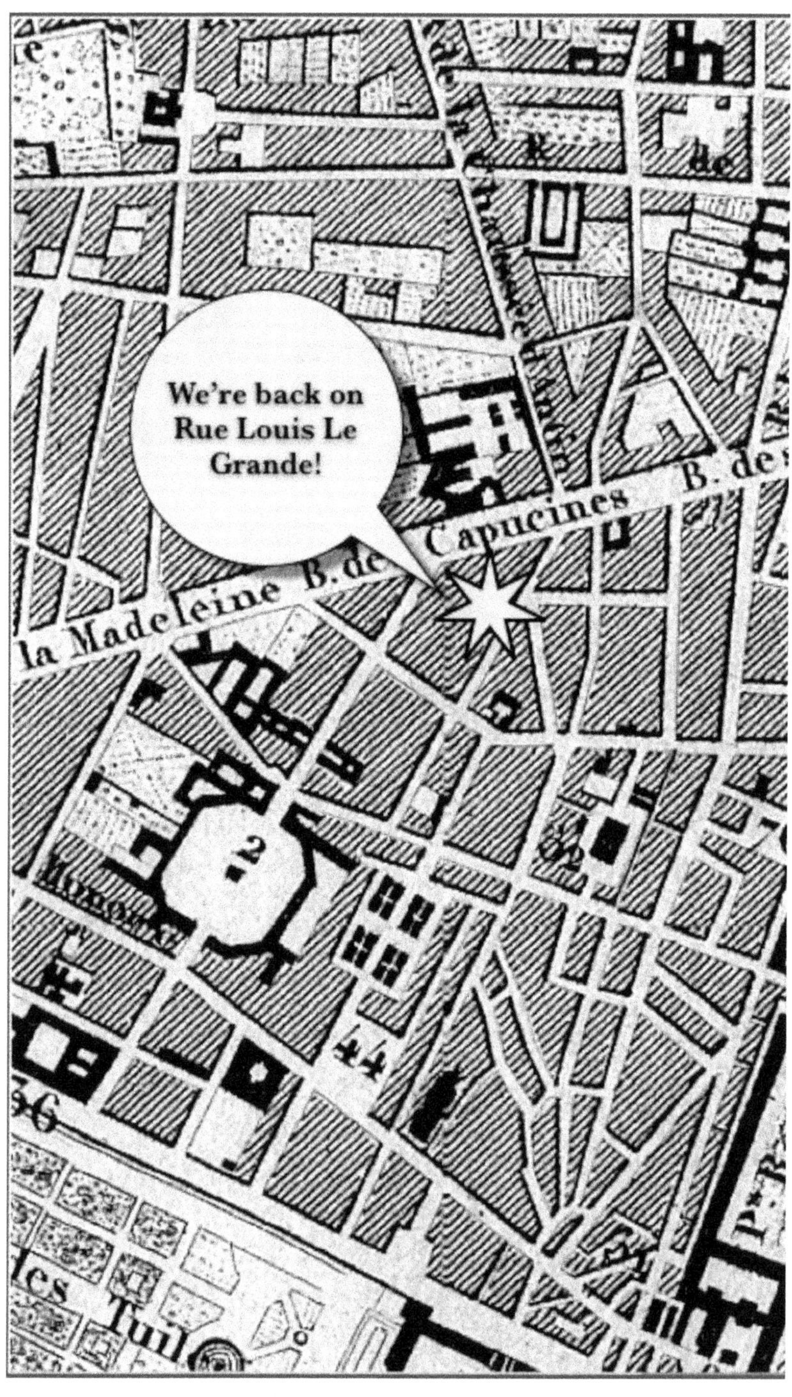
We're back on
Rue Louis Le
Grande!
la Madeleine B. de Capucines B. de

Lucien was so tired, as he threaded his way among the crowds on the streets that evening that he felt sure he must have wandered far and wide over the whole city since morning. Truth be told, he had been wandering in a circle, and was at no time far from the new house guarded by the old soldier, in which he had passed the previous night.

It was late, when the child and the dog, both footsore and weary, strayed onto Louis Le Grand Street and found themselves in front of the dark, unfinished house. Unfinished or not, it was like meeting a good friend. He ran up and knocked upon the loose boards that filled the doorway. The old soldier's familiar, "Who goes there?" rattled out from behind the boards.

"Oh, it's you is it?" the old man said when he heard Lucien's voice, and Fox's friendly bark. He hurried to remove the planks blocking the door and let them in. "What makes you so late, child?" asked the old man. "I expected you long ago."

"Expected me?" exclaimed the boy lighting up, grateful to even be remembered.

"Of course," answered Father La Tuile, as, with Lucien's help, he replaced the planks. "Where else could you sleep, with no money to pay for a bed? But come along, your's is ready, and here's a bite of supper for you," said the old man pointing to a neat little spread on top of a barrel. A piece of clean paper served for a table cloth.

"Oh, thank you, Father" said the child much touched by this fresh evidence that he was expected, "but I've got some supper here," holding up the basket as he spoke.

"Keep it for morning child, and eat this. Sit right down to it," said the old man, rolling up two empty nail kegs for seats for them both. "While you are eating, you can explain to me why you refused the work the builder offered you this morning. You were in the right the way you talked to him but that's no way to get work to do."

"I know it, Sir, but my uncle wouldn't want me to be a servant. He wasn't educating me for that."

"A body must eat and drink, and have clothes to wear, that's about all I know," returned the old soldier, "and I don't see that an education helps you to that."

"Oh, yes, it does," began Lucien, who, now he was getting rested and refreshed, wanted to talk, and was ready to pass on to Father La Tuile the arguments in favor of an education, which he had so often heard discussed by his uncle and his tutor.

The old man cut him short, though not unkindly, by saying, "if you've finished your supper, we'll go to bed, and talk in the morning. I'm tired and sleepy," he added with a loud yawn. In truth, although it verged on midnight, he had not been able to close his eyes for thinking of this child wandering about the streets alone, and perhaps coming to harm.

"Mind you set the little dog to watch," he said to Lucien as he hobbled behind the curtain. "The good Lord watches, but, I'll take a brave dog any day."

"If he's half as tired as I am," laughed the boy, "I'm afraid nothing short of a cannon shot would wake him."

"Tut, tut, child, what do you know about cannon shots? Just wait till you've been in a battle, helping good souls on to their reward; then you can talk! As for my Austerlitz, he was never too tired to have one eye open to keep watch for me," growled the old soldier from his pallet.

Lucien tumbled into the straw with a cheerful laugh. Fox cuddled up close to him, and in a few moments, they were all asleep.

Early next morning, when the workmen appeared, they welcomed Lucien as an old friend. He asked them with diffidence if they would teach him to work.

"What of the builder?" asked one laughing.

"I suppose I'd have to hide when he came," replied the boy with an answering smile.

"You're not strong enough for our kind of work," said one of the masons.

"But I must live," persisted Lucien.

"That's true, but you would have to pay to be apprenticed to our trade, and you have no money."

"No, I haven't any money but if you would teach me to work, I would teach you what I know."

"And what do you know?"

"Let me think," began the child; "I can play the violin."

"That's no use to us," interrupted one of the men, "What else can you do?

"I can write."

"That's no good," replied the mason, "I can't even read."

"Very well then, I'll teach you to read and you can teach me your trade."

"Listen to that!" exclaimed the old soldier with pride. "There's a smart one for you. When I was young, it never entered my head to teach anyone how to read. For that matter, I never knew how myself".

"I'd be glad to teach you, Sir," said Lucien quickly.

"Can't teach an old dog new tricks," returned the old man with a laugh. "But perhaps you might read to me. It would hearten me up to hear about the battles of my Emperor."

"Yes, indeed, I'll read whatever you want me to," said the boy.

"A fine idea, comrades!" cried one of the men. "This chap isn't strong enough for a mason but what's to hinder his giving us reading lessons when we're resting. We can give him his meals, and Father La Tuile his lodging." So it was settled.

At noon Lucien gave his first lesson using his Robinson Crusoe for a text book, and reading a little of it aloud to his class, to whom it was new, and very entertaining.

When they had returned to their work the old soldier produced a file of old newspapers. "Now I'm ready to hear about my battles, little one," he said. "That's what I like."

With a smile, Lucien asked, "You don't want me to read about those where our side got beaten, do you?"

"Yes, yes, read everything. Even though the tide of battle was against us, those were good old times. I'd give my other leg to live them over again!" Father La Tuile cried with enthusiasm.

Although the boy did his best to put spirit into his voice as he read the long-drawn newspaper accounts of almost forgotten events, he could not help laughing to see how soon the old soldier was nodding off.

Many days passed this way in this uneventful routine, Lucien giving his lessons or reading aloud when the masons or Father La Tuile could listen. When the builder appeared, he and Fox slipped away till he was gone. They had plenty of play time, and the boy was gaining in health and strength, due in no small measure to him helping the builders with their lugging, when he could. As for Fox, he quickly regained his strength, but also was gaining in other ways, for he had all these new friends, besides a lot of new accomplishments taught him by his young master. But, best of all, he had his freedom to go and come as he pleased - although he would never go far without Lucien by his side.

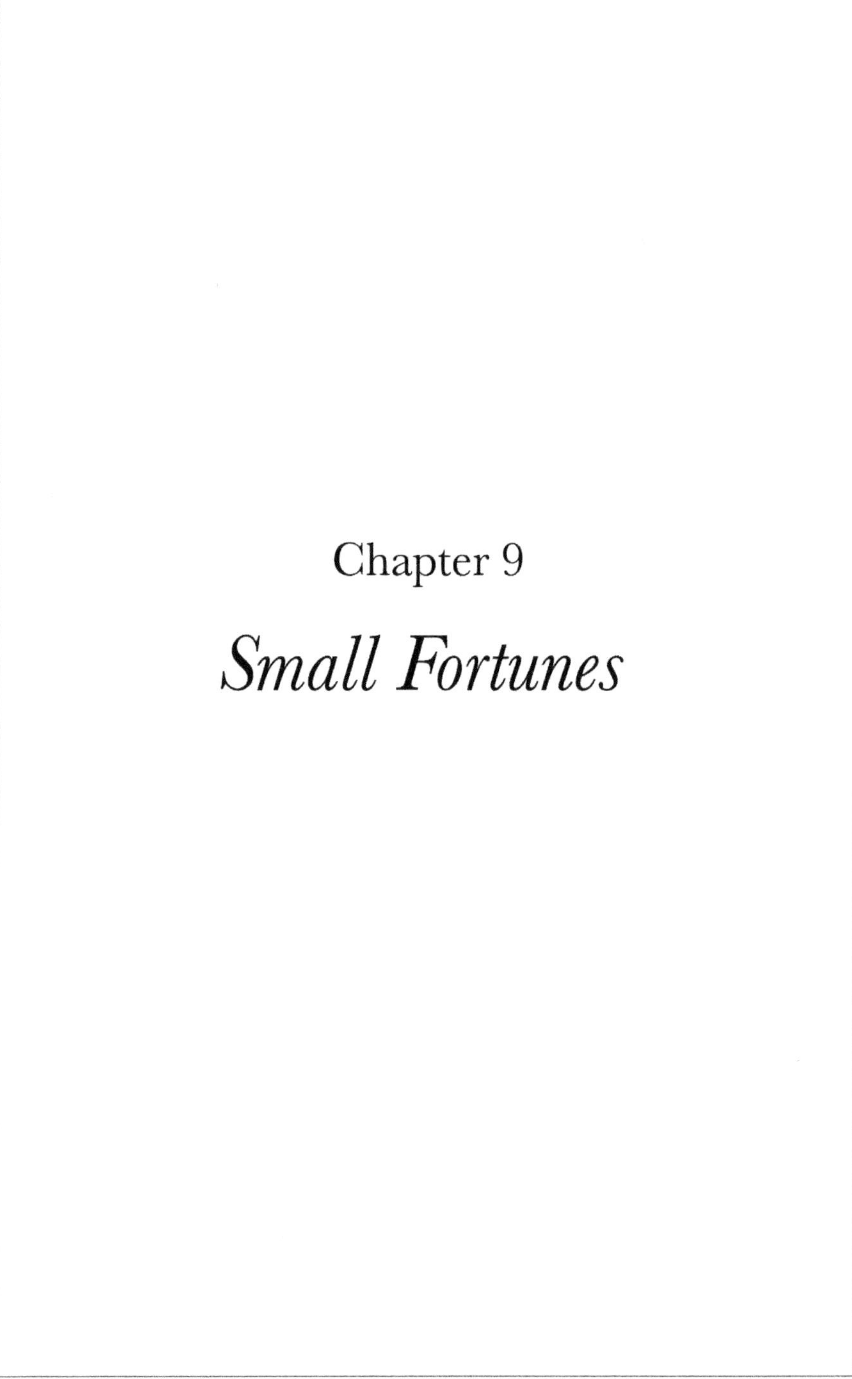

Chapter 9

Small Fortunes

Where's Lucien?
(Turn the page to see.)
That settled, he put on a brave front while bidding them good-bye, but it was a very desolate little boy who walked back through the Arc d'Etoile.

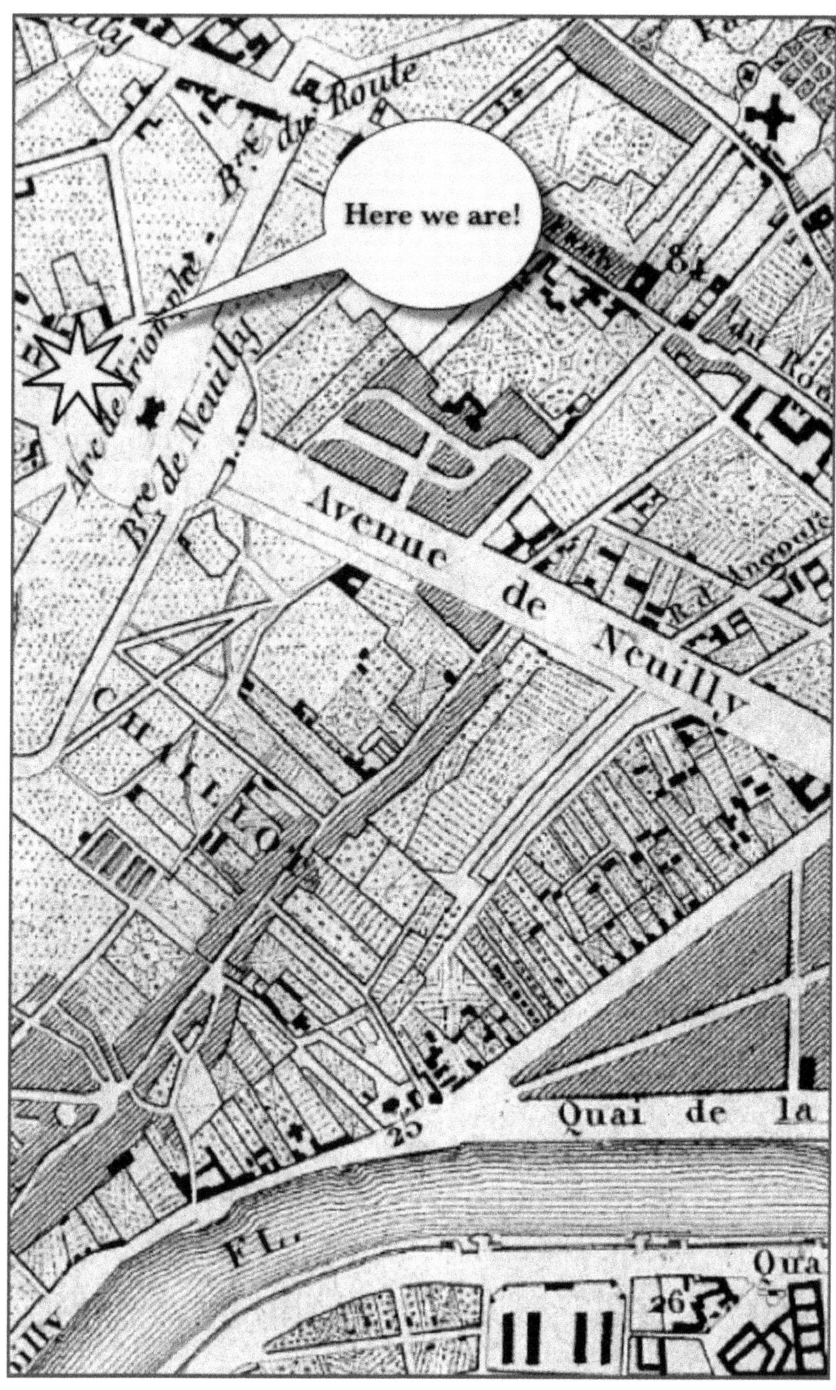
Here we are!
Avenue de Neuilly
Quai de la
25
26

The work of the masons upon the new house was rapidly approaching completion. Lucien knew that the home was almost ready for the fine carpenters to begin their work, but it had not entered his head that the entrance of a new set of workmen meant the departure of his friends, the masons. So, when on one fine Sunday morning when the masons appeared in holiday attire, with their walking canes and bundles, saying they had come to bid him good-bye, Lucien was shocked and surprised.

"Good bye?" cried the boy in bewilderment. "Why, where are you going?" he asked mechanically shaking the hands they held out to him.

"We're going home to see our people first, and then we've got a job of work to do in Lyons," replied one of the men.

"Why didn't you tell me?" asked Lucien, much distressed by this sudden severing of their pleasant relations.

No one answered. In fact, the men were sorry to part from the boy, and none of them had had the courage to speak of it to him.

"I'll tell you what, boys," said one of the masons presently, "we're out on a lark today and don't expect to start on our journey right off; what's to hinder our giving the little chap a good time before we go? Let's take him with us now, and bring him back this afternoon."

"Agreed!" they cried in chorus.

"Hold on, I've got something to say to that," said the old soldier, to whom Lucien had been reading when the men came up.

Lucien and Fox were dancing about in a hurry to be off, but the boy stood still to listen as Father La Tuile said to the masons, "If you take the boy, you must see him safe home again, and mind you, he gets no liquor to drink, and you mustn't take him where you wouldn't take your own little brothers."

"All right!" answered the workmen laughing. "Come along, little schoolmaster, and don't forget Fox."

"Wait a minute," said the old soldier, as he began turning Lucien about and looking him over with a critical eye. "He must pass inspection before he goes. "Why, bless me, child, you've got on a clean shirt, where did you get it?" he asked. "Did you wash it yourself?"

"No Sir, I don't know how to wash. I paid to have it done up."

"Paid! What do you mean?"

"I shelled peas and prepared vegetables for a laundress who was good enough to wash my clothes for me," replied the boy.

"Good then! I think you'll do!" exclaimed the old man heartily. "Be off, and a good time to you," he added patting the child's shoulder fondly. "Don't be out late, and take good care of him," he said to the masons, with a full measure of paternal concern.

"Trust us for that," they called back, as they started off with Lucien and Fox in tow.

To their questions as to what he had already seen of Paris, the former answered with a smile, "Very little except

Louis Le Grand Street, and the Boulevard where the Café is. Oh, yes, and the Tuileries," he added with a sigh.

"Isn't that where you were deserted? Should you like to go there and see the place?" asked one of the men.

"No, no!" cried the boy in sudden distress. "I never want to set eyes on it again."

"How about the Champs Elysees?" asked one of the masons.

"Yes, yes, let's go there," Lucien answered eagerly.

"The very thing," they all agreed, and arm in arm, with the boy in their midst, the masons sauntered along the Avenue Champs Elysees till they reached the Arc d'Etoile. Talking and laughing together they quite forgot Lucien. He was lagging behind now, for he found himself far less at home with these friendly masons in holiday dress and manners than when associating with them at their work. Their talk was all about their friends and families, whom they expected to see in a day or two. Each seemed to know the others' sisters and female cousins, and sweethearts as well. The girls names seemed to fill the air, held there by endless streams of compliment and flattery. Lucien didn't know quite what to make of it. He thought they must be very upstanding girls, but he got awfully tired of hearing about them.

It made him lonesome, and drawing in Fox's leash, he caught the dog up and held him close to assure himself that he had a living, loving friend all his own. "Listen to them, Fox," he whispered half crying, "they've all got somebody who cares for them, but I'm all alone." The dog, feeling his emotion, said by his affectionate demonstrations as plainly as if he had spoken, "I love you, dear little master. How can you be alone when you have me?"

"Yes, that's so, and I'm very happy for it," answered Lucien, who understood him perfectly, and was ashamed to seem so ungrateful. He wiped his eyes and hurried to catch up with the masons, giving Fox the length of the string whenever there was a chance for him to take a run or a roll on the grass.

When the masons had set out in the morning they had fully intended to begin their journey immediately after taking leave of Father La Tuile and Lucien: hence their bundles and staffs. The sight of the boy's surprise and distress had caused them to change their plans. They impulsively proposed giving their little teacher the "day's pleasure" they had talked of. It was a mistake all around, as such hastily formed schemes often turn out to be.

After the men had taken a drink at a saloon on the way, they became loud and boisterous in their talk and poor Lucien felt quite out of his element among them. He still trudged in their wake, because he did not know what else to do. Besides, he thought their feelings might be hurt if he should ask them to take him home to Father La Tuile.

Near the Arc d'Etoile, they filed into a cheap restaurant and began noisily giving orders for their midday meal. They gave Lucien the seat of honor at one of the tables, and laughed uproariously to see Fox leap into a vacant chair on his left. The sight and smell of the hot food put fresh courage into the boy, and he laughed and chatted happily with the rest.

"Eat your fill, little schoolmaster," one of the workmen said kindly, "it's a long walk back to the new house." "Fill up the dog, too," added a comrade, "dogs are always hungry."

"That's so!" barked Fox, whose greedy catching of morsels tossed to him called forth renewed peals of laughter from the half-tipsy masons.

Wine flowed freely, and, for a time, the men became steadily more hilarious, but after awhile, Lucien looked on in dismay to see one after another settling to sleep on their stiff chairs, or with their heads bowed upon the table.

Nobody had said a word about leaving, and as he looked at these men now, they seemed so unlike the friendly masons, with whom he had set forth in the morning, that he could not muster courage to question any of them. Before they all fell asleep, he had gone to the door several times and looked out, but no one took any notice of his restlessness except Fox, who was becoming very uneasy himself. He kept running in and out, and sniffing at the masons, but they were too drowsy to notice his restlessness either.

So the day wore on till lights began to twinkle away among the trees of the Champs Elysees, and in distant buildings. At last the landlord, finding that he was getting no more orders from his sleepy guests, brought in lit candles, and began arousing the artisans.

"Come lads, isn't it time you were on your way?" he asked.

"It is that," answered one of the masons, stretching and yawning. "Come on boys."

They paid their score, and then, still only half-awake, stepped out into the night air, which soon began to revive them.

"It isn't that late, is it?" they cried, at sight of the rising moon.

"Yes, it's awfully late," returned Lucien quickly. "Please take me home: Father La Tuile will be so worried."

"What's that you say?" asked one of the masons in a surly tone?

The boy repeated his request to be taken home.

"Sure enough!" cried one of the men, stupidly scratching his head, "What's to be done boys?"

"I have it, comrades," said another, entirely ignoring him and Lucien. "It's a fine night, and we're already outside the walls: let's start right off for home. We'll be there by sunrise."

"Hear! Hear!" cried the men, tossing up their caps.

"But, what will become of me?" exclaimed Lucien in alarm.

The masons cast puzzled looks his way. "That's easy settled," said one. "Let's pass around the hat for our little schoolmaster."

The child looked on troubled and bewildered, not realizing that the money he heard dropping into the hat had any connection with him. He was only waiting for the hat to finish its round to ask again to be taken home.

"Ten francs," said the foreman counting the collection, "that isn't so bad. Here you are, little one, put that in your pipe and smoke it," he said jocularly, as he tried to thrust the money into Lucien's hand. The hand closed against it, as the boy said indignantly, "I thought you were my friends, and now you treat me like a beggar."

"Nonsense, child," replied the foreman, "didn't you read to us, and teach some of us to read, and try your best to teach some of the men to write?"

"You already paid me for it," answered the child with dignity.

"Just a bite to eat, that's all. You got mighty little for your trouble. We always meant to give you a tip when we went away."

"Look here," put in another workman, "it don't pay to run about with a straw on your shoulder, youngster. You've got to look out for number one, so just take your money and say no more about it."

Lucien, still holding back, looked so much "the little gentleman," which was what they all called him behind his back, that the masons stood looking at him irresolutely. "Oh, come," said one, whom drink had made irritable, "we can't stand here all night. It is time we were off."

"Take the money, child," spoke up another kindly, "and get a cab to take you back to Louis Le Grand Street. It is too far for you to walk at night, and besides, you might get lost."

The foreman stepped close to Lucien and slipped the money into the boy's pocket. "You can't get home without some of it," he said in reply to the child's look of protest.

"Just think that we are giving you a ride. You didn't mind our paying for your dinner."

"That's true," returned Lucien too frightened at the thought of being left alone and penniless in this strange place to refuse further.

That settled, they all shook hands with him, and he put on a brave front while bidding them good bye, but it was a very desolate little boy who walked back through the Arc d'Etoile. Fox pattered beside him with drooping tail and such a dejected hang of the head that his long ears trailed in the dust.

A Fox In Paris

Chapter 10
The Strangers

Where's Lucien?
(Turn the page to see.)
"A odd young one that!" said the puzzled driver. "I guess he's a runaway and I ought to have taken him home, whether or not," added the man, hailing a more promising fare.

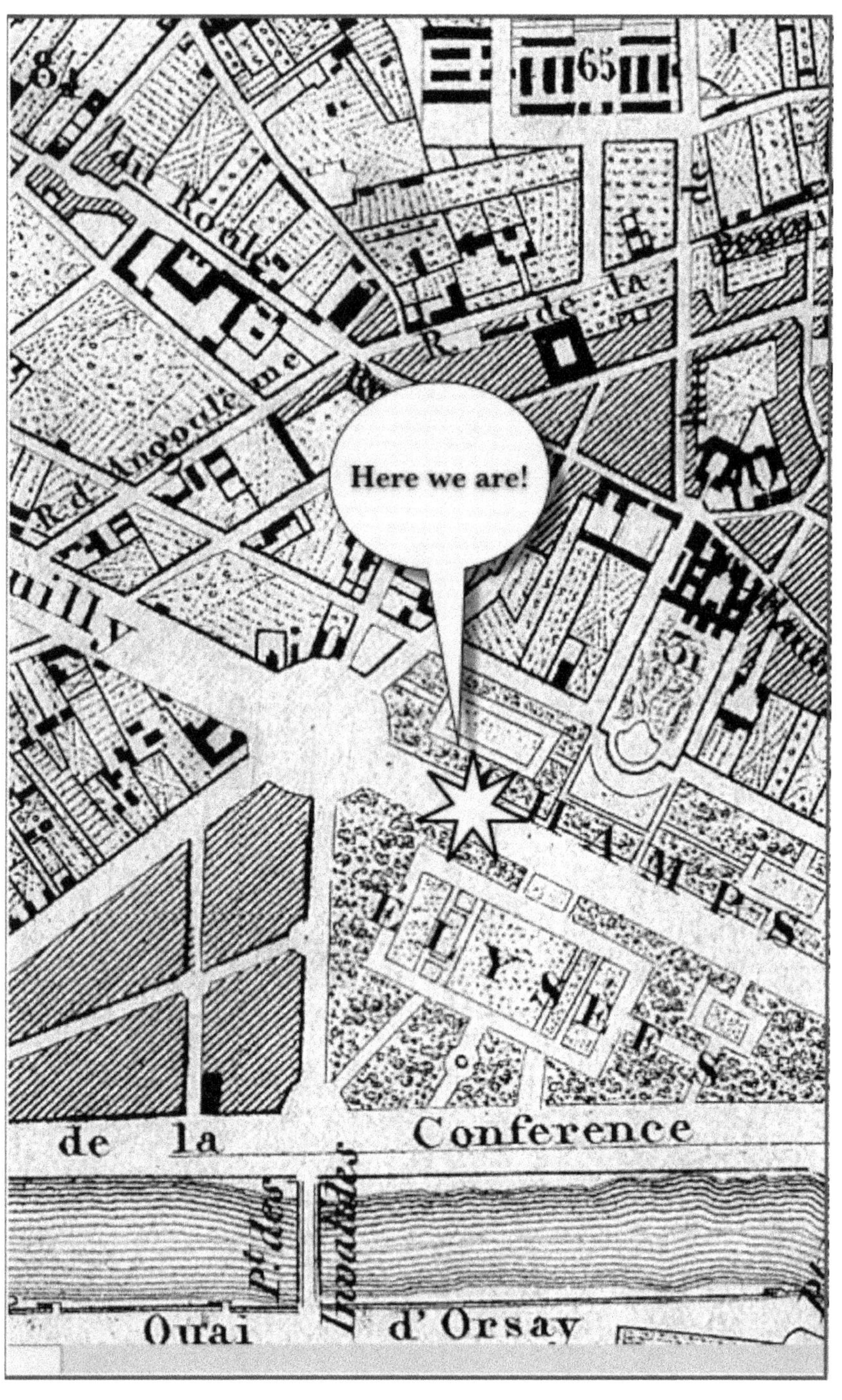
Here we are!
65
du Roule
R. de la
R. d'Angoulême
CHAMPS
ELYSEES
de la Conference
Pt. des Invalides
Quai d' Orsay

The fare to Louis Le Grand Street, when he had learned it from a cabman, seemed to Lucien too wasteful, given his current financial state and that he thought he might so easily walk.

"I could buy Father La Tuile a new pipe and some tobacco with that money," he thought. "It is a fine moonlit night; I can find my way. I'll walk."

"Well, are you coming?" asked the driver impatiently.

"No, I'll walk," Lucien replied.

"I suppose you haven't any money," returned the man quickly. "Never mind that little one; jump in. Your parents will be glad enough to pay my fare, with a good "pour boire" to boot, you bet," he added laughing.

"No, it isn't that," stammered the child, suddenly remembering his talk with the police officer about lost children and prison, and in a panic, lest this man might land him in prison, if he knew the facts, seized Fox in his arms and hurried away.

"An odd young one that!" said the puzzled driver. "I guess he's a runaway, and I ought to have taken him home, whether or no," added the man hailing a more promising fare.

The child was already out of sight.

In the weird shadows cast by the moon and the lights gleaming among the trees, he could find no resemblance to the way so gayly traveled by the masons in the morning. He wished now that, instead of giving way to depression, as he had done after the men began to drink, he had been more alert, and used his eyes better. Do his best, he could recall nothing familiar in his present surroundings. Slackening his pace, he looked anxiously about him. As he did so, Fox, who had been trotting at his heels ever since they got out of sight of the cab driver, gave a growl and sprang in front of him with such suddenness as almost to trip him up.

"Hold on, what's your hurry?" said Lucien pulling the dog's leading string up short. Fox barked, and showing his teeth, growled and bristled. The boy supposed him to be warning some beggar dog, of whom he stood in fear, to keep his distance. "Oh, you silly Fox, what are you afraid of?" he said, stooping to pat the dog.

He was now in a very lonely part of the Champs Elysees, and he was startled, as he straightened up, to find two rough-looking men confronting him. Unknown to the child, he had been followed by this evil-eyed pair from the moment the mason had slipped the money into his pocket.

"Please, young Sir, could you tell me the way to Orleans Street?" asked one in advance the instant Lucien looked up. "I'm a stranger," the man added, affecting a foreign accent.

"So am I," replied the boy frankly, "the only street I know is Louis Le Grand, and I was just going to ask you how to get there."

The second man now stepped forward, saying, "What was it you wanted to know, gentlemen? Perhaps I can be of service."

"I want to find Orleans Street," replied the first speaker, "and this young gentleman is looking for Louis Le Grand Street."

"It's lucky you met me then. Those streets are near together, and I live in that neighborhood. I'm on my way home, and if you will come right along, I'll show you the way. I'm in a bit of a hurry," he added with a hoarse laugh that set Fox growling again.

"You're very kind," answered the second stranger, "I'm a rich American, and I'll pay you well for your trouble. I'm just over here to sell a couple of gold mines. I don't suppose this child has any money. I saw him hail a cab, but he didn't ride."

Lucien, who knew so little of America as to suppose it still inhabited by Indians, was studying the man with much childish curiosity.

"Oh, yes, I've got ten francs," he exclaimed starting, "but I didn't want to spend it on carriage hire."

"Sensible boy!" said the wealthy American. "Have you been long in Paris? I suppose your parents are rich, but how do you happen to be out alone in the evening in so lonely a place as this?"

Lucien briefly told his story. The two men drew aside, and it did not strike the boy as odd that the two professed strangers should link arms, and suddenly become confidential. He overheard them saying something about ten francs and asked quickly what they meant; for some reason, associating it with that sum in his own pocket.

"I was just telling this American gentleman that I'd see you safe home for ten francs," replied the second stranger. Lucien was too polite to say that they could ride for less, but that was what he was thinking. He remained silent, with Fox tugging at his string, as if trying to drag his master out of danger.

"Let's go over there where the lights are so bright, and there are so many people," Lucien said presently.

He was only thinking of buying something to eat at one of the stands, but the men exchanged meaning glances, as he spoke.

"What does it matter?" said one, "It is getting late, and the crowd will soon be gone."

Lucien was puzzled, but he was glad to find them acting upon his suggestion and moving toward the lights, the boisterous crowds, and most importantly to him, food. He led them along apace, wandering among the vendors, trying to decide what he would like. As they walked along, passing an empty by-path, they heard groans. Lucien, pulled forward by the dog, ran toward the sound and came upon an old man lying on the ground.

"Did you fall, Sir?" the boy asked with eager concern.

"Yes, heaven help me! I'm blind and I've lost my way."

"Oh, gentlemen," Lucien cried out to his two companions, "let's take this poor blind man along with us."

"Come along yourself," said one of the strangers, seizing the child by the arm, "it isn't our business to look after every beggar you meet," he added, giving a vicious backward kick at Fox, who was trying to rip his trousers.

"Oh, Sir," said Lucien, shaking off the man's detaining hand, and addressing the supposed American, "You said you were rich; surely you will not refuse to help this poor man. If you can afford to pay this gentleman ten francs to show us the way, couldn't you pay him a little more to see the blind man safely home? I'd be glad to do it for nothing, if I only knew the way," said the boy.

"It is for me to say what I'll do with my own money," retorted the man sharply.

Despite the impatience of his two companions, Lucien lingered beside the blind man.

"Do you live far from here, Sir?" he asked kindly.

"Yes, but that isn't what troubles me, my child," replied the frail old man.

"What then?"

"Come, come, young man, we must be going," said the first stranger brusquely. "The guard will take care of this man. Come along."

"Wait just a minute, Mr. Wealthy American," replied the boy, and then turning to the blind man he asked, "you didn't come here alone did you?"

"Never till today," answered the blind man. "My good, faithful dog always brought me."

"Where is he now?" asked the boy looking around in search of him.

The old blind man sighed deeply, then replied solemnly, "Dead. He got run over by a tram when he was running from a big dog that was chasing him."

"Come, boy, we can't wait for you any longer," said the second stranger crossly, putting out his hand to grasp

Lucien's arm again. The boy dodged, and stepped to the other side of the blind man.

"Just a minute more," he pleaded. "You've been kind enough to want to show me the way home, and you must want to help this poor old man, too. We can't go away and leave him like this." Turning to the blind man, Lucien asked "shall I lead you to a cab, Sir? You could easily ride home."

"No, no, I don't want to go home," the man answered in despairing tones. "Oh, my poor wife and daughter! What shall I do!"

"We've had enough of this," said the first stranger roughly to the boy. "Now you must come with us."

"But, I couldn't go and leave this poor man alone here, gentlemen. I know what it is to be alone and in trouble, but I am not blind like him, thank heaven." "Neither is your arm broken, I hope," moaned the old man.

"Oh, Sir, is yours?"

"It feels like it. I got a bad fall here. I came down on my arm, and I can't move it, it hurts so. It's my right arm, too," wailed the blind man. "How shall I play my violin? Without that, how shall I earn anything to support my family?"

"Your violin?" asked the little boy eagerly. "Did you earn money playing on a violin?"

"Yes, my child. I've played for thirty years, though I only know one tune. Folks are very good to me, though, and everyone gives me something. My wife is a cripple, but she gets a little serving to do, and our girl does what work she can find to do. That is how we manage to live. I've got a son as well," the blind man added in a lower tone of voice, "but he drinks. He's no help to us,"

The strangers had stepped aside and were talking together angrily while the old man was speaking. They glowered at Lucien as, turning a bright face to them, he said with animation, "Why, this old man says he earns money playing the violin, and he is so unhappy because he has hurt his arm so he can't play. He only knows one tune, but I know four, and if you will be good enough to wait a few moments, I'll take his violin over there where all those people are, and see if I can't earn some money for him with my four tunes."

"You're a born idiot!" cried the first stranger, dropping his foreign accent. "We've waited too long for you already. Come right along this minute."

"Why, what good French you speak!" exclaimed the astonished boy.

"My child," said the blind man, "I thank you from my heart for your kindness, but you must do as your guardians say."

"Guardians?" cried Lucien, "they're nothing to me. They offered to show me the way home, that's all. I don't have to go with them unless I want to, and now that I have seen how unkind they can be to a poor blind man like you, I don't want to. Good-bye gentlemen, I'll stay where I am."

"Not much you won't," growled one of the men as they both grabbed at Lucien to pull him away.

At the first sign of threat to his young master, before they could take a step Fox was on them, throwing himself at the legs of the American, and sinking his teeth into the mans ankle. So sudden was the assault that the one man almost lost his balance and to let go of Lucien to keep from falling. As he kicked at the dog to dislodge him, the other man was still working to drag Lucien away with him.

"Let go of me," cried the boy, "or I'll call Murder! Thieves!" In his excitement, he had raised his voice, which rang out shrilly upon the evening air. At its first clear pipe, the men vanished like smoke on a clear day, with Fox right at their heels. Lucien laughed, rubbing the arm where he had been grabbed, as he watched the dog trot happily back to him and the blind man.

"What a brave dog you are Fox," he said, as he scooped him up and hugged him. "Isn't that queer?" he said turning to the blind man. "They have completely disappeared."

"I'm sure your little guardian there gave them pause, but I wonder, have you any money with you, my child?" asked the old man anxiously.

"Yes, ten francs."

"Where is it now?"

"In my pocket, Sir," replied the child, after assuring himself the money was safe.

"Did they know you had it?"

"Yes, I told them."

"That accounts! Those men are thieves. Thank God, dear child, for putting it into your heart to come to my relief. Heaven only knows what evil fate might have overtaken you and your dog, but for your kind heart."

Lucien turned pale. "Thieves!" he exclaimed, "Oh Sir, perhaps they'll come back! Let's go over near those people; it is so dark and lonely here. I'll do my best to help you." And he did.

The old man groaned as he finally rose stiffly to his feet, "My arm. I am afraid it must be broken."

Lucien picked up the violin which, luckily was not injured by the fall, but he would not have found the bow, had not Fox sniffed it out where it had fallen among some shrubbery. When he had them both, he took the old man by his left hand, and called Fox, who was using his free time for a frolic on the cool grass.

"Is this your dog?" asked the old man eagerly, as Fox ran up and began jumping upon him in friendly fashion.

"Yes, indeed. I wish you could see him, Sir, he's so cute. It's very strange the way he takes to you: he did not like those two men at all. But what in the world has he got in his mouth?" Lucien had not observed that the blind man was bareheaded.

"Why I do believe it is your cap, and he knows it," said the child taking the cap from the dog's mouth, and giving it to the old man.

"Dogs know more than people think," said the latter. "He likes me because he sees that I am your friend."

Seeing Fox sitting up with the cap in his mouth had put a new idea into Lucien's head, and made him inattentive to what his companion was saying.

They walked for a moment in silence, then the blind man asked, "Did you say you lived on Louis Le Grand Street?"

"Yes, Sir."

"Then you'll get home all right. I live near there myself, and when my girl comes to fetch me home, she will show you the way. But you haven't told me how you came to be so far from home in the evening."

Lucien told his story, as they ambled slowly toward the Café Des Ambassadours, and the blind man, in his turn, told him something more of his own troubles. "If I don't take home twenty-six francs tonight," he said, "we shall be turned out of our only home tomorrow. That is why I was feeling so terribly when you found me: I thought I should never be able to earn anything more. My poor wife is paralyzed, and my daughter, Marie, knows nothing but trouble for our sake."

As they drew near the crowd of pleasure seekers, Lucien began to feel very timid about playing for them, and he tried his best to think only of the blind man's great need, but it seemed as if his last measure of courage was ebbing out at his toes when the old man whispered, "Here's the place to play, stop here. There are children close by, I hear them laughing, and they are our best friends."

"Why so?" asked the boy wishing to gain time.

"Because children love music, and they don't know whether it's good or bad."

"Thank you," replied Lucien laughing, "I see you think I don't know how to play." The old man smiled absently, "Now begin," said he, listening nervously as the child drew the bow across the strings.

"What are they laughing at?" he asked in Lucien's ear.

"My dog," answered the boy, laughing to himself in spite of the stage-fright that had him in its grip.

"What's he doing?" asked the blind man anxiously. "You mustn't let him take people's attention away from the music."

"No danger of that" replied Lucien, as he was trying to tune the old violin. "He is sitting right in front of me with my cap in his mouth, and when anybody comes near he sits up so funny, just as though he had been used to doing it always."

The old man laughed with unaffected delight. "That was a lucky thought of yours, my child," said he. "Now begin to play."

The boy tried the strings and giving a toss to his fair hair, and taking a deep breathe to steady himself, began the Marseillaise. There was a sudden silence round about him, which startled him, and then from a hundred throats burst forth the words of the song. The child was strangely moved, but he bravely played on, though the tears were running down his cheeks.

As he played on, there was a movement toward the dog, and coppers and small change began to rain into the cap he held, till to the amusement of the bystanders, he dropped it with an impatient bark. Lucien laughingly emptied it into the blind man's pocket, and returned it to Fox, who took it meekly, holding it as before.

For a young boy, Lucien played fairly well, but it was not his playing which drew the little crowd about him, and kept the coins rattling down into the hat. His appearance was so interesting and so striking that the onlookers saw at once that he could not belong to the blind man. Curiosity was active among them, but no one liked to ask any questions, as both the man and the boy seemed so happy. As for Fox, he was evidently enjoying himself. The children laughed and clapped their hands at his antics, and soon emptied their fathers' pockets for his benefit.

Lucien stopped to rest himself, and Fox, when he had played his four tunes, as well as to give the latter a chance to eat the cakes the children were offering him.

"Shall I play any more?" he asked the blind man.

"Yes, if you're not too tired, my child. It takes a great many pennies to make twenty-six francs, and without that we're lost."

Lucien began again. He was tired, and ill at ease with so many looking at him, but he played on with Fox sitting by, patiently holding the hat. The dogs amusing way of dropping down to rest, and sitting up again, when he got ready, made every body laugh, especially as he held fast to the hat.

"Shall I stop now?" asked Lucien at last. "Nearly everyone is gone, I must have driven them off," he added laughing, as he rubbed his aching arms.

"Yes, stop now, my child, and may Heaven bless you!" said the old man fervently.

Just then the proprietor of the restaurant came forward, inviting them both to be seated and have some refreshments. The blind man accepted eagerly, but said, as he did so, "Why Sir, you never offered me anything before."

"Good reason!" answered the man with a loud guffaw. "My customers always fled the moment you drew the bow, but this young gentleman helped to swell the crowd tonight. Eat and drink your fill, all three of you, and come back tomorrow."

And so it was here that the weeping and astonished daughter of the blind man came upon them. She had been seeking her father for more than an hour, not dreaming of his venturing so far alone.

"Fill her up, too," said the smiling proprietor when he saw her, "she's a good daughter. Eat all you want, and remember me when you say your prayers." Giving one of Fox's long ears a tweak, he went in to count his gains and lock them up in his strong box.

"I've been so worried about you, Father," began the girl. "Whatever made you come clear out here alone?" Then looking curiously at Lucien, who politely lifted his cap, as she did so, she lowered her voiced asking "and who is this young gentleman with you?"

"Have patience, Marie," answered her father gaily, "and I'll explain. I came out here alone because you couldn't leave your work to bring me, and I hoped to make more money here than anywhere else. No one knows better than you do, daughter, how much we stand in need of it just now."

"Yes, Father," responded Marie sadly.

"I knew you would come out here to look for me, Marie, after you found I was not in the other places, so I felt safe enough coming alone. But I took a bad fall, and I thought my arm was broken," said the blind man.

"Oh, poor Father!" exclaimed the girl, starting forward.

"It is better now," he added, "and I hope it is only bruised. I was heartbroken to think I could never play again, and that my last hope of keeping our home was gone, and I lay on the ground crying like a baby when this angel came and helped me." The girl gave a quick sob. "It's a long story, Marie," the old man said.

"Please don't tell any more of it," interrupted Lucien.

"I must, my child, but since you don't want to hear it, I'll only tell Marie now that you have saved us all by your beautiful playing and your dog's cunning tricks."

"Oh, please don't say any more, Sir. It was you who saved me from the robbers. They might have murdered me," said Lucien with a shudder, and drawing nearer to these new friends.

"That's very true, my dear," returned the blind man.

"Here, Marie, count our gains," he added cheerfully, as he began to empty his pockets. Marie gathered the change into her apron, and was soon sorting it into piles upon the table. She counted it over and over in silence. At last her father, out of patience, asked, "Isn't it enough, Marie?"

"No, Father, we have only seventeen francs here."

Lucien had been watching the girl, as with a look of despair growing upon her face, she counted and recounted the money.

"And ten more makes it twenty-seven," he said simply, as he laid his own money beside the rest.

"Oh, you kept part back, did you?" returned Marie thoughtlessly.

"Kept it back!" cried the boy indignantly, "That's my own money. I put it with yours to make enough for your rent. I'm glad I didn't spend any of it on a cab hire, or I should not have found your father, or been able to help him."

Her face flushed with embarrassment, Marie cried humbly, "I beg your pardon! I spoke out of turn."

"That's all right," replied Lucien with a bright smile. "I was only mad for a second."

"Your money!" exclaimed the blind man, just coming to understand what was going on, and almost in tears, "No, no I won't take it! It is all he has in the world, Marie; give it right back to him. Where is he?" he said groping for Lucien. "Give me your hand, my child."

The boy slipped his hand into that of the old man, who raised it to his lips and kissed it. "May God reward you for your kindness! We shall never cease to pray for you," he added, with tears streaming down his cheeks. Lucien was crying, too, now. Marie regarded them in astonishment, not yet knowing the whole story of the evening.

Lucien was the first to break the silence that had fallen upon all there. "You said your landlord was going to seize your furniture and turn you out tomorrow, if you hadn't the twenty-six francs you owed him. Now if I only got seventeen francs when I tried to raise it for you by my playing, it isn't kind not to let me make up the rest with my own money."

"You are in the right, my son," answered the old man with emotion, "I will take it."

"But, Father," Marie was protesting, but her father cut her short with "Do as I bid you, my daughter; take it. I accept it as a loan until we can repay it. And that isn't all we owe him. Half of this evening's receipts are rightfully his. If we have enough for the landlord, we must use it all, but if we haven't, you must give the boy his share of the receipts, and return his own money."

"When you hear the whole story, Marie," spoke up Lucien, "you will see that, if I have perhaps saved you from being turned out of your home, your good father saved me from those wicked men. My dear Uncle always said we ought to help one another," added the child, his voice growing sad, as it always did when speaking of his uncle.

None of them had observed that a middle-aged gentleman at a neighboring table was listening to their talk. While Lucien was speaking, he came and stood beside them.

"You needn't have any scruples about taking the boy's money," he said sitting down by the blind man, and giving the other two so plainly to understand that he wished to speak to him alone that they withdrew to another table.

"Excuse my listening," he continued, "but I was sitting close by, and that is a very interesting child. Who is he?"

"I don't know, Sir," replied the blind man, and he then told the gentleman what the child had told him of himself.

"We mustn't spoil him," returned the other. "Take his money that he may feel that he has helped you. I'll see that it is repaid, so you need not worry about the obligation. It is too late to say more tonight; I'll see you again."

After taking the blind man's address, he arose and called "Francois!" At the sound of his summons, a private carriage came gliding to the curb and stopped.

"Here Francois," said the gentleman to the coachman, "take these people home. They will tell you where to go. I'll walk."

The blind man and his daughter were too astonished to speak, as the gentleman helped them into the carriage. It was the first time such a thing had ever happened to them, and Marie, who could see how finely appointed it was, was almost afraid to sit upon the soft cushions. Not so Lucien. It was like a touch of home to him, and he saw nothing unusual in the carriage being placed at their disposal. Lifting his cap to the gentleman, he sprang in after Marie, calling to Fox to follow.

"That boy has been raised in luxury, that is evident," said the owner of the carriage to himself. "The dog is used to carriages, too," he added, as he saw Fox's graceful leap after Lucien. He laughed when he caught sight of the look of consternation upon the girl's face when the dog, jumping upon the seat beside Lucien, barked fancily out of the window. Before closing the door, the gentleman had shaken hands with them all. The poor blind man, finding voice, began to thank him for his kindness.

"Don't thank me," was the reply. "I should have done nothing if this young man had not set me the example. Thank him."

He shook hands with Lucien again as he bade them good night. To Marie's consternation, Fox put his paw imperatively upon the gentleman's arm.

"So you want to shake hands, too, do you, doggie?" said the latter laughing. "Well, give me your paw."

Lucien laughed, too, and the blind man and his daughter began to feel more at ease, though they were both sitting on the edge of the seat, looking far from comfortable. They came near falling over when the impatient horses started off, and Lucien had hard work to keep from laughing at their nervousness. He and Fox took to the luxurious carriage and rapid driving like ducks to water.

Occasionally, the dog thought it well to bark out of the window to let outsiders know he was passing, but most of the time he wore the air of saying, "I'm so used to this, it quite loves me!"

A Fox In Paris

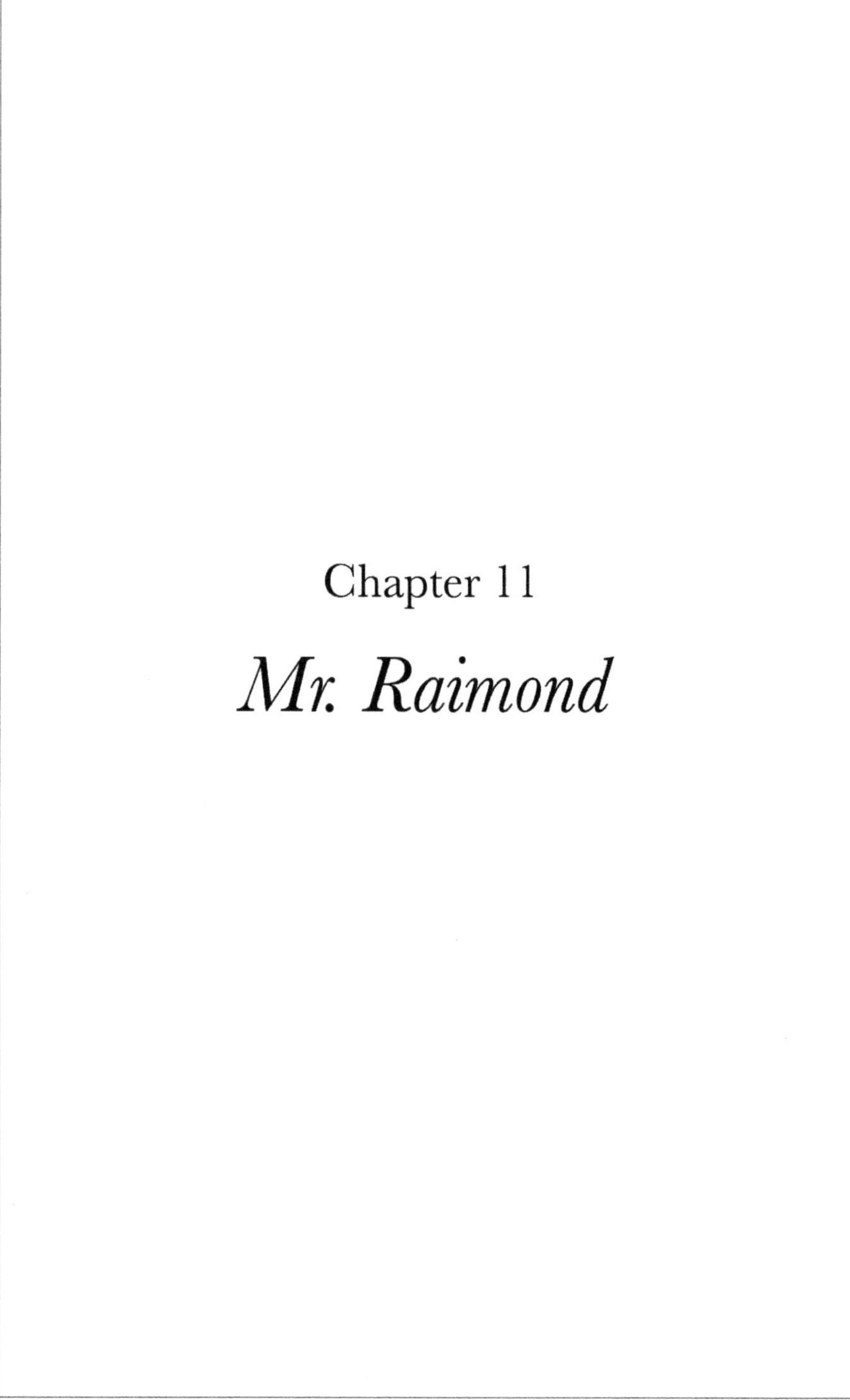

Chapter 11

Mr. Raimond

Where's Lucien?
(Turn the page to see.)
When he awoke, he heard voices, and in the stranger talking with the old soldier, he recognized the owner of the carriage.

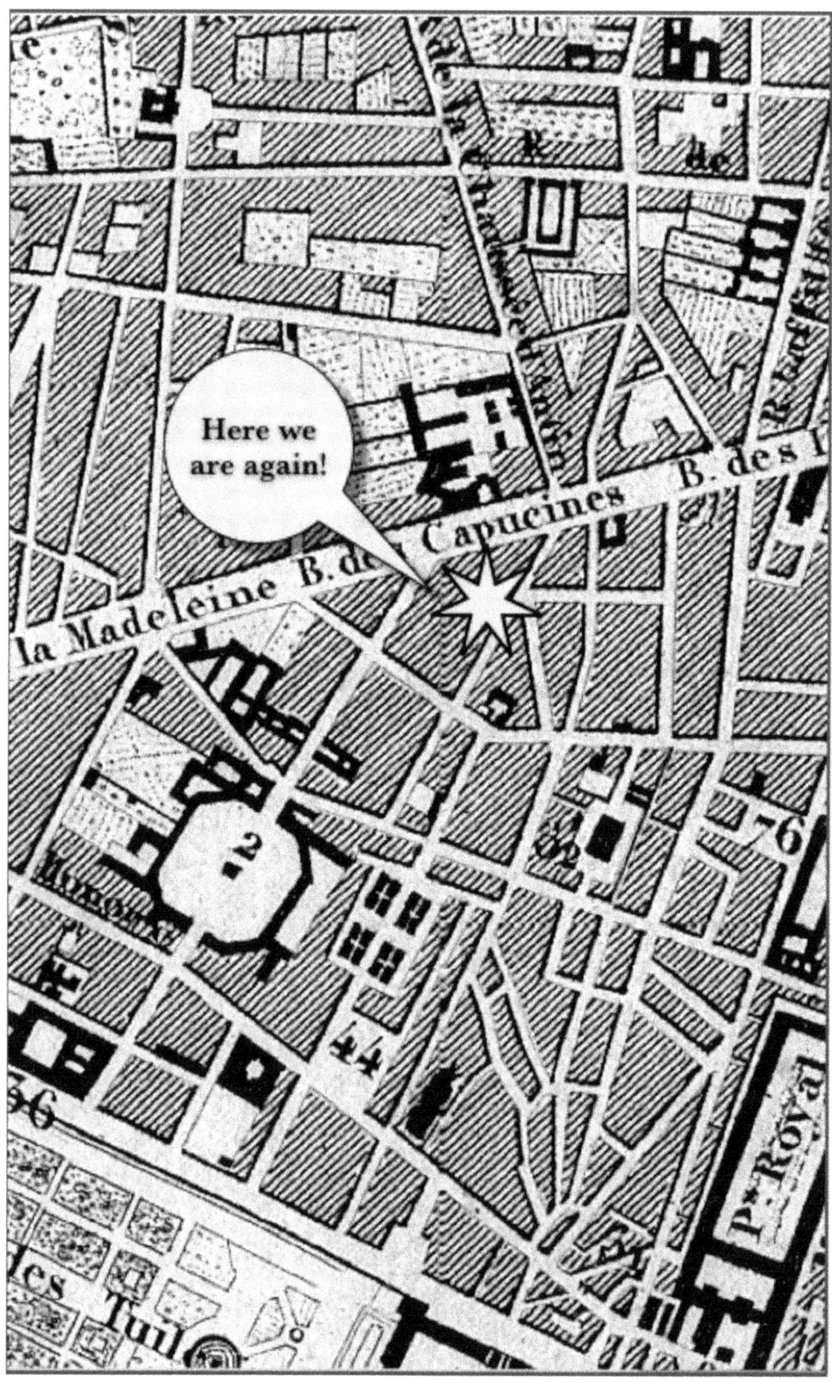
Here we
are again!
la Madeleine B. de
Capucines
B. des
P.^al Royal
les
Tuil
76
2
44

Father La Tuile, meanwhile, was putting in a very anxious time. He was filled with self-reproach for having been so easily persuaded to allow Lucien to go off with the masons. As evening gave way to night his imagination took wild flights, and he conjured up visions of all sorts of dreadful happenings to the child, of whom he had become very fond. At the sound of each passing vehicle, he anxiously hobbled to the door, only to find it already gone. The footsteps all turned out to be false alarms as well. At one point, he reached the door just as the bearers of a motionless body on a litter paused to rest a moment. His heart stood still, and he grabbed the lintel for support, but the still form and its solemn bearers passed also.

He trimmed his smoky lantern, and waited a long time before another came near enough to catch his ear. This time it was the clatter of steel carriage wheels on the pavement, and by the time he got to the door, they were already stopping before it. Great was his relief to see his two new wards springing from an elegant private carriage.

"Bless my soul," he said to himself, not liking to come forward when he saw the liveried coachman, "that child must be a kind of Cinderella."

As soon as Lucien came in he began at once in childish fashion to rattle off the story of his adventures, but he looked so pale and tired that the old man insisted upon his going to bed. He was indeed worn out and slept late the next morning. When he awoke, he heard voices, and in the stranger talking with the old soldier, he recognized the owner of the carriage. Seeing him awake, the gentleman said to him, "Your friend here tells me that you have been deserted by a relative, whose name you are not willing to disclose."

"Yes, Sir," replied Lucien, looking up into his face with boyish frankness.

The gentleman looked at him thoughtfully for a moment. "My name is Monsieur Raimond, and I have your ten francs for you," he said, giving Lucien the money. "I have settled it with the blind man. Now what can I do for you? Better still, what can you do for yourself?"

"Thank you, Sir," said the child taking the money. "I can read and write and cipher, and play a little on the violin; perhaps you heard me last night."

"Yes, I did."

"It was dreadful at first to have everybody looking at me," Lucien ran on, "and I could hardly play at all when I began, but every penny that dropped into the hat for the poor blind man made me ashamed to be thinking of myself. It was very silly of me to be so scared, but it was the first time I had ever played before strangers."

"Not silly at all, my child, but very natural," the gentleman answered kindly. "It would be a poor way for you to earn your living, however. It was your youth and not your playing that brought in the money. You haven't enough talent for music to make it worthwhile to spend the time and money it would take to make you into a musician. We must think of something else for you," added the gentleman. Lucien smiled.

"I always told Uncle I should never make a good player," he said, "but he was so fond of music himself that he made me take lessons."

"That was natural enough, my child, he was giving you the education of a gentleman, but now that you seem to be a poor boy all alone in the world, you need something quite different."

"That is very true, Sir," returned Lucien sadly.

"See what you think of this plan," said his new friend. "I have some property just beyond the Champs Elysees, which needs looking after." He hesitated a moment, looking intently at the child, "I am retiring from business, and due to the ill health of my wife, she and I are going to spend some months in traveling. We lost a little boy about your age last year," continued the gentleman with emotion, "and my poor wife has never been well since. That is the reason I cannot take you home with me. The sight of a child near his age is more than she can bear."

Lucien slipped his hand into that of his new friend, who went on to speak of his plan for the boy.

"There is an old stone wall around the land I was telling you about," he said, "but it doesn't keep out the marauders, who break my bushes and fruit trees, and create an awful mess. There's plenty of good building material there, too, to put up a little house for a watchman, and I don't want that stolen either. Would you be afraid to look after such a place? It would give you a home, and a chance to get steady work outside."

"Afraid of what, Sir? I've nothing but this money," responded the boy, "and I'd soon find a good hiding spot for it."

"If you like," said the gentleman, "and I'll take you right out there, if you're ready."

"I beg your pardon, Sir," put in the old soldier respectfully, "but what will you give him for looking after your property?"

"Not much!" returned Mr. Raimond laughing. "I am going to give him a chance to show what stuff he is made of. There isn't even a bed for him to sleep on, let alone a roof to cover it, for there is no house there. But, as I said before, there is plenty of building material, and he can soon knock together some sort of shelter. He'll have plenty of spare time, until he finds work. As for food, he'll find enough fruit to begin upon, and I'll give him seeds to make a garden, if he wishes. I may even see that he doesn't starve," added Mr. Raimond with a cheerful wink to Father La Tuile, who had been looking rather concerned. "He has his ten francs, to begin with," he continued, "for I transferred the blind man's debt to myself, you see."

"Yes, Sir, it's all right," exclaimed Lucien eagerly. "I'm not afraid to trust you, and I'm ready to begin right away to look after your place. But if you don't mind," he said, glancing at Father La Tuile, "I'd like to do an errand before I go with you," and without waiting for a reply the boy hurried out into the street with Fox bounding beside him.

Mr. Raimond and the old soldier looked after him as Lucien disappeared. "A fine child that," said Mr. Raimond, "we must look out not to spoil his fine independent spirit."

The old soldier said nothing. He quickly wiped his eyes and then rolled one of the nail kegs over for Mr. Raimond to sit down on while they waited for Lucien to return from wherever it was he had disappeared to.

When Lucien came running back with a parcel in his hands, Father La Tuile and Mr. Raimond were sitting upon the kegs and passing the time in idle conversation. They stopped when Lucien walked up to the old soldier and presented him with the parcel.

"Here's something to keep you company when I'm gone, Father La Tuile," he said, thrusting into the old man's hand a paper of tobacco and a new pipe. "Just look at your Emperor on that pipe," he added laughing, "isn't that fine? I picked it out on purpose to please you."

The old man turned aside to hide his emotion.

"The reason I got lost last night," continued Lucien, embracing him, was because I wanted to save the cab fare to buy you these."

The old soldier was crying outright. "This is a fine gift indeed," he added.

"Please don't feel bad, Sir," said the child trying hard not to join tears with him, "I'll come to see you," he said, "can't I, Mr. Raimond?"

"Certainly, whenever you want to, so you look after my place," he said to Lucien, "and your old friend must visit you and look after you," said Mr. Raimond smiling, as he shook hands with Father La Tuile at parting.

His carriage was waiting outside and they quickly departed, Francois, the coachman, driving rapidly to their destination.

"What book is that you have with you?" asked Mr. Raimond after they had sat in silence for some time.

"Robinson Crusoe, Sir," replied Lucien, "my uncle gave it to me on my last birthday. I think I'm like Crusoe, don't you, Mr. Raimond? Paris isn't a desert island exactly, but you can be pretty lonely here. I guess you could starve to death here too," said the boy thoughtfully. "Robinson Crusoe was all alone, and so am I," he added.

"Not quite," Mr. Raimond said under his breath, but all Lucien heard for reply to his chatter was "Humph!" He was afraid Mr. Raimond thought him forward, so he said no more.

A Fox In Paris

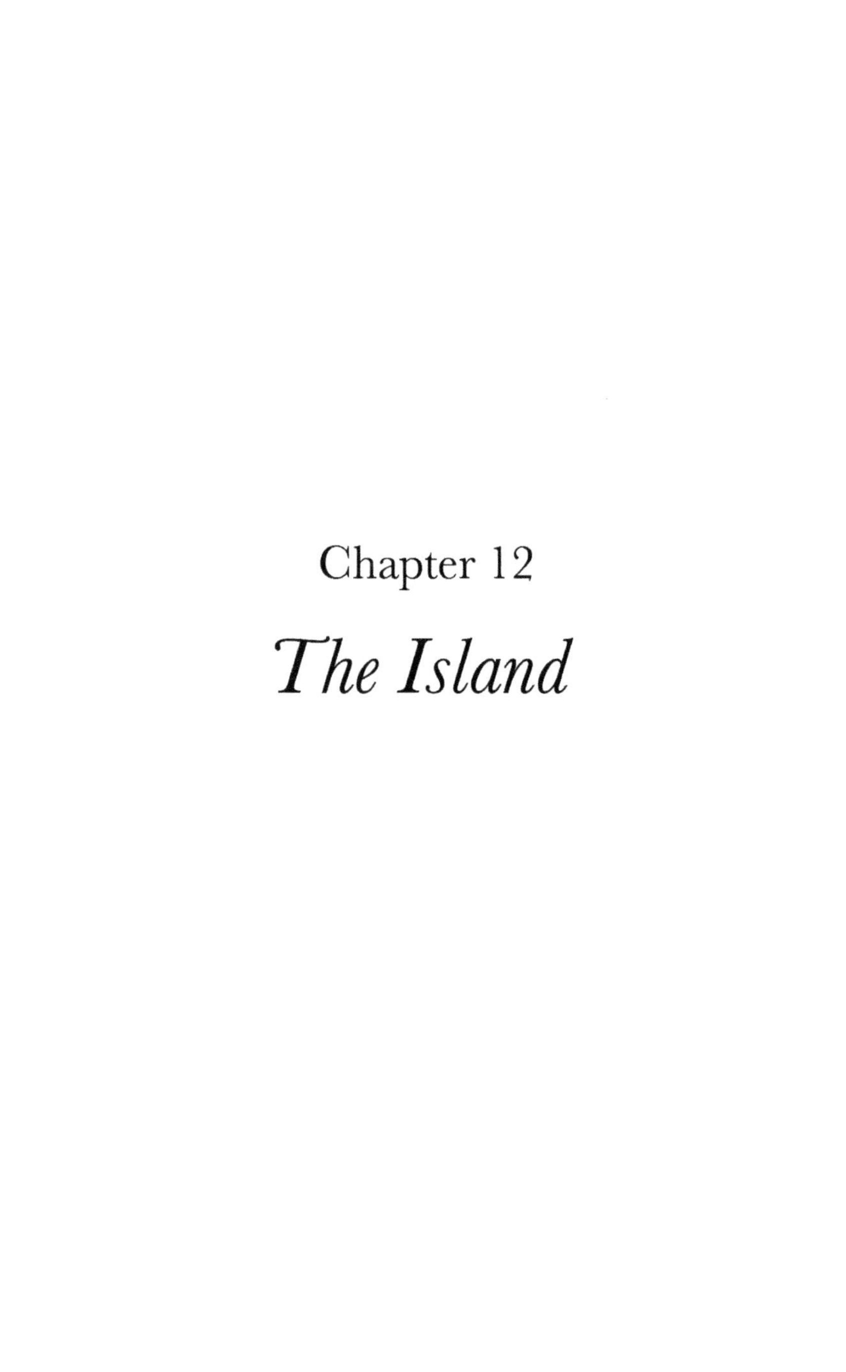

Chapter 12

The Island

Where's Lucien?
(Turn the page to see.)
Lucien looked about the place with great interest, while Fox dove right into the chaotic old garden as if it were ordered up just for him. It was very large, and much overgrown with grass and weeds.

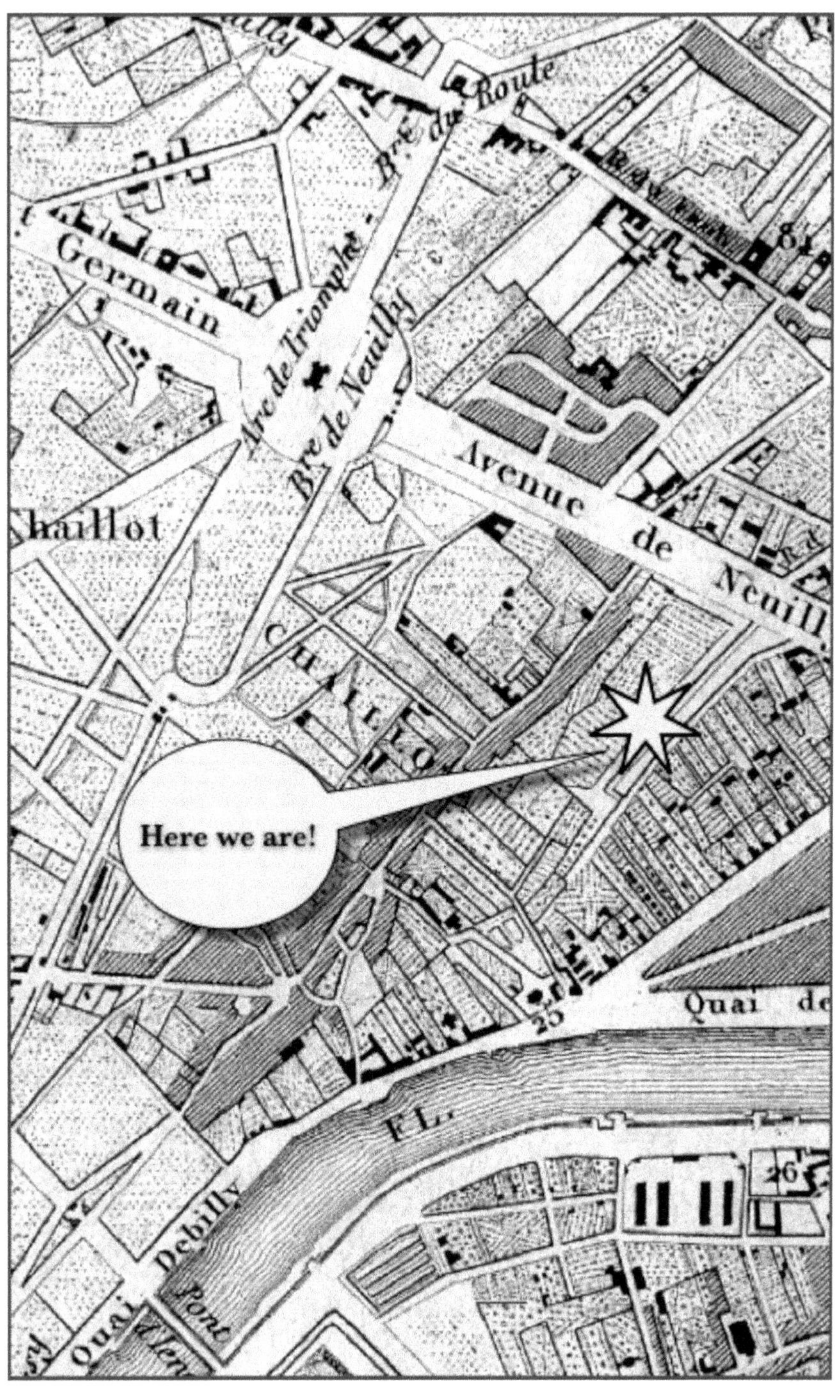
Germain
Bre du Roule
Arc de Triomphe
Bre de Neuilly
Avenue de Neuill
Chaillot
Here we are!
Quai de
25
Fl.
Quai Debilly
Pont
26

The carriage jerked to a stop in front of a roughhewn door set in an old crumbling wall.

"Here we are," said Mr. Raimond cheerfully, as he and Lucien got out, with Fox at their heels.

Taking an old black iron key from his pocket, Mr. Raimond unlocked the ancient door, and led the way into the enclosure. Lucien looked about the place with great interest, while Fox dove right into the chaotic old garden as if it were ordered up for him alone. It was very large, and almost square, and much overgrown with grass and weeds. There were also, planted round about, a good many fruit trees and bushes. Here and there were clumps of lilies and roses and old fashioned flowers scattered amongst them. Lucien's heart gave a bound at sight of it all, and his eyes filled with tears at the memories they evoked.

Mr. Raimond watched him in silence till he saw the boy's face brighten as his thoughts took a more cheerful turn. "It's a regular Crusoe's Island," the child was saying to himself.

"Well, my boy, what do you think of it?" asked his new friend.

"Oh, Sir," answered Lucien, with a long-drawn sigh, "it is almost too good to be true."

Mr. Raimond looked relieved, and pointing to a big pile of lumber and stones, he said, "There's all you'll need for your house," then talking a few steps away into a patch of bright sun and weeds, added, "and here's a fine spot for your garden. I'll send you some seeds and other things tomorrow."

"You don't mean to give me everything here, do you, Sir?"

"I don't mean to give you anything but the use of it all."

"And can I do what I like with it?" Lucien asked eagerly.

"Yes," came the reply.

"Then I'm just like Robinson Crusoe, and this is my island. Oh, Mr. Raimond, how can I ever thank you?"

"By taking good care of my property. If you have any trouble you must call the police right away. They have a station on that corner over there. My nephew is the lieutenant, and I'll speak to him about you."

"I'd better begin right away to build my house," said Lucien eager to get to work, Crusoe-fashion.

"It is fortunate the weather is warm," replied Mr. Raimond. "You will have plenty of time to build a house before you need it to shelter you from the cold. I advise you to put it in that corner, where the wall will give you shelter from the North wind, as well as make two sides of your house, said Mr. Raimond enthusiastically. But checking his excitement, he suddenly gave Lucien a hard look, "How old are you child?" Mr. Raimond asked abruptly.

"I was eleven last March, Sir."

"You are very young to be alone," said Mr. Raimond in a troubled voice. "You were taking such good care of the blind man last night that I didn't realize how young you were. To be sure, you reminded me of our boy, and he was only ten," he added sadly. "Perhaps I ought not to leave you here."

"Oh, yes, Sir," cried Lucien, seizing his hand in both his, "please let me try it."

The elder considered the situation for moment, rubbing his chin thoughtfully. "Very well," replied Mr. Raimond, "I don't see anything else to be done, I must leave town tomorrow afternoon, and I don't know when I shall be back. I wish I could take you home with me, but you see I can't on account of my poor wife."

"I understand, Sir," said Lucien drawing nearer to Mr. Raimond. "My dear Uncle is dead, too."

"Well, well," answered Mr. Raimond, kissing the boy's upturned face, "we must do the best we can. This is far better for you than running the streets and sleeping in empty houses."

As he went out, a fine young woman curtsied to him and he recognized her as Marie, the blind man's daughter. He had told her father of his plan when he saw him that morning, and she had come hoping to find Lucien here.

"My father sent me to thank you for all of your help to us last night," she said to Lucien, "and to tell you he will pay you your half of the earning just as soon as he can."

"He doesn't owe me anything. Mr. Raimond was kind enough..."

"...To give you back your ten francs," interrupted Mr. Raimond, "and to lend this lovely girl's father that amount himself, but that has nothing to do with the other debt. I'm afraid you have a great deal to learn, Lucien."

The boy made no reply.

As Mr. Raimond was getting into his carriage, he said to the coachman, "Wait a moment, Francois," and began searching for something.

"Here it is!" he exclaimed, producing from under the cushions a tin horn, upon which, to the astonishment of Marie and Lucien, he blew a lively blast. He then put the horn down and took out his watch and marked the time.

After a minute or so, two police officers came running down the street toward the sound.

"That's what I like," said Mr. Raimond to them. "You made good time, boys. Now whenever you hear this horn, you are to run for your life to protect this young man and my property. Don't forget," and he quietly slipped a tip into their hands.

"There are no robbers this time," Mr. Raimond added, "I just wanted to try how the alarm sounded."

The policemen went off laughing.

"Now, Lucien, be sure to blow that horn first thing, if you need help. Better the police should run for a false alarm than that any of my fruit should be stolen."

Marie and Lucien laughed.

"Now, goodbye, and take care of yourself," said Mr. Raimond, leaning down from the carriage to shake hands with Lucien, and telling the coachman to go directly home. He had a sneaking hope that his wife might be willing to listen to the story of this child, to whom he felt wonderfully drawn, and perhaps be persuaded to adopt him. He was confident that nothing could more surely prevent her drifting into confirmed melancholia than to reawaken her interest in children. That interest seemed now to lie in the grave of their only child.

When Mr. Raimond reached home, he was so full of enthusiasm for his project that he ran lightly upstairs to his wife's room, and addressed her so cheerfully that she, bursting into tears, accused him of heartlessly forgetting their great sorrow. Hastily dropping the lid on the trunk she was packing, she left the room before her astonished husband could reply.

He stood at the window a moment pulling at his bushy mustache, and then went out quietly, to order the garden seeds, tools, and some other little things for Lucien.

Chapter 13
The New Natives

Where's Lucien?
(Turn the page to see.)
"Look," was Marie's reply, as she eagerly pulled out a pair of snow-white pigeons, that she held out to Lucien. "They are for you," she said simply.

Bre du Roule
Germain
Arc de Triomphe
Bre de Neuilly
Avenue de
Here we are!
Quai
25
Fl.
26
Quai Debilly
Pont

Fox was showing a lively interest in Marie's apron. She did her best to shoo him off, while waiting impatiently for Mr. Raimond to take his leave. The moment the gate swung closed after him, she gently pushed Fox away again and turned to Lucien.

"What do you think I have in my apron?" she asked.

"It's something alive, I see it move," answered Lucien eagerly.

"Put your ear down and listen," said the girl.

"Birds. Doves? Is it doves, Marie?" asked the boy, as he bent over the apron to listen.

"Look," was Marie's reply, as she eagerly pulled out a pair of snow-white pigeons, that she held out to Lucien. "They are for you," she said simply. "I wasn't sure I'd find you here, but I thought I'd bring them anyway. I wanted to give you something myself, and these were all I had."

"How did you know I loved pigeons?" asked Lucien fondling one of the birds, and much touched by the gift.

"I didn't, but I love them myself, and I had nothing else to offer you," answered the girl.

"Well, I do, Marie; I had ever so many at home. My dear Uncle was very fond of them, and when he and I called them, they would light upon our shoulders, and eat from our hands. I wonder who feeds them now," said the boy with a far away look in his eyes, now filling with tears.

"I hope you will like these," said Marie anxiously.

"Indeed I shall," replied Lucien, recovering himself, and chatting cheerfully with the girl, as they planned a shelter for the doves.

Fox was intensely interested in these new arrivals, but the birds took little notice of his antics. They strutted about picking up the crumbs Marie scattered for them, as much at home in their new environment as if they had known no other. Marie and Lucien laughed as they watched them.

"I was afraid Fox would be jealous," said the latter. "Yes, I mean you, old fellow," he added as the dog, hearing his own name, jumped upon him.

"Oh, he's too good a dog for that," returned the girl. "They'll be company for one another. I must be going now, but I'll come back tomorrow to see how you're getting on."

Lucien escorted her to the gate and bid her farewell, then, as soon as the gate had clapped shut he turned to the dog, "Look here, Fox," he said, I'm a regular Robinson Crusoe now. My island is surrounded by a stone wall instead of the sea," he laughingly ran on, "but I guess I like it better, don't you?"

"Yes," answered Fox, as plainly as could be, and the child caught him up and hugged him.

"We're better off to start with than Crusoe was," Lucien went on. "There's plenty of nice fruit here, and everything ready for a house; it's fine isn't it old chap?"

Fox got another hug for saying "yes!" so pat.

Despite the advantages he was counting, however, Lucien soon began to feel lonely, and Fox and the pigeons had to listen to an endless stream of lively chatter, not uttered because of his interest in them, but to bolster his failing courage as the day wore on.

When he suddenly remembered that he had no shelter to sleep under, he tried to set up some boards in the corner of the wall, but it was hard work. It was late when he began, and the boards were long and heavy, so night overtook him before he had enough in place for his purpose. His tender hands were filled with splinters, and he ached all over, but he knew he must still prepare some sort of a bed to lie on. Remembering the jungle of dry weeds, and coarse grass at the other side of the old gardens, he groped about in the dim light gathering armfuls. Lightly piled under the slanting boards, the tired child thought they made an excellent bed to turn into. He was hungry, as well as tired, for he had eaten nothing since morning.

"Are you hungry, too, Fox?" he asked the dog, while considering whether he ought to go outside and buy goods for them both. Fox said, "Yes," emphatically, but Lucien was too deep in thought to heed him. He was thinking of his adventures the previous night, and especially of the two thieves.

"It wasn't so far from here where we met them," he said to himself. "Suppose they should see me: they would never let me off, if they caught me a second time. No, I think we'll stay here now, and just go to bed. Come Fox." Fox obeyed, but he looked very much disappointed. They crawled under the lean-to, and into the rustling bed, and in less time than it takes to tell it, were both in the Land of Nod.

Lucien's sleep was not so refreshing as it might have been, for the weeds did not prove a very comfortable bed after all.

They mashed down too easily, and were full of prickers besides. He awoke stiff and lame, and "hunger" didn't come close to describing the gone feeling inside of him, so the first thing he did was to sally forth with Fox in search of their breakfast. With money in his pocket, it was easy to find, and "Crusoe" and "Man-Friday" returned to their island in better spirits.

Lucien bought food for the pigeons, too, and after attending to their wants, he began to think about putting up a better shelter for himself. "I must begin this morning; it is hard work," he said looking at his lacerated hands. "No, Fox, I wasn't talking to you," said the boy with a laugh as the dog capered about him at the sound of his voice, "I was talking to myself. But let's play you are my man-Friday, and I will talk to you."

"All right," answered Fox as plainly as a dog could speak. Then picking up a stick he tossed it up, and, catching it again, dared Lucien to chase him. So in a grand game of tag, they forgot all about house building.

"Oh, Fox," cried the little boy, quite out of breath, "you're too bad. Go off and play by yourself: I must get to work."

He examined the piles of building material. "I don't believe I'll have a frame house," he said, "there's plenty of stone here, and a stone house is warmer in winter."

"So it is!" barked Fox, who was sitting up cocking his ears at Lucien.

"Oh, you funny dog," cried the latter, hugging him. "Let's go outside to the fountain and get a drink. I'm thirsty, aren't you?"

"Certainly. I'm everything you are," Fox replied by barking and jumping around his young master.

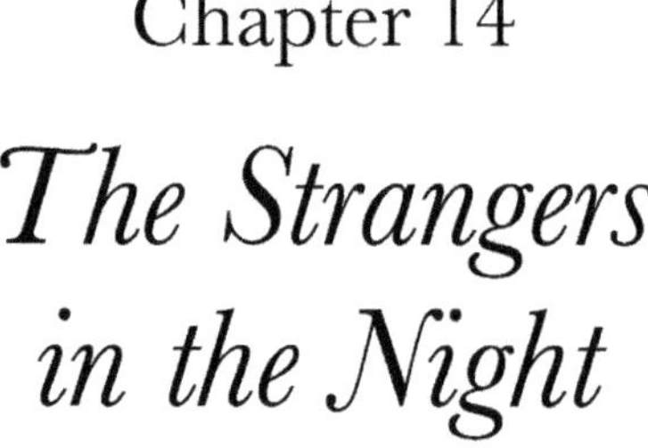

Chapter 14
The Strangers in the Night

It was on this evening, after Jean had ceremoniously presented Lucien the key to his new front door...that Lucien called Fox inside and closed and locked the new door behind them.

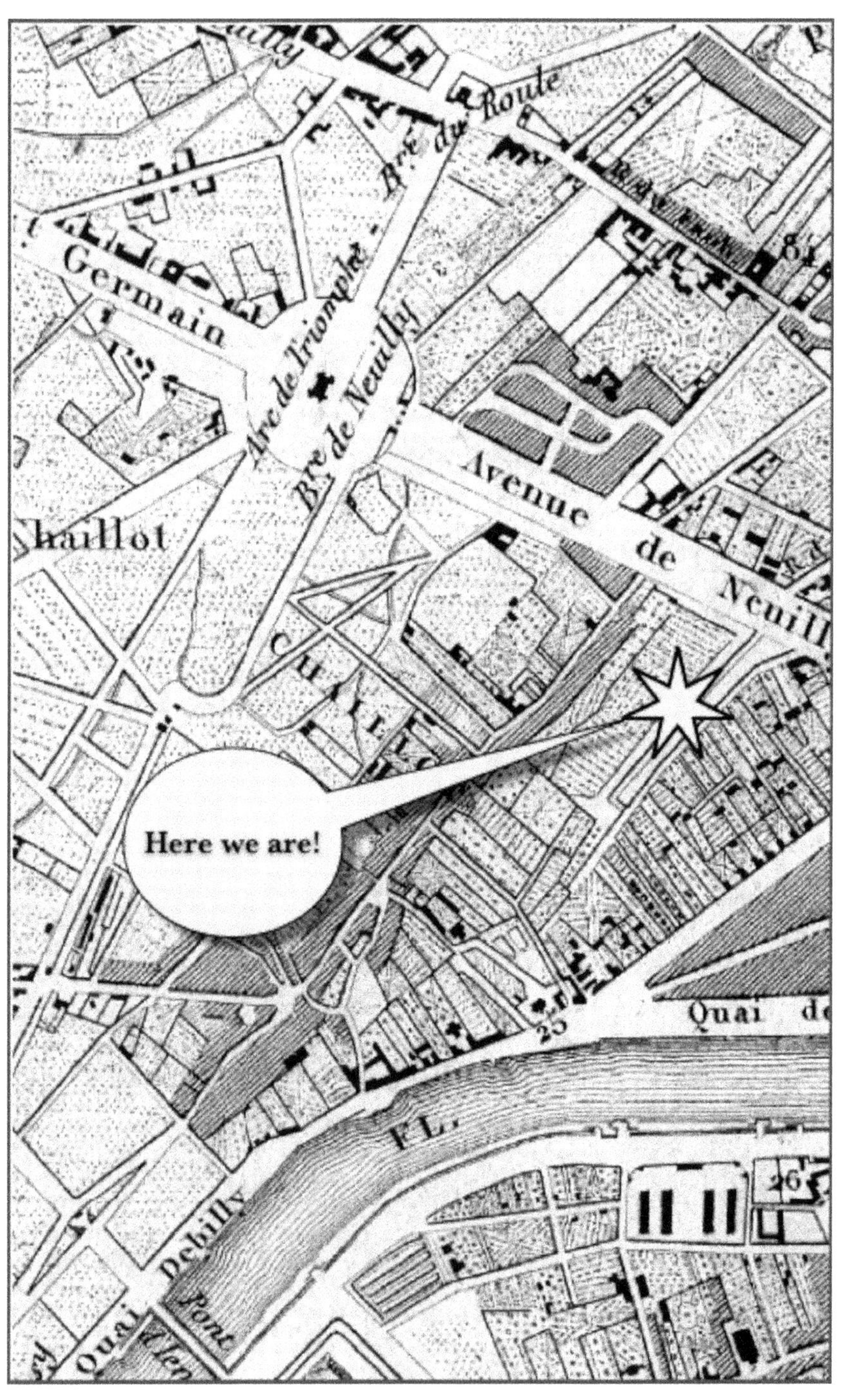
Here we are!
Germain
Arc de Triomphe
Bre du Roule
Bre de Neuilly
Avenue
de
haillot
Quai
FL.
Quai Debilly
Pont
25
26

As it happened, several masons were talking together near the fountain when Lucien and Fox arrived there for their drink.

Because of his friendship with the masons at the house on Louis Le Grand Street, these men did not seem like strangers to the boy, and seeing them look at him with curiosity, he went up to them and began to ask their advice about building his house. Supposing him to be joking, they began teasing him. Lucien was for a few moments much confused and distressed, but his courage soon returned, and as soon as they would listen, he said, "We are here in this world to help one another; my dear uncle always told me so. I'm not asking something for nothing. I don't know how to build a house, but I know how to read and write, and play on the violin, now if..."

"Much help that would be in building a house!" interrupted one of the men with a sneer.

"I know it wouldn't put up a house," returned Lucien, "but if any of you will help me with my house, I'll teach you what I know."

"Clear out of here with your nonsense, or I'll kick you," snapped the surly tradesman, to whose remark the boy had just replied. At that instant a gentle voice came from behind the group.

"Brother, surely even you would not kick a poor child."

Spinning around, the men regarded a young woman, and instantly recognized her. "Why, it's Miss Marie!" exclaimed some of the other masons, evidently very glad to see her.

"And why shouldn't I kick that youngster, if I feel like it?" asked Marie's brother, advancing defiantly toward Lucien.

But, before he could take another step, and with a sudden storm of anger flashing in her eyes, Marie quickly dropped the basket she was carrying and sprang to the boy's side throwing her arm about him. "I'll tell you why brother!" she exclaimed defiantly. "Yes, and since you drive me to it, I'll tell these gentlemen the whole story, and if there's a man among them, he'll kick YOU if you dare to lay even a finger upon this child." She paid no attention to Lucien's embarrassed efforts to keep her from speaking, and the men listened in serious silence, as she went on with her story.

She spared no detail of the extremity to which her family had been reduced, and of the great service rendered them by this boy. As she proceeded, the men drew nearer to Lucien, looking at him with honest admiration. The moment she ceased speaking, they crowded about him, begging his pardon for ridiculing him at first, and they all insisted upon shaking hands with him, that is, all but one, Marie's brother. The rest of the masons turned upon this one with reproach.

"Don't say a word more," he cried. "I see now what a wretch I am. I'm not fit to live. I've made trouble enough. I'll go drown myself," he said pulling his cap over his eyes and starting for the river.

"Don't be a fool, Paul," said an older man, laying a detaining hand upon his arm. "None of us has always kept the straight and narrow, and besides, that would bring the worst kind of trouble upon your family! Why can't you make a man of yourself, and support your poor old blind father, I'd like to know?"

"That's so," chimed in some of the others.

"Now we know your weakness, we'll help you to keep straight after this," the older mason added.

"Better eat your breakfast while it is hot, brother," said Marie retrieving the basket and starting to unpack it.

"I don't deserve it Marie, give it to him," returned Paul pointing to Lucien.

"I've got something for him, too," replied Marie, throwing a light smile over her shoulder at the little boy, now standing behind her.

That smile almost got tangled up on the way in the ardent glance of a handsome fellow, whom the other masons called Jean. He seemed to have no eyes or ears for anyone but Marie since she appeared on the scene. The distracting thing to him was that, despite all this, she didn't seem to know he was there. He thought it a great waste of her smiles to bestow them upon a mere child, even if that child were saying, "Oh, Marie, how good and kind you are!" He himself couldn't muster courage to speak to her after his, "Good morning, Miss Marie," when she arrived.

"I was just wishing for something hot," said Lucien, giving Marie great pleasure by eating with evident relish all she had brought him.

"This is my second breakfast," he said with a laugh, "but the first didn't taste like this, did it, Fox?"

"Not a bit," Fox managed to bark for answer while catching the tidbits tossed him by Marie and Lucien. She had easily guessed at the fact that the boy, fearing to spend his capital too freely, had bought only dry bread for himself and his dog that morning.

He was fast learning the value of money.

The masons had been talking apart while Lucien and Paul were eating. Presently, one of them, speaking for all, told Lucien not to bother himself about his house. "We'll build it for you all snug," said the mason. "There'll be near three hours of daylight after we finish our job this afternoon, and we will come back and help you."

They were as good as their word. They marched through the old gate right on time; set their tools down and asked where he wanted his house put. Then with practiced eye, they examined the building material on hand, and selected the most suitable. When he offered to help, he was laughingly dismissed, and told to run about whistling, with his hands in his pockets, and the house would grow of itself.

"I never go about with my hands in my pockets," returned Lucien, taking it seriously.

"Do what you like then, play with your dog; we don't need you," was the reply.

It did seem like magic to the little boy; they worked so fast. Nevertheless, night overtook them long before the house was completed, but they promised to return every day they could and finish it; which they did. All the time, Lucien had supposed that he was to give them lessons in return, as in the case of the other masons. These men only laughed when he broached the subject, and said they had done the work as much for the sake of the blind man as for himself.

Jean, the handsome young mason, had evidently done his share for the sake of the blind man's daughter. He had been especially kind to Lucien, who was loud in praise of him to Marie afterward. Jean was a carpenter, as well as a mason, and it was he who made the snug pigeon house, put up out of the reach of cats. He also did most of the carpentry work about the little house, and ended by fitting a good lock to the door. All of these things took time, and gave Jean the chance he coveted to be present about the place in order to see Marie during her frequent visits. He was rewarded by occasional glimpses of the girl, but she was very shy about speaking to him.

It was on this evening, after Jean had ceremoniously presented Lucien the key to his new front door, and left for the day, just as the sun was setting, that Lucien called Fox inside and closed and locked the new door behind them. He turned to the dog, saying, "Well old boy, here we are all locked away in our Crusoe Castle. It seems a bit lonely now with the door locked and everyone gone. What shall we do to pass the time? Shall I read to you from Robinson Crusoe?" Fox seemed content with this idea, and sat down on the floor beside Lucien's chair.

Lucien had barely gotten into the book, which he almost didn't need to read at all, he knew it so well by now, that Fox began to growl and bristle. He kept running uneasily to the door. Carefully peeping out of the window, Lucien espied two men moving stealthily about among the fruit trees in the quickly fading daylight. He watched them awhile with much alarm. As they slipped in and out among the shadows cast by the pale moonlight, he saw that their present object was to steal the fruit, but he did not know how soon they might turn their attention upon his little house and himself. "Oh Fox, what shall we do?" he whispered to the dog. He suddenly remembered the horn given him by Mr. Raimond. He crept quietly to the door and slipping it from the peg Jean had placed beside the door to hold it. Then easing the door open, he crept outside, and suddenly blew a shrill blast upon it, while Fox barked and growled for all he was worth. The men, startled at the sudden commotion, made a rush for a gap in the wall and slipped through. Lucien could here them cursing and running along the street outside. The next moment a voice cried "Halt!" There was noise of a scuffle, and then a triumphant "We've got them boys!"

As Lucien ran out to see what had happened, he approached the two, now being handcuffed by the police officers, who had answered his call. As he got closer, the light from a street lamp struck full upon the faces of the two men, and Lucien stopped short, "Why, they are my two bad men," he cried breathlessly.

"What do you mean?" asked the police lieutenant, who had just come up. "Wasn't it you who blew the horn? You're the chap my uncle, Mr. Raimond told the boys about, aren't you?"

"Yes, Sir," replied the child.

"Well, considering your size, you're pretty plucky," returned the other laughing. "But what do you know of these men?"

Lucien told him.

"That is only part of your story, sonny, my uncle told me the rest," said the officer kindly. Then turning to the other officer, and the two unwilling listeners in their midst, he rapidly recounted the story of Lucien's connection with the blind man.

"That was nothing," said the boy when he got a chance to speak. "Wouldn't any of you have done the same if you could play on the violin? As for my money, what better use could it be put to? One of the masons told me that giving it to the blind man was a fine investment, and that the house they have put up for me was interest from that investment. Come see my new house," added the boy, taking the police lieutenant by the hand.

"Your house?" cried the officer. "You'd be lucky if my uncle let's you roost in one of his trees, let alone giving you a house to live in."

"Come with me, Sir, and see for yourself," replied Lucien, pulling him along with childish familiarity.

The rest of the party, except those guarding the prisoners, followed them into the enclosure.

"You don't mean to say you live here alone?" exclaimed one of the policemen, looking at Lucien in astonishment.

"Indeed I do," answered the boy, "and I'm thankful enough to have such a home now," adding sadly, "it is only a month since my uncle died. If you knew all I've been through since then, you wouldn't wonder that I'm glad to be here. Besides, Mr. Raimond told me I had only to blow the horn if I needed help, and you would look after me. You see he was right," said the child smiling up into the faces of the men, "and there's nothing to be afraid of."

"You're right there, little one!" responded one of the men heartily.

After examining the little house and the the rest of the place, the policemen drew away from Lucien and talked together in low tones awhile, then the lieutenant came forward and offered the boy ten francs as a token of good will from them all.

"I can't take it, Sir," said Lucien drawing back. "Why does everybody offer me money? It makes me feel like a beggar. I'd be glad enough to earn some Francs though, if you will tell me how."

"Let me see," replied the lieutenant, pulling at his mustache thoughtfully. "I believe I might find something for you to do. Can you read and write?"

"Yes, Sir," Lucien answered eagerly.

"It's odd," said the lieutenant to his companions, "but only yesterday Mr. Germaine was asking me if I couldn't find him a boy for the printing office, 'a good respectable boy,' he said. I guess you'll do," he added turning to Lucien. "Meet me at the Station House tomorrow morning at seven o'clock, and I'll see what I can do for you."

"Thank you, Sir. I hope you gentlemen are not offended with me because I couldn't take the money," said Lucien anxiously looking from one to another of the policemen. "Not a bit," was the hearty reply, "but you'd better take it as a loan."

"That's so," said the lieutenant. "Take it as a loan, my boy, and you can pay it back when you get ready."

"You'll be sure to let me pay it back?" Lucien said, hesitating.

"Of course," replied the lieutenant.

"Then I will take it. Thank you all very much," said the boy shaking hands with his new friends, and adding, "it's just wonderful how kind everybody is to me."

This sent the policemen away laughing but there wasn't a dry eye among them.

Chapter 15
The Printshop

Where's Lucien?
(Turn the page to see.)
Their destination proved to be a printing office, where Lucien was introduced to a very kindly old gentleman, named Mr. Germaine, who agreed to take him on trial.

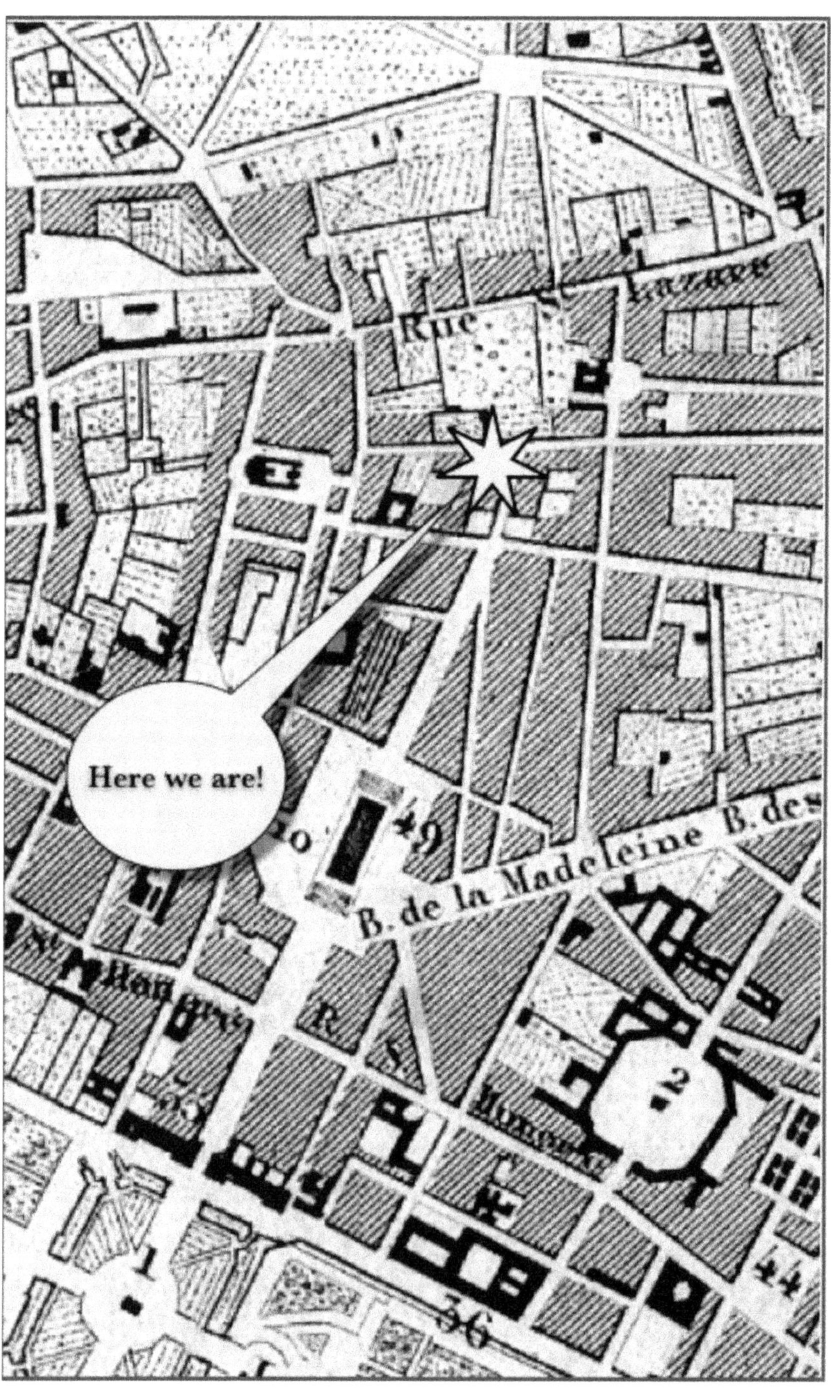
Here we are!
Rue
B. de la Madeleine
B. des
36

The excitement of the evening, and the prospect of earning his own living, had Lucien tossing and turning all night, waiting for the sunrise.

When morning finally arrived, he and Fox had shared their meager breakfast, and the pigeons had been cared for, long before it was time to meet the lieutenant. The officer, as he came sauntering out of the door of the station house, laughed at the sight of Lucien. He looked at his watch, "Twenty minutes of seven," he said, "have you been here all night?"

"Not quite, Sir," answered Lucien, laughing in his turn, "but I was up very early."

"So you were! Come on, I'm all ready. We are not going to walk this time," said the officer pointing to a light wagon by the curb. "Jump in, my boy, while I unhitch the horse." Laughing at Fox's frantic efforts to follow his master into the high wagon, the officer quipped, "What, you don't mean to make your dog work, too, do you?"

"Oh, Sir, I couldn't leave him alone all day, could I? He'd be so lonesome, and he's all I've got in the world," said Lucien timidly, fearing the officer did not favor Fox's attendance.

"Of course you couldn't," was the reply. "Here goes!" said the lieutenant, tossing the dog into the wagon. He sprang in himself, and they were off at such a pace that it was all Lucien could do to keep his seat, while Fox gave up his scheme of barking at everything they passed, and was glad to cuddle down between the boy's feet and keep quiet.

To be starting out to earn his own living made Lucien feel so grown up that he wished he could sit up with more dignity, but he enjoyed the drive too much to be troubled about anything.

"That's a fine horse of yours," he said to the officer.

"Oh, he isn't mine, he belongs to the Chief. That's why I'm in such a hurry; he wants him at eight o'clock. He doesn't mind my giving him a bit of a spin like this occasionally though," said the lieutenant smiling, "so I thought you and I might as well enjoy a drive. I wish that uncle of mine would leave me one of his horses when he goes away, but he got mad when I asked him the other day," added the young man. "He seems to have taken a fancy to you though, or he wouldn't be trying to help you."

"Yes, Mr. Raimond has been very kind to me," said the boy simply.

"Well, I don't seem to be on the right side of him," returned the nephew with a light laugh, "but perhaps, if I look after you, I'll get there."

"I hope so," replied Lucien, puzzled by the other's bantering tone, but glad that he had so capable a protector on his side.

Their destination proved to be a printing office, where Lucien was introduced to a very kindly old gentleman, named Mr. Germaine, who agreed to take him on trial. After the lieutenant was gone, Mr. Germaine gave the boy careful directions for the simple work he was to begin upon.

"Do you think you understand, my son?" he asked.

"Yes, Sir."

"Then sit here by me and begin. I'll help you if you need help."

Before the day was over, they were fast friends, and Lucien had told Mr. Germaine all his adventures. He was surprised and delighted to find that he was to receive nine francs a week for his work from the start, his wages to be increased as he became more useful to his employer.

He trudged off home at the close of what had been a very happy day for him and just outside the wall he met Marie.

"I've been waiting for you," she said with animation. "You must let me blindfold you," she added, producing a large handkerchief.

"What for? To play blind man's bluff? I'm afraid I'm too tired and hungry," returned the boy, as Marie bandaged his eyes.

"No, something better than that: it's a grand surprise. Come along," said the girl leading him by the hand.

"You forgot to blindfold Fox," cried Lucien with a ringing laugh as he heard the dog barking right and left, as though greeting friends. The handkerchief over his eyes did not prevent Lucien from hearing smothered laughter, and hurried whispers all around him after they had passed through the gate. He could hear light footsteps, too, but he knew Marie did not want the surprise spoiled, so he lent himself to her guidance as though he were indeed blind, and threw deaf into the bargain.

When she brought him to a stand still, there was a hasty scuffling of feet upon a bare floor, and the sound of muffled laughter, dying away into silence that could be felt. Lucien's heart beat fast as Marie, with fingers trembling with excitement, removed the handkerchief. He assumed he was in his own house, because his was the only house on his "island." But, once his eyes were doing full duty again, he wasn't so sure. A peal of laughter, in many keys, greeted his puzzled expression, but, he seemed not to hear it.

"Well," said Marie at last, disappointed at his long silence, "how do you like it?"

"Like what? It's all a dream, Marie. I wish we could wake up, I feel so queer". He rubbed his eyes.

"You're awake sure enough," said a friendly voice, which he recognized as that of Marie's admirer, Jean, "just tell us how you like it, boy."

"If you're sure I'm awake, I can tell you that it beats any fairy story I ever read. But, what does it mean? I'm all turned around, and I can't understand it."

"It means that you've got a good many friends who wanted to give you a surprise," came the shouted reply, from Marie's father, who was sitting in the corner with tears coursing down his cheeks.

"They've done it, that is sure!" exclaimed Lucien, beginning to examine the room. The rough boards of the walls and ceiling had been covered with a pretty paper. In one corner stood a little stove, and on the wall beside it, hung such simple cooking utensils as he might need.

In short, what had been Lucien's barren quarters, was now a proper home, small, but comfortably furnished, even to a good bed and bedding.

Lucien, after inspecting everything, rubbed his eyes again, saying with childish abandon, "I don't care what anybody says; I believe I'm dreaming."

At the sound of the fresh laughter this evoked, he started like one out of sleep, and looked around the room again, noticing for the first time that he really was in the midst of friends. Here were the masons who had built his house, and with them some men whom he did not recognize, but he saw Father La Tuile seated next to the blind man. To his greater surprise there was his new friend and employer Mr. Germaine standing in front of everyone else.

"Well, my boy," said the kindly old gentleman, "you do seem to know how to make fine friends. I was asked here by the Lieutenant to meet some of them this evening."

Observing that Lucien was looking with a very puzzled expression at the strangers standing with the masons, Mr. Germaine said with a laugh "Don't you recognize the officers that came to your rescue last night? You see all they have to do, if they want to disguise themselves, is to leave their uniforms at home," he said with a smile.

"Then they will excuse my not knowing them," said the boy with a happy laugh, in which every one joined.

Mr. Germaine called Lucien's attention to some things which had escaped his notice. Among others, there was a press for his clothes, and a provision closet, which was well stocked.

"But tell me, Sir," Lucien said clasping Mr. Germaine's hand, "how can these things be mine?"

"They are yours, my boy," replied Mr. Germaine, "because your good friends have made them so. They have all found out that you seem very averse to taking money you have not earned, but in a case like this, where each of your friends puts in a little towards making you comfortable, it would be very ungracious of you to decline the gifts."

Lucien was silent until he became conscious of an uneasy movement among the assembled company. "I suppose you are right, Sir," he said looking up into Mr. Germaine's face. "You must know a great deal better than I about such things. I have been thinking it over and I don't find that I feel the same about accepting all these things from my friends as I do about taking money. I am very grateful to them all."

There was a great clapping of hands at this, and Lucien tried to laugh, but his eyes were full of tears. Leaning his head against Mr. Germaine's arm, he said, "Couldn't you tell them all for me how I thank them every one, Sir? I can't do it."

"You've thanked us enough, give us your hand boy," cried one of the masons setting a hand shaking fashion, which spread through the room in no time. There was laughing and talking, and in the midst of it, Mr. Germaine took his leave.

Lucien felt like crying when he saw him go. The child's heart was full to overflowing, and he longed to give it ease by talking with this old gentleman, who seemed more like the people he had always been surrounded by than did anyone else he had yet met in Paris, with the exception of Mr. Raimond. He wanted to run into his arms and weep upon his breast, but he knew he must control his feelings, so as not to wound the feelings of his other kind friends. So he bade Mr. Germaine a cheerful good night, promising to return to work in the morning.

"You hardly looked in here, Lucien," said Marie, taking his hand and leading him back to the little cupboard, "here's meat and bread, and what do you think of this big pie? Here's cheese, too, and jam; oh, there's so many good things."

"You found them out, didn't you, Fox?" said Marie laughing at the way the dog was sitting up beside her begging.

"Why can't we all have supper?" cried Lucien. "I'll be Robinson Crusoe, and we'll play you came in a boat to see me." His friends joined in the laugh, and then somebody said, "You've got a good table, but only two chairs for all to sit on."

"Let's take the table out of doors," said Marie. 'It is bright moonlight, and you can make seats out of those long boards. There's plenty of big stones to rest them on."

"I believe you think of everything, Marie," said Lucien looking at the girl with new respect.

"Everything but me," muttered Jean, taking the table out of doors in his strong arms. He left it for some of the others to place suitably, and hurried in again not to miss a chance of helping Marie with the dishes and provisions. He left it to his mates to arrange the temporary seats.

Marie took little notice of him, though he waited upon her assiduously. She was no coquette, but she knew that, while she was so necessary in her house, she ought not to think of marrying, so she gave little thought to a beau.

Jean was a good fellow and it was Marie's real worth which attracted him so strongly, and made it impossible for him to give up the hope of winning her. He had given Lucien a hint or two on the subject, while at work upon the house, and the child was troubled now to see that Marie scarcely spoke to Jean, despite the way he ran back and forth to wait upon her, but he did not venture to say anything on the subject to either of them.

When everything was ready, Marie summoned them all to supper.

Lucien took the blind man out and seated him at the head of the table; the rest, amid much merriment, seating themselves as best they could.

"Fox acts as if it were his party, instead of mine, doesn't he?" said the boy laughing to see the way the dog was taking toll from all hands.

"It is partly his," returned the blind man, patting Fox, as he jumped on him at the moment. The old man had a warm corner in his heart for the little dog.

Marie and Jean set everything in order after supper, and at ten o'clock the little party broke up. Then, for the first time since his arrival in Paris, Lucien slept upon a bed. "Isn't this fine?" he said as he got in. Fox gave a sleepy little grunt in reply. Lucien laughed. "You see, Man-Friday, it is only since I haven't had any bed to sleep on that I've learned to appreciate one," said he drowsily, as he slipped away into the Land of Nod.

Fox had made himself so comfortable on the chair with a cushion that he only yawned and stretched himself when Lucien spoke to him early the next morning.

"You appreciate a nice bed too, don't you old fellow?" said the boy laughing, as he got up and began to dress. "You'll have to get up, all the same, if you are going to work with me, I can tell you."

Fox was ready when it was time to set out, but before that they made a fresh discovery: a wooden coop containing two rabbits. Fox was for treating them as intruders, but Lucien put a stop to that. "Behave yourself, Sir!" he said. "Is that the way you treat strangers when you were a stranger yourself just days ago? And, look at me, I'm only a stranger in this great city of Paris, though now I have all these fine things." Fox sat up and begged. Lucien threw back his head with a merry laugh. "Yes, I'll excuse you," said he, "but we mustn't spend time talking. I've got to pull some grass for the rabbits to eat while we're away. My, but you're a funny dog!" he exclaimed as Fox began dashing about chewing grass.

"Come, old fellow, it is time we were off," he said, starting for the gate a few moments later. He went with a light heart to his work, thankful to have found a way to earn his own living, and because of his liking for Mr. Germaine. Fox had plenty of reasons to be in good spirits and they were a pleasant pair to look at as they hurried along.

On the way, Lucien stopped at a little shop where Marie often worked, and where she happened to be this morning.

"Who gave me those beautiful rabbits, Marie?" he asked the moment he saw her.

"Jean's grandmother."

"Has she more for herself, Marie?"

"Yes," she replied.

"Then you can tell her that I'll try to keep her supplied with fresh grass for them."

"That will please her," returned Marie, "for she can't always get enough for the rabbits to eat, but she is so fond of them that her family likes her to have them. How did you sleep on your new bed?"

"Oh, fine! It's a wonder that I awoke this morning at all," replied Lucien.

"I could hardly sleep at all last night, I was so happy," said Marie. "My brother, Paul, feels so ashamed of the way he has behaved that he promised our parents last evening that he would turn over a new leaf. He seemed in earnest, and we owe it all to you, dear Lucien."

"Marie," said the boy, changing the subject hastily, "I stopped to ask you about getting my washing done. Now that my good friends have given me a change of linen, I'll own up that it makes me miserable to wear soiled clothes. I can afford to pay for my washing now, if I knew anybody to do it for me."

"Leave that to me," replied Marie. "I'll fetch them every time, and have them mended for you, besides."

Lucien thanked her and hurried away to the print shop, eager to get back to his new job.

A Fox In Paris

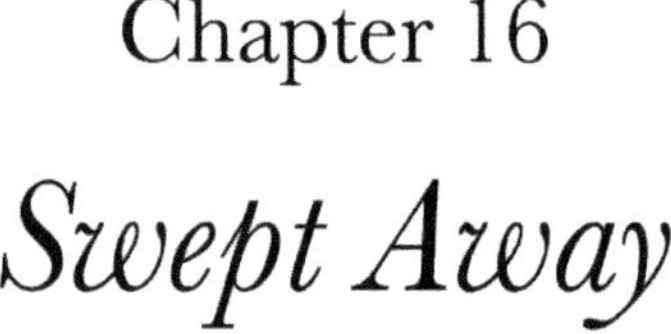

Chapter 16

Swept Away

Where's Lucien?
(Turn the page to see.)
He had attended services at Saint Roch that morning, taking Fox with him as usual. Coming out of the church he lingered to watch the large congregation disperse.

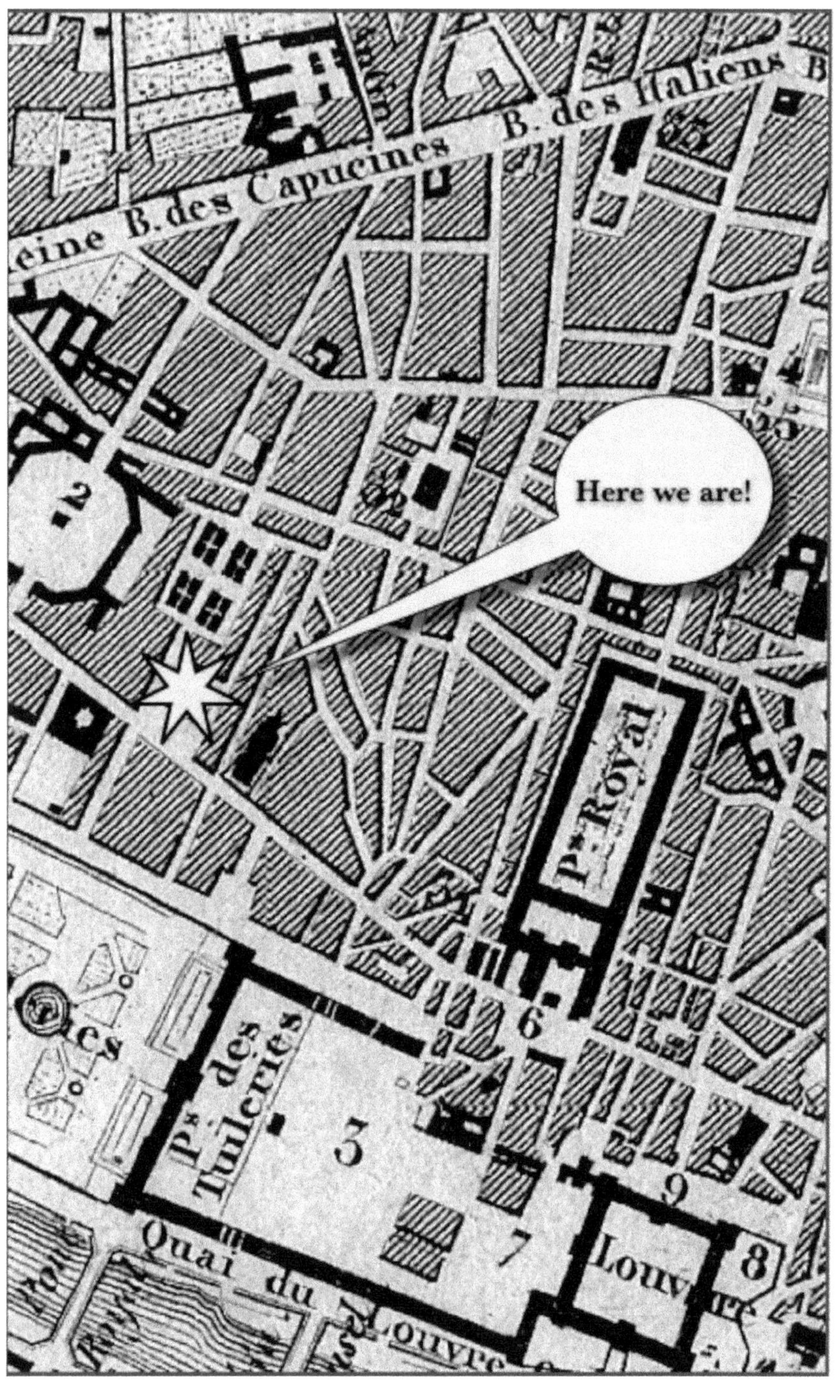
B. des Capucines
B. des Italiens
Here we are!
Pᵃ Royal
Pᵃ des Tuileries
Quai du Louvre
Louvre

Lucien's life settled into a welcome monotony after the party. There was always his day's work, which, like every one's work, was trying some days, but he stuck at it faithfully. Mr. Germaine took him home with him to lunch every day, and the boy had become very dear to the old man and his kindly wife.

Marie's brother Paul had turned over the new leaf, as he promised, and as it stayed turned, there was joy in his parents' home. Paul's gratitude to Lucien for being the means of his reformation, through what he had done for his father, knew no bounds, and he was never so happy as when spending his spare hours in the boy's service. Lucien had many spare hours himself, for Mr. Germaine had wisely fitted his work to his years, so he and Paul mended the gaps in the old wall, pruned the fruit trees, and worked in the garden, getting it ready to plant in spring.

The whole place was so improved, that, when Mr. Raimond returned, after an absence of four months, he hardly recognized his own property. The rough wooden gate, freshly painted green by one of Paul's friends, seemed to return his stare of astonishment. Even the rusty old lock had been oiled and shined up like new. He walked up and down in search of one of the old gaps in the wall, that he might look over, but there wasn't even a peep hole left, so he went back to the gate.

He pulled out the old iron key for the lock, and looked pleased when it slipped easily into the new oiled lock. But, before he turned it, he hesitated, then drew it out and returned it to his pocket. He then proceeded to knock loudly on the gate. As Lucien was away at work, there was no response to his knocking. In utter bewilderment, he sought out his nephew, the police lieutenant, to make inquiries about his young protégé. What he heard of him gave him lively pleasure, but he asked his nephew not to mention his visit to Lucien.

"The boy is doing splendidly," he said, "and it is better to let him work out his own salvation. I'm off again tomorrow on another trip, and I'll see him when I return."

So Lucien knew nothing of his visit.

The pigeons and rabbits had begun to multiply, and the sale of them, added to his weekly wages, made the boy imagine himself growing rich.

Months passed with little of importance occurring in his life, but he had reason to remember one Sunday in February 1838. He had attended services at Saint Roch that morning, taking Fox with him as usual. Coming out of church he lingered to watch the large congregation disperse. The street was blocked with vehicles, many of them fine private carriages, and Lucien watched with interest to see the latter come up in turn for their owners, then escape skillfully out of the crush and drive rapidly away.

He and Fox were quite unconscious of the interest they themselves elicited. Many a passerby exclaimed, "What a handsome boy!" at sight of Lucien. And so he was. He was growing into a fine, healthy lad, his natural refinement showing itself in personal neatness and good manners. Fox with his Sunday bow of red ribbon on, was attracting more attention than Lucien liked, for he kept dancing in and out among the carriages, raising the ire of the coachmen by jumping and barking at the spirited horses. Lucien kept calling him out from under carriages and horses but he ran right back again without allowing the boy to catch him, till Lucien was out of all patience with him. He wanted just to go home and read a new book, lent to him by Mr. Germaine, and began to move on with the crowd, whistling to Fox to follow, but the dog kept making fresh sallies into the crowded street, so they made slow progress.

Suddenly a dark, well polished carriage came pulled up out of the throng and stopped near by. It stood there for a moment, motionless, and then, a woman's voice from within called out, "Fox." Then the door was thrown open and the lady inside called out again, "Fox, come!" and without an instants hesitation, the dog sprang into the carriage. The door slammed, and the horses were off at a brisk trot before Lucien fully realized what had happened. Then he tried to overtake the carriage, calling wildly, "Fox! Fox! Stop thief! Stop thief!"

As he needed breath for running, and no one seemed to pay any attention to his cries, he soon hurried on in silence.

Presently he realized that amid the throng of carriages, all looking much alike to him, he had lost sight of the one to which he had given chase. Sitting down upon a doorstep, he cried as he had not done in many months. The only ray of light in the darkness that enveloped him was the hope that Fox might escape, and find his way home.

He tried to comfort himself by remembering what a very knowing little dog Fox was. It was not much comfort, though, to remember how faithful and loving he was, and to think that perhaps others might now claim his love and devotion. It was bitter going home, bereft of the friend and companion of his lonely hours. As he passed through the Champs Elysees, he ran up and down the paths calling "Fox! Fox!" and giving his familiar whistle, but there was no response.

He tried to think he might find the little dog awaiting him at the green gate, and hurried forward, peering about him with sharpened vision, as he ran. If the dog was there, he must try to make him understand what a dreadful fright he had given him, and that it must not happen again. Sadly, there was no Fox at the gate, and it was with a heavy heart that Lucien turned the key and went ashore on his now lonely island.

The pigeons came cooing and fluttering around him, and the rabbits did their best to attract his attention but he took no notice of any of them. Missing the quick intelligence of Fox, these creatures seemed to him too stupid and commonplace for notice. From force of habit, he attended to their wants, however, and then sat down to read. The words blurred, and he could make no sense out of them when they straightened out. "Mr. Germaine told me he knew I'd like this book," said Lucien, "but I don't. I think it's stupid. I guess I'll get something to eat," he said closing his head upon the table in an abandonment of grief.

He ate no dinner. The fire died out, and he went to bed at dark, cold and hungry, but with ears straining to catch every sound. Many times since his return he had run out to the gate, thinking he heard Fox bark, and each time the disappointment seemed the harder to bear. He slept little, and the night appeared endless. It had new voices, too, that terrified him. He was out of bed at dawn, and ran to the gate first thing, hoping for sight or sound of Fox, but met only disappointment.

With lagging feet he went back to feed the pigeons and rabbits and got his own breakfast, but he felt no interest in anything. On the way to work, he stopped to tell Marie his trouble, and they wept together. Lucien's first words to Mr. Germaine were, "Oh, Sir, I've lost my dog."

"I'm so sorry, my boy," was the reply, "but you must work all the harder. There's nothing like work to cure trouble."

The poor boy worked hard enough that day, but he seemed principally to be making work for others, for he spoiled everything he tried to do. "I'm afraid you will have to get another dog," said Mr. Germaine smiling, while he was patiently trying to undo some of Lucien's tangles.

"No, Sir, I don't want any dog but Fox," replied the boy, bursting into tears, to the astonishment and distress of Mr. Germaine.

"Well, well, my son," he said kindly, "never mind; I see your heart isn't in your work today, and I don't blame you. Fox was a good little dog, and we were all fond of him, and should be glad to see him back again. Put on your cap and spend the rest of the afternoon looking for him. Who knows but he is looking for you, too?"

This brought the first smile to Lucien's face. He thanked Mr. Germaine, and hurried off, running hither and yon, following ladies and carriages, but he saw nothing of his lost friend.

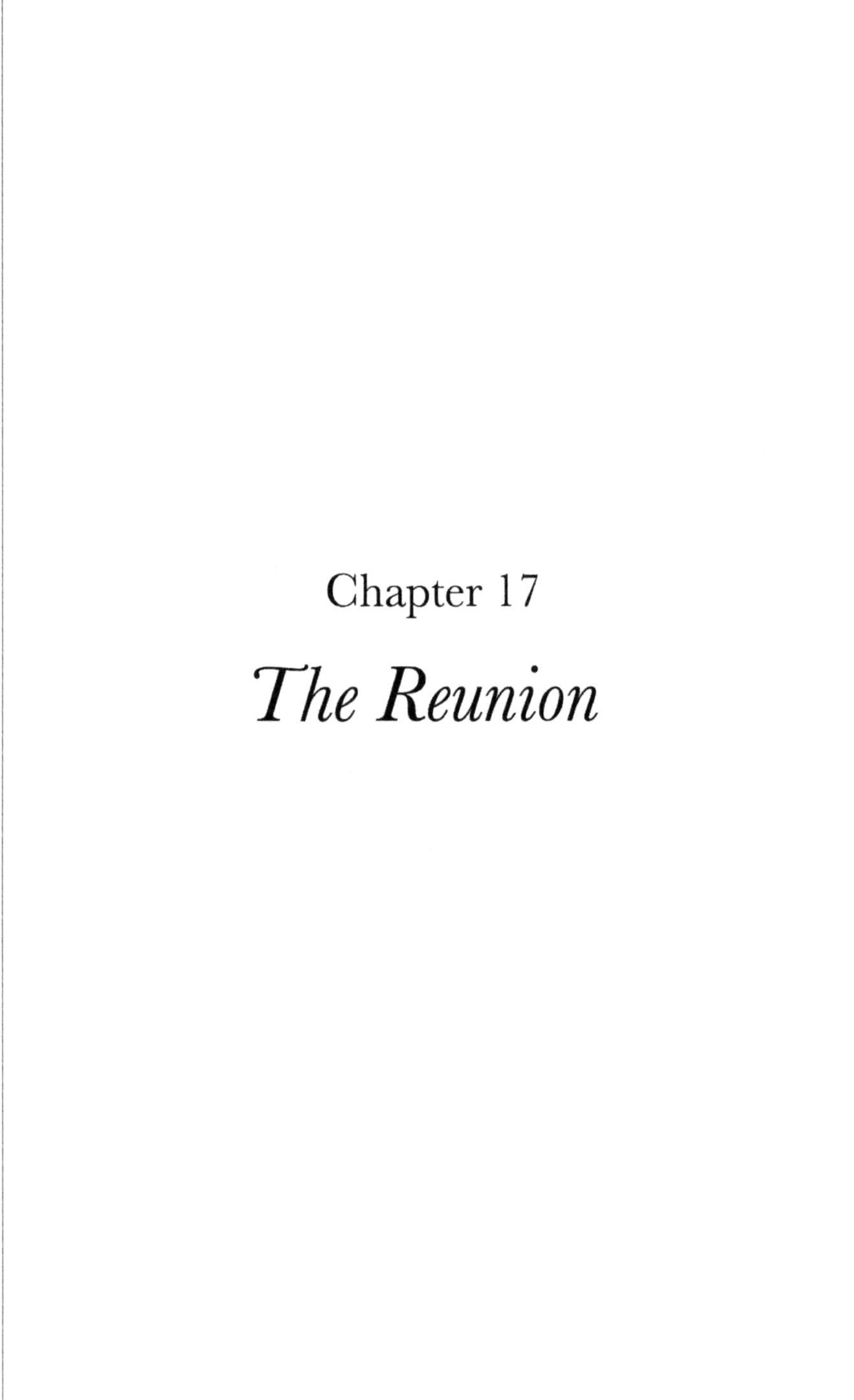

Chapter 17

The Reunion

Where's Lucien?
(Turn the page to see.)
"What place is this?" he cried, startled at sight of the high wall, and the big key Lucien was turning in the lock.

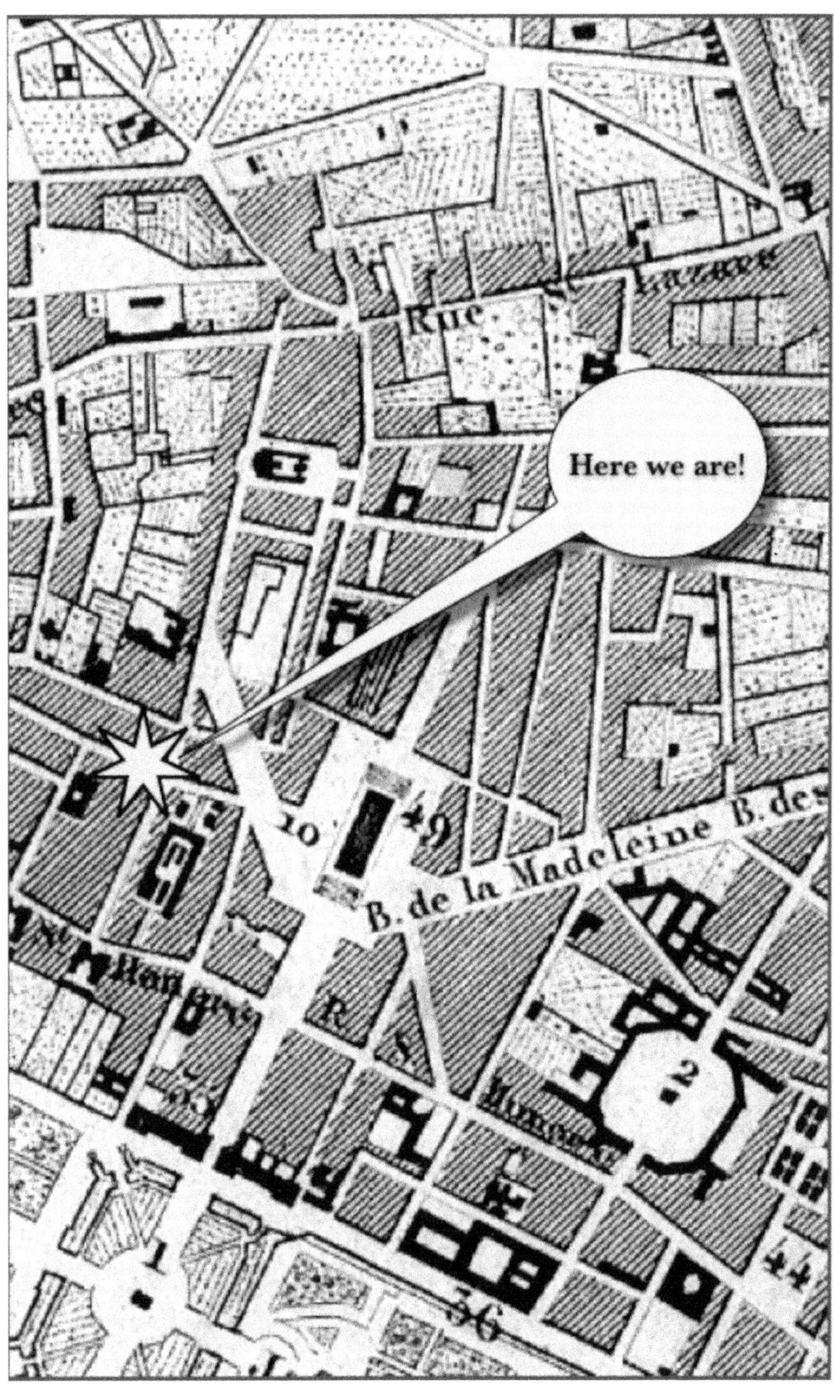
Here we are!
Rue
B. de la Madeleine
B. des
10
9
36

On a cold evening, not long after, with the ground covered by a thin, early snow, a shabbily dressed young man standing outside of a cheap restaurant caught Lucien's eye as he was passing on his walk home from the print shop. Something familiar in beggar's appearance attracted Lucien and he stopped short to look at the panhandler more closely. As he stepped forward to accost a passing gentleman for some change, his face became plainly visible, in the lamp light.

The gentleman quickly dropped something into the outstretched hand, and went on his way. Neither of them perceived Lucien, who had drawn back into the shadow of a house, and stood spellbound watching the beggar. A beggar he certainly was, for he asked alms of everyone coming his way. A few obliged him, but more turned the cold shoulder, and Lucien saw him shake a clenched fist at many of the latter after they had gone by. At last, he broke into abusive language to a gentleman who had not only refused to give him anything, but had exclaimed, "What is a great, hulking fellow like you doing begging? Why don't you go to work?"

His reply sent the gentleman hurrying around the corner, but at the sound of his voice, Lucien finally stepped out of the shadows and walked slowly up to the man. "Gustave? My god, then it is really you! How can it be? I must be dreaming."

"Who knows my name here?" answered the beggar in alarm. "Who are you anyway? I don't know you." Lucien touched the young man upon the arm; "Keep your hands off me!" almost shouted the latter, pulling away from the boy and starting up the street.

"Wait, wait, Gustave," cried Lucien hurrying after him. "I don't want to harm you. Don't you remember me, Cousin? I'm Lucien." The young man stopped dead in his tracks at these words.

"You lie!" he cried turning to the boy. "He's dead, and, besides, he was only a little boy."

"Yes," replied Lucien, drawing nearer to where the other now leaned, quaking with fear against a wall, "You are right, Gustave, he was only a little boy when you deserted him in the Tuileries. But he is not dead, as you will see, if you take a good look at me," he added, trying to smile in order to reassure his cousin.

"Well, you seem to thrive on being deserted," snapped Gustave, trying to hide his fright and embarrassment by bravado.

"Yes," answered the boy quietly, "your dear father told me that God would help us if we helped others, and I have found it true. Now I should like to help you, Cousin, if you will let me."

"What? When I deserted you...?" began Gustave.

"Never mind," Lucien interrupted. "I have forgiven you. I know you meant to injure me, but you did not succeed. Come home with me now and I will tell you the tale while we have our supper."

While he was speaking, Lucien had started to walk towards home, and his cousin had kept by his side.

After a short walk, Lucien stopped before his familiar green gate. "Where are you going?" asked the latter as Lucien stopped and took the big key from his pocket. "What place is this?" he cried, startled at sight of the high wall, and the big key Lucien was turning in the lock.

"It is my island," replied the boy, "It is where I live." He walked into the compound and held the gate for his cousin to follow.

"Yours! You don't own all this fine land, do you?"

"No, but I take care of it. Come into the house, and we'll have a fire and some supper."

Once the door to the house was unlocked and they were inside, Lucien lit the candles and Gustave looked about in astonishment. "Whose house is this, anyway," he asked uneasily, as his glance wandered around the neat, well-trimmed room. "I don't want to be seen by anybody likely to know me, mind you," he said.

"There's no danger," answered Lucien. "This is my house and nobody comes here but those I choose to let in."

Seeing that his cousin was chilled through, the boy was hurrying his preparations for supper and working over the fire to make it burn hot. Gustave sat close beside the stove, sullenly watching him, saying nothing further after he found they were safe from intrusion. His brain was in a whirl. He realized that he no longer had the innocent child, whom he had deserted, to deal with, but a well-grown lad of uncommon intelligence. He could not muster courage to tell him the truth about himself, and he was busy making up a plausible story against the time when Lucien should demand an explanation of his changed circumstances. He intended to unfold a melancholy tale, which, no doubt, would work upon the sympathies of this generous boy, but, one look into

Lucien's frank eyes convinced him that it would never do to contradict himself. He was still trying to straighten out his story when Lucien called him to supper.

Lucien, much saddened at finding his cousin in such a plight, ate little, but Gustave was like one famished, and soon cleared the table of eatables. After supper Lucien asked again the meaning of his cousin's altered fortunes.

"Oh, it's easy enough explained," replied Gustave, monopolizing the warmest corner, and the most comfortable chair, "I met with bad luck, that is all."

"And I with good," returned Lucien, "but as there was a cause for my good luck, so perhaps, there is one for your bad luck."

"What do you mean? Explain yourself," said Gustave gruffly.

Lucien gave him the main points of his story, modestly keeping in the background his own good deeds.

"Humph!" said his cousin, shrewd enough to read between the lines. "Now see what you think of my bad luck. When I got home from Paris, after," here he paused, "our trip. I found someone waiting for me who made me a lot of trouble. She..."

"She?" asked Lucien in surprise. Who was "she?"

"You wouldn't know if I told you," snapped his cousin, pulling up suddenly. "That wasn't what I started to tell you about. Let me see, oh, yes, it was the servants I was thinking of; they bothered me so, asking questions about you, that I cleared them all out of the house."

"What! All of Uncle's old servants, who were so fond of him?" cried Lucien with flashing eyes.

"Yes, to the last one," replied Gustave defiantly. "I guess a man has a right to do as he pleases in his own house."

Lucien was silent, his eyes upon the floor. His companion went on glibly, "When I tell you that I ran through my whole fortune in six months, don't imagine I did anything really wrong. Naturally, you are astonished, but what does a boy like you know about such matters?" said Gustave patronizingly.

Lucien did not speak. Gustave gave him a suspicious look and continued, "To begin with, the new servants proved a set of rascals. They robbed me right and left. Then I had a host of false friends who borrowed money of me and never returned it. They ate and drank me out of house and home: Of course, I had to give balls and parties and keep fast horses to please them; in short, I lived like a prince," said Gustave swaggering.

Lucien sitting with averted eyes, still said nothing, and his cousin began to feel uneasy about the possible effect of these revelations upon him. After all, they were not so very far from the truth, for he had not succeeded in making up the tale with which he had intended to deceive the boy. With another sidelong look at Lucien, he forged ahead, "I suppose I did wrong to gamble," he said with simulated meekness, "but I was driven to it by others. Keep out of bad company, whatever you do, Lucien; there's no telling where it will lead you."

The boy shot a pointed glance at his cousin which made the latter hurriedly catch up the dropped thread of his story,

"Of course I lost," he said, "for I was in the hands of swindlers. When I found I had only ten thousand francs left in the world, I closed the house and came to Paris, hoping to retrieve my fortunes. Unfortunately, some of my false friends came, too, and they persuaded me to gamble again. I staked my last dollar and lost, and my friends deserted me when they found I had nothing more to give.

Lucien interrupted sadly, "And what of my uncle's house? Have you lost my old home as well?" Hearing about it now, so many good old memories of his life there with his uncle, and playing in the garden they both loved so well, came flooding back into his head and set the tears coursing down his cheeks, that he could not help but ask.

"My house is still my house, for now," replied Gustave with hollow authority. But wanting to keep Lucien's attention on his current condition, he continued his story. "Yesterday I was turned out of my room, because I could not pay the rent. What is more," continued Gustave, looking furtively at Lucien to see how he was taking this part of the story, "my landlady seized my trunk and my clothes. I had had nothing to eat all day today, or I should never have lowered myself to beg."

"It was well I met you," said Lucien quietly, but he did not look at his cousin.

"You see how it all happened, don't you?" asked Gustave.

"No, I'm afraid I don't," replied the boy.

"But you have no ill-feelings against me, have you?"

Lucien hesitated; "I'm afraid I did have," said he, "while I thought you were rich, but you seem to have been punished for what you did to me. It was your dear father who told me we reap as we sow."

"I suppose you think yourself very virtuous because you've got all these fine things," sneered Gustave. "I wonder where you would have been if you hadn't met your Mr. Raimond, and the masons you tell about who built your house?"

"That's very true, Gustave. If I hadn't met Mr. Raimond, the comrades of the blind man's son would never have put up this house."

"And what about your dog?" Gustave asked triumphantly. "Without him, you would have had none of your adventures and good fortune, that I can see."

"That is true too, Gustave. If I had not taken pity upon him, others would not have wanted to help me."

"I'm sick of all this foolish talk," said Gustave abruptly. Stretching himself with a yawn he added, "I'd like to go to bed. Where do you expect me to sleep?"

"With me. You are welcome to half of my bed. That's the best I can do for you," answered Lucien.

"All right then, I'll turn in," suiting the action to the word, and making no attempt to undress, further than to toss his shabby coat on a chair and to kick off his damp boots.

This was a fresh shock to Lucien, who remembered his cousin as a very fastidious person.

While he himself was preparing for bed, he heard something that sent his heart into his mouth. He flew to the gate and flung it wide, and Fox bounded into his arms.

Hastily slamming and locking the gate, he hurried into the house, hugging and kissing the spaniel as he ran.

Entering their little house, he heard his cousin say with an oath, "Shut the door, can't you? What do you mean by freezing me out this way?"

Fox bristled and growled at sight of a stranger in Lucien's bed.

"Hush up, you little beast, or I'll make you," said Gustave angrily.

"No, you'll never lay so much as a finger on Fox," cried Lucien lividly. The next instant with his face buried against the dog, he was weeping bitterly, Fox whining in sympathy.

Gustave rose on his elbow to look at them. "I do believe the fool is crying," he said to himself, then aloud he added petulantly, "I wish you'd stop that noise and come to bed. What kind of a way is this to treat a visitor!"

Lucien made no reply. He intended to look after the dog's every comfort before he retired for the night. Fox had a very good bed of his own, a box with some soft old carpet inside, but Lucien had put it out of sight after he was lost. It took him some time to get it out now and arrange it to the dog's satisfaction, Gustave talking the while, in the most disagreeable way, because, as he claimed, his comfort was set aside for that of a good-for-nothing dog.

"The reason I don't answer you back, Gustave," said Lucien at last, "is that I am too happy over having Fox back again to care what you or anybody says, but I should like to remind you that you said a while ago that a man had a right to do as he pleased in his own house."

"A man, yes, but not a boy."

Lucien laughed, as he gave Fox a final good night hug, and blew out the candle

Chapter 18

Wanted!

Where's Lucien?
(Turn the page to see.)
The next morning, as he and Lucien were crossing the Place de Le Concorde, they saw a number of people stop to read a notice put up in a prominent place.

Here we are!
de la Madel
Jardin
des Tuil
Quai des Tuileries
36
28
33

"It is very odd, Gustave," said Lucien the next morning, "but Fox doesn't seem to take to you at all." The dog had growled every time the elder cousin came near him, and once or twice had showed his teeth in a way that surprised Lucien.

"So you think dogs have their likes and dislikes, do you?" Gustave asked, kicking a bit of wood at Fox. The dog snarled as it hit him.

"None of that, Cousin!" said Lucien hotly. "It's a case of love me, love my dog. Now you are in my house, and Fox is part of my family. Certainly, I believe that dogs have their likes and dislikes. If not, why was Fox so glad to get back to me? For that matter, why did he come back at all? Tell me that, Fox," said the boy fondling the little dog gamboling about him.

Fox replied with an enthusiastic bark, and they laughed together.

"But, we must be thinking of your affairs, Gustave, and how I might help you," said Lucien turning to his cousin.

"Thanks, you have quite the air of being my guardian, Lucien, but, I imagine I am old enough to manage my own affairs," Gustave said loftily.

He was trying to freshen his shabby garments by the aid of a brush and soap and water.

"I am going to see some friends, who may prove useful to me. Suppose you lend me a clean shirt and a fresh tie; that is the best service you can render me at present. Give me a clean handkerchief, too, while you're about it," he said to

Lucien, who was obligingly looking over his wardrobe to supply his cousin's wants, "put some cologne on it, too."

"You're asking too much," returned Lucien with a laugh, "I haven't any toilet luxuries at present. I suppose I must have had plenty of such things when I was a little boy," he added thoughtfully. "When you left me in the Tuileries, Gustave, I must have been very handsomely dressed, for every one took me for a rich man's son."

"No doubt!" answered Gustave disagreeably. "My father wasted a lot of money on you; I wish I had it back now."

Lucien wheeled round and faced him, saying sharply, "I should think you were getting back some of it right here and now."

"Of course, of course," replied Gustave quickly in a conciliatory tone. "I was only joking. Yes, indeed, Lucien, it was lucky I met you, and you are a friend in need, but I wish you'd chain up that brute," he said, jumping aside to escape Fox's snap at his heels.

There was a resolute air about Lucien, where the dog was concerned, that kept his cousin from venting his spite upon Fox, but there was no love lost between them.

"If you let him alone, he will not bother you," was all the satisfaction he got out of Lucien, who was quietly putting the room in order.

"By the way," said his cousin nonchalantly, "I must borrow some money from you."

"How much do you want?"

"As much as you can spare."

"I've got thirty francs," said Lucien producing an old purse, "I'll divide with you. I can't let you have it all."

This was much better than Gustave had expected, and he showed his satisfaction. "You're a good chap, Lucien," he said patronizingly. "I'll return it soon."

When the boy was ready to go to work, his cousin set out with him, but soon excused himself, and Lucien saw no more of him that day. When he reached home that night, however, he found Gustave waiting at the gate, and seemingly in good spirits, but he said little, and went early to bed.

The next morning, as he and Lucien were crossing the Place de Le Concorde, they saw a number of people stop to read a notice put up in a prominent place.

"Let's see what it is," said Gustave drawing near and looking over the heads in front of him, he read it out for Lucien's benefit.

> "Lost Dog.
>
> Fifty Francs Reward
>
> Lost, a small black spaniel, with long ears, tan feet and tail, and a white spot on his breast. Answers to the name of Fox. He was lost about two years ago, and recovered by his owner last Sunday, but has since disappeared. The above reward will be paid for his return to Madame Marboeuf, 37 Lafitte Street."

"Madame Marboeuf! How strange!" muttered Gustave, rejoining Lucien, who had caught Fox up in his arms and was hurrying away.

"That is all about you dear little Fox," he was saying to the dog cuddled in his arms, "but I shall not give you up to anybody."

"Well, good bye, Lucien," said his cousin, making no reference to the notice. "I'll see you later," he added jauntily. "I suppose you peg away at your work all day. It must be an awful bore."

"No, I like it," answered the boy as he went his way, still carrying the dog.

When he entered the printing office, he told Mr. Germaine about the advertisement first thing. "It was a great big bill," said he, "so that everybody could see it. It was well printed, too. I know good work when I see it now, thanks to you, Sir. I grabbed Fox up and hurried away as soon as I found out what it was about," added the boy with a lighthearted laugh.

Mr. Germaine looked grave. "What are you going to do about it?" he asked, shooting a keen glance at Lucien from under his shaggy eyebrows.

"Do about it?" echoed the boy slowly, not understanding.

Mr. Germaine turned back to his writing.

Lucien eyed him a moment, and then asked hesitatingly "What do you think I ought to do about it, Sir?"

"My advice is that you return the dog to his rightful owner," replied Mr. Germaine, not looking up from his work.

The boy turned pale, and then flushed deeply. "Never!" he cried in excitement. "Nobody shall ever separate Fox and me again. I'm his rightful owner. He would have been killed by the police but for me. Then where would that lady's dog have been?" he asked triumphantly.

Mr. Germaine, who was sharpening a pencil, neither looked up, nor replied.

"Besides," continued Lucien, still on the defensive, "I've been his 'rightful owner' for two years. It's just the same as though that lady's dog had been killed, and this was a new one," he added positively.

"Don't be too sure, my boy," returned Mr. Germaine, darting another glance at Lucien, "suppose you should be accused of stealing him."

"I? Steal a dog? Oh, Mr. Germaine, what a dreadful thing to say."

"My dear Lucien, your good uncle surely taught you that it was theft to take or keep what was not your own."

"He did indeed, Mr. Germaine, and if that is the way it looks to you, that settles it," answered Lucien sadly. "I'll take him back to his mistress now, if you'll excuse me, Sir. I couldn't work today."

"That's all right, my boy," said Mr. Germaine, giving Lucien an approving pat on the shoulder. "We must worry along without you this time."

On his way out, Lucien told the story to the printers, who expressed much sympathy with him and the unconscious dog. One man suggested his trying to buy back Fox, and as the rest thought it a feasible plan, it gave the boy a ray of hope as he started on his sad mission.

It was, however, so faint a gleam, amid the gloom that enveloped him, that poor little Fox whined and shivered in his arms, affected by his dejection. It almost seemed to Lucien as if he were pleading with him not to desert him.

"And poor me, what shall I do without you?" he said, kissing the dog's head. "You will have a good home and kind friends, but I shall be all alone – or worse," for just then he remembered his cousin.

A Fox In Paris

Chapter 19

Madame Marboeuf

Upon seeing the grand house, Lucien looked down at Fox and remarked sadly, "Well, at least I know you will have a grand place to lay your head at night."

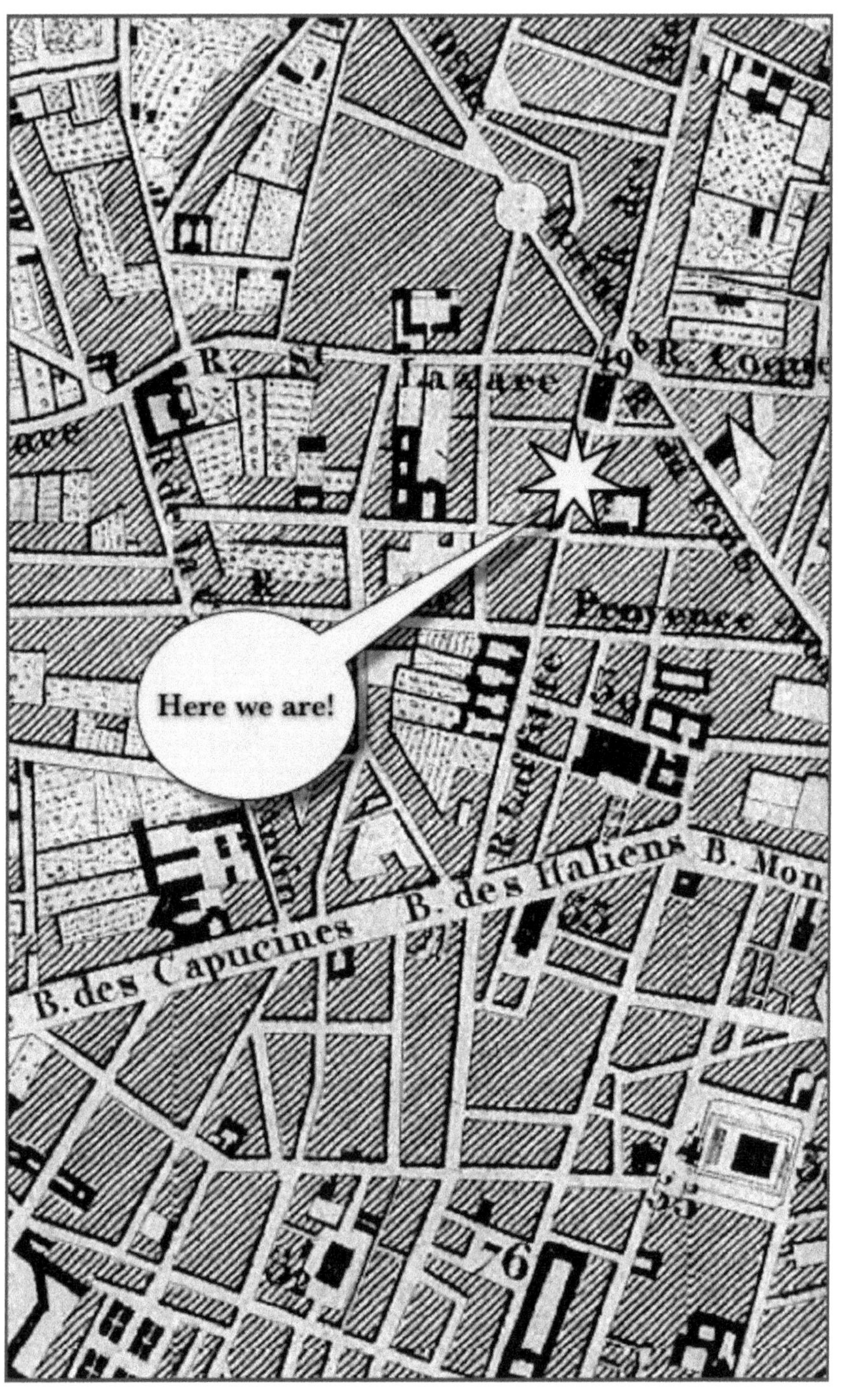
Here we are!
B. des Capucines
B. des Italiens
Provence

Upon seeing the grand house, Lucien looked down at Fox and remarked with sadness, "Well, at least I know you will have a grand place to lay your head at night, even if it is not with me." Fox looked none to happy at the prospect. As they drew nearer the house, Lucien was surprised to find Gustave standing at the door. To his eager, "What brings you here Cousin?" Gustave was too startled to reply at once; then he said mockingly, "and what brings you may I ask?"

"To return my dog to his rightful owner," Lucien answered promptly, but with saddened voice.

"To get the reward, I suppose," returned the cousin with a harsh laugh.

"Not I!" Lucien exclaimed indignantly. "I wouldn't touch a penny of it; it would be like blood-money to me. All the rewards in the world couldn't tempt me to part with my Fox."

"What then? You seem very independent," said Gustave inquisitively.

"I am. Your dear father taught me to be honest, and I intend to keep so."

Gustave winced. "Look here youngster," he said, "don't say anything about me to Madame Marboeuf, as you'll get yourself in trouble."

"Why? Do you know her?" asked the astonished boy.

"That's nothing to you. Just remember what I tell you," was the curt reply as Gustave turned on his heel and walked quickly away.

The servant summoned by the concierge took Lucien to Madame Marboeuf's apartment, which was on the second floor. "You're in luck," said the man to Lucien, as they were going upstairs, "I wish I had found Fox. A body doesn't pick up fifty francs every day." Lucien was silent.

Passing through richly furnished rooms, hung with heavy draperies it gave him a sense of suffocation to think of his dear Fox being shut up in there after the free, happy life he had had with him. Instead of trying to spring from his arms, the dog seemed to cling the closer to him after they entered the house. At the open door of Madame Marboeuf's boudoir, the servant paused, saying, "Madame, here is your dog."

"Fox?" cried the lady, casting aside a piece of elegant embroidery and putting out her arms to Fox, as Lucien brought him near. "Come Fox," she said, overjoyed, "Come to your own mistress, who loves you so." The dog gave an apologetic little whine and a shiver, but made no move to leave Lucien. "Why, you ungrateful little beast!" said his mortified mistress. "Put him down boy," she commanded. "What do you mean by holding him so tight that he can't come when I call him?" Lucien gently set the dog on the floor, but Fox refused to leave him, even when the lady, in desperation, offered him a tempting bonbon.

"The dog is bewitched, what have you done to him?" she said sharply to Lucien.

"Saved his life two years ago, Madame, and taken care of him and loved him ever since," he replied with a simple directness that she would have found charming at another time, but now she was mortified and angry; too much so to find words at once to reply. "You see for yourself, Madame," Lucien resumed respectfully, "how he loves me and begs you not to separate us."

"Nonsense, you silly boy," cried the irate lady, "I see nothing of the kind. He is my dog, and he'll be all right as soon as you are gone. You can buy another dog that you will think just as much of. Here, Pierre, give this boy the reward and show him out."

Lucien did not move. "What are you waiting for?" asked Madame Marboeuf, impatiently. "Isn't the reward large enough?"

"It isn't that, Madame," said the boy with gentle dignity, "I don't want any reward, but I should like to ask a favor of you," he added, his voice beginning to tremble.

"Well, what is it," asked the lady, looking bored.

"It is that you let me keep Fox. I don't want the reward; it would seem like selling a friend to take it. He is all I have in the world. I implore you, Madame," Lucien said in supplicating tones, seeing that the lady appeared quite unmoved.

She was a handsome woman of about fifty, and looked like a person accustomed to having her own way, and upon whom fortune had, quite obviously, smiled. She was looking at Lucien now as though he were a curiosity. "You are certainly a very odd boy," she said brusquely. "The idea of your supposing that I would give away my darling Fox!"

"I didn't expect you to give him to me," rejoined the boy, catching at straws, "I meant for you to sell him to me."

Madame Marboeuf threw her hands up with a ringing laugh, "And how much did you expect to pay for him?" she asked.

"You set the price yourself, Madame, when you offered the reward. I haven't the fifty francs with me, but I can get them, and I'll cheerfully pay you that amount, and more, if you ask it, for my dear Fox." His dear Fox, crouched at his feet, was looking up into his face as he talked, and taking no notice whatever of his mistress. Lucien, who understood him so well, could not see how she could harden her heart to the dog's mute pleading to stay with him.

She no longer addressed Fox, as she had done at first. In truth, his indifference mortified her so much that she did not want to give him a chance to make further display of it before Pierre, the servant who had brought them to her. Within the past two years she had had an experience which had shaken her faith in human nature, and this, perhaps, made her doubt the sincerity of Lucien's appeal. At any rate, it left her quite unmoved, and his strenuousness bored her. "I've had enough of this," she said abruptly to Pierre, "you may double the reward, since he doesn't seem satisfied, and send him off." Catching Fox by the collar, she held him fast, despite his wild struggles and prolonged howls when Lucien turned to go.

Dazed and heartsick, the boy followed Pierre down stairs. "Here's your money," said the latter, offering him the one-hundred francs.

"Not my money!" cried Lucien, indignantly. "Do you think I'd touch that wicked woman's money?"

"My mistress is not a wicked woman," returned Pierre, but he did not speak as though troubled by the boy's vehement words.

"I suppose you call her good," Lucien retorted with scorn.

"Not that either," replied the man thoughtfully. "She hasn't a chance to be one thing or the other. She has plenty of money, and everything she wants, and always has her own way. I don't believe she ever had any real trouble," continued Pierre, "so she thinks money is the great cure-all. That's why she told me to double the reward, and now she thinks you are fixed all right."

The servant's talk gave Lucien a few more moments under the same roof with his beloved dog, so he was glad to listen as the man went on, "Now, if you needed help, she'd give you money, but she doesn't seem to have any sympathy or pity to give to anybody. Ladies like that make the greatest fuss over dogs," said he, "while it seems they wouldn't lift a finger to do anything for a poor child."

"She may keep her money for all me," said Lucien. "It wouldn't be honest for me to take it anyway, for the first time Fox gets out, he'll come straight home to me, just as he did before."

Pierre laughed. "I hope he will," he said quietly, "for we don't want him here. He's a perfect nuisance to what he used to be, and Madame keeps us on the jump looking after him."

Pierre opened the front door for Lucien. "Good day." He pauses a moment. "You know, perhaps Fox will get home before you. Stranger things than that have happened," he added, closing the door, and giving Lucien a quick wink before it latched shut.

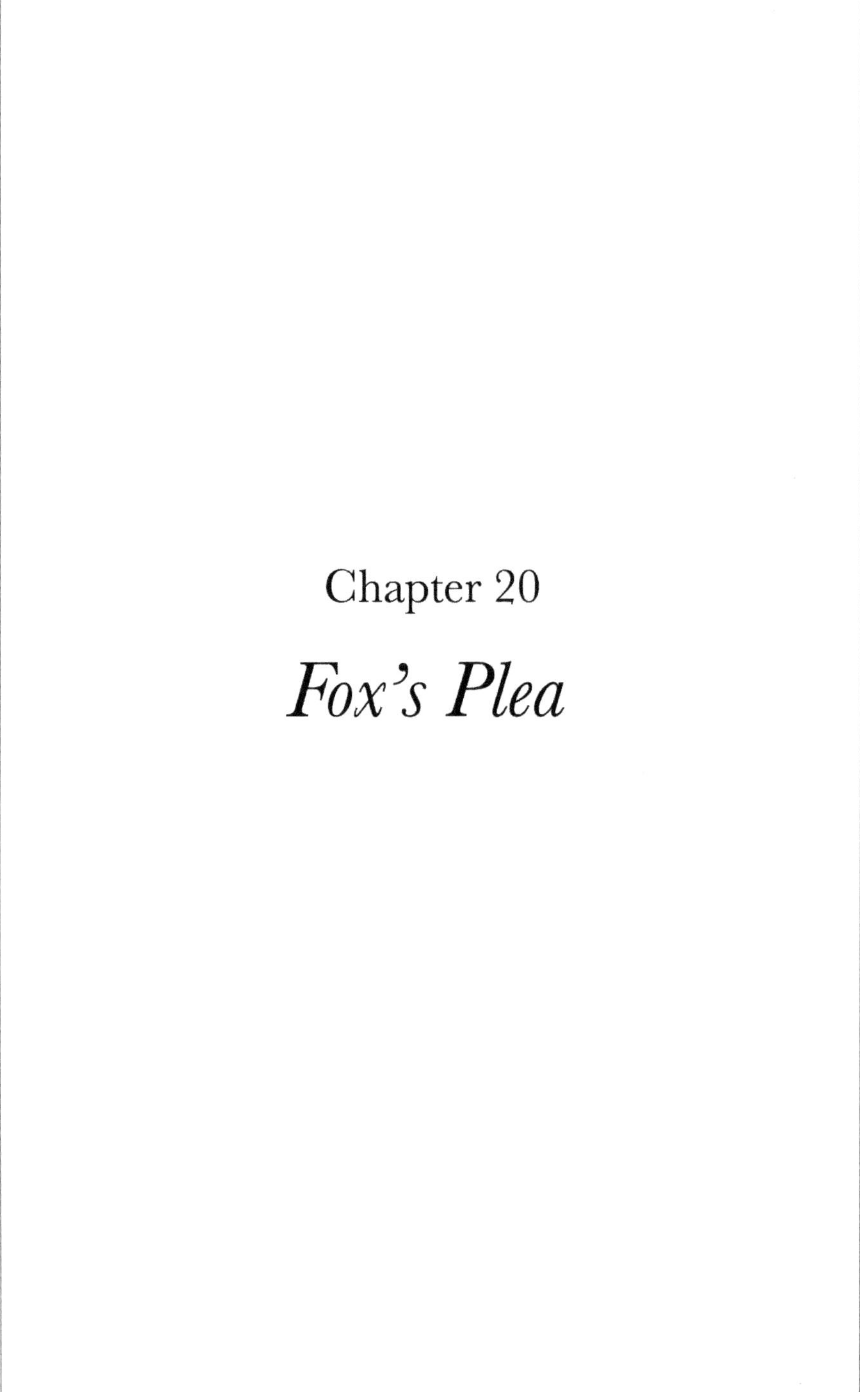

Chapter 20

Fox's Plea

Where's Lucien?
(Turn the page to see.)
"All right my boy, and when it is ready we'll print it on good paper, so the lady will have no excuse for not reading it," said Gaspard laughing.

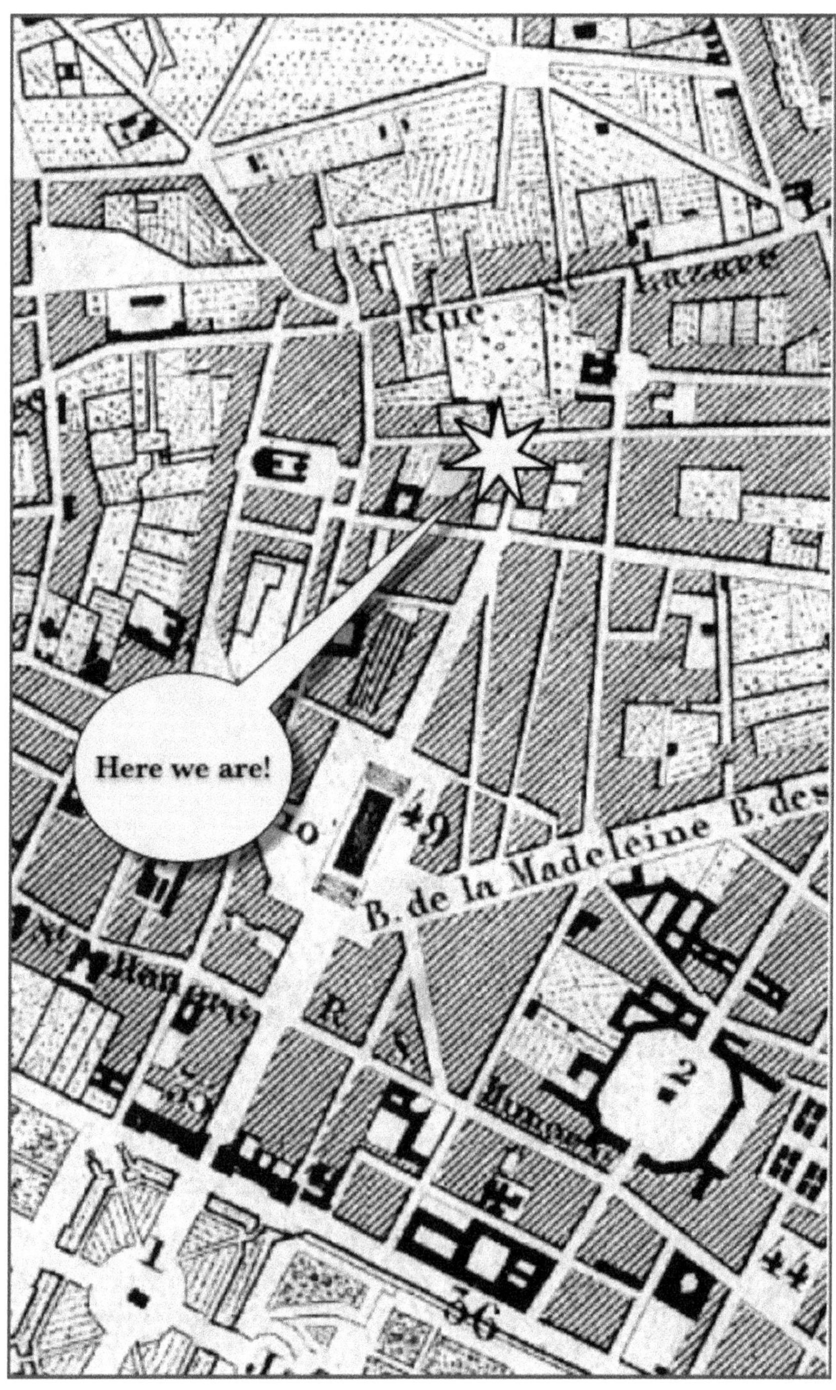
Here we are!
Rue
B. de la Madeleine B. des

As the heavy, ornate door latched behind him, Pierre's words and manner put a new idea into Lucien's mind. He smiled as he noticed that the house stood on a corner. "So much the better for Fox and me," he was saying to himself, as he darted off the steps and onto the side street, and ran bump into a man.

Before he could ask pardon, the voice of his cousin exclaimed loudly, "Look what you're about, can't you? You nearly knocked me down. I'm no ten pin!"

"What! You here again, Gustave?" cried Lucien.

"And why shouldn't I be here again?" retorted his cousin. "Victoria Street is free to the public, isn't it? Besides, I wanted to see how you were coming on. Did you get the money?"

"Of course not!" replied Lucien with spirit. "Do you think I'd take this woman's money?

"Idiot." muttered his cousin under his breath, and then aloud, "How did you like Madame Marboeuf?"

"I think she's horrid," was the curt reply.

Gustave looking relieved asked, "What are you going to do now?"

"Stay where I am. Mr. Germaine gave me the day, and I'm going to spend some of it here near Fox," answered Lucien resolutely. His cousin was visibly annoyed by the boy's stalwart determination, but he merrily said, "I'm off then. I've some pressing business to attend to."

When Lucien was sure his cousin had gone he began to pace beside the house, whistling. He knew well enough what would happen. He had only to wait until his faithful little friend, hearing his familiar whistle, found a way to get out. It did not seem to him that he had to wait very long. Perhaps old Pierre was not so watchful as his mistress expected him to be, and carelessly left the door open a crack, or possibly he was tenderhearted and could not resist the dog's struggles to be let out, and opened the door on purpose. At any rate, in short order, there was Fox jumping and tumbling all over Lucien and they were laughing and crying together as they hastened to the printing office.

"So, you changed your mind did you?" was Mr. Germaine's greeting as they entered.

"No sir," volunteered Lucien.

"But you've brought back your dog; how's that?"

"Yes sir, and I will tell you all about it, but, it will save for all of us, if you will let me call the printers in to hear it. I want everyone's opinion or advice, for the matter isn't settled yet."

"Very well my boy, but we must not take too much time to it, for we are short one of our best hands today you know," replied Mr. Germaine, looking pointedly over at Lucien. The boy declared, "Never mind that Sir" he said, "I'll make up the for the lost time; see if I don't, just as soon as this is settled."

With that, he called in the printers who gathered around him and interrupted his story with many comments and angry interjections, telling him what he ought to have said, and what they would have done, and all manner of things. "It is easy enough for you to say what you should have done," said Lucien, "but it is no joke talking to a high and mighty lady like that. Anybody would think she owned you, the way she shuts you right up if you try to answer her. It was all I could do to keep from crying when I begged her to let me keep Fox; she made me so unhappy."

"What did she say when you asked her?" replied Mr. Germaine.

"She told her man to double the reward. She thought I was after money," answered Lucien indignantly.

"Why didn't you offer her the one hundred francs for the dog?" asked one of the printers, who evidently thought this a very original idea.

"I did, and she laughed at the suggestion," returned the boy.

"That's because it was her own money," replied the man. "I suppose she thinks you haven't any of your own."

"But, I told her I could easily get it," interrupted Lucien.

"Oh, a bird in the hand is worth two in the bush," put in another printer. "The thing to do now is to take the one-hundred francs, and go straight back to her and say, 'Here's your money madam, and I'll keep my dog.'"

Lucien astonished the printers by doubling up with laughter.

"Excuse me, Gaspard," he said, when he could speak, "but you don't know the lady. She isn't here," he added with a furtive glance around the office, "as I shouldn't be laughing," and he gave another ringing laugh, which set them all off.

"By this time tomorrow you won't be able to say that I don't know the lady, my boy, " said Gaspard, evidently on his plan. "Now look here comrades," he went on "I'll tell you what we'll do; let's raise that money among ourselves, and Lucien can pay it back when he's ready. If you'll do it, I'll tackle the lady, and I bet she'll take the money for the dog."

Gaspard was soon striding away to Madame Marboeuf's with the money jingling in his pockets, leaving Lucien to do his work in the printer's absence. In a very short time Gaspard was back again, looking very much crestfallen. "Here's your money boys, help yourselves," he said spreading the money on a bench. "You're right about the lady, Lucien," was all they could get out of him as he went stolidly back to his work.

Later, he was willing to tell Lucien about his interview with Madame Marboeuf. "She laughed in my face," said he, "and asked if I took her for a fool and what did I think she wanted with your paltry money! Yes, and she said, to tell 'that boy' that when she gets Fox back, she'd see to it that he didn't run away again," added Gaspard.

"She has the law on her side," said Lucien downcast, "but I am very much obliged to you Gaspard, and to all of you for raising the money. Fox and I have certainly got good friends."

"You always will have," said Gaspard as he laid a big hand on the boy's shoulder and turned to go back to work.

"Oh Gaspard, please wait a minute. You have seen the lady, and I want your advice."

"Go ahead," said the other printer to Lucien.

"I have an idea," Lucien said brightening. "Madame cares more for dogs than for people; she just laughed at my sorrow over parting with Fox, but she talked to him first as if the thoughts he had were deep feelings; that was before he let her see that he cared more for me than he did for her," added the boy retrospectively, and quietly to himself.

"Well," asked Gaspard puzzled, "I don't see what you're driving at?"

"I'll tell you," announced Lucien. "Now suppose we write her a letter signed by Fox. We can tell her his side of the story, don't you see? She would read the letter when she wouldn't let one of us talk to her."

"Very true," returned Gaspard.

"We must all have a hand in it, for you are all Fox's friends," Lucien went on. "I'll jot down what each one thinks we ought to say in the letter, and then I'll ask Mr. Germaine to put it into good shape for us."

"All right my boy, and when it is ready, we'll print it on good paper, so the lady will have no excuse for not reading it," said Gaspard laughing.

The letter, when finished read as follows:

"To my dear and respected Mistress, Madame Marboeuf, When you lost me in the Tuileries two years ago the guards set upon me, and I should not have escaped alive but that a little boy, lost like myself, had compassion upon me. Gashed and bleeding, as I was, he took me up in his arms, and washed and dressed my wounds. He tore his handkerchief in two, binding up the worst of my wounds with one piece and tying the other to my collar to keep me safe near him. He is an honest little boy and would have returned me to you, if you had had your address upon my collar as you should have had for such a valuable dog as I am.

Perhaps you advertised for me, as you are doing now, but this little boy, was a stranger and knew nothing about such things then. His home was in Bordeaux, and he had never been in Paris in his life 'till that very day, when he was cruelly deserted by his only relative. You may well believe how glad he was to find a brave little dog like me to love him and keep him company. The poor child had but one penny in the world, but he shared with me the bread he bought with it.

Don't you see dear Mistress, that no one with a heart could forget these things? I may be only a dog, but I have a heart. I have heard you say it yourself, dear Madame. That poor boy and I have never been separated since that day. He was poor enough, and eager to earn his own living, but he would go nowhere to work where he could not have me with him.

He is not my master in the sense that you are my mistress. He and I are close friends, sharing one another's joys and sorrows. In short, we understand one another. Surely you must have seen that the day he brought me back to you. Wherever I may be, my heart will always be with him, and every chance I get my body will follow it.

You may tie me fast with a silken cord, or a golden chain, but I shall surely get away. Can't you understand that? My friend and I are flung together; we lead a free and happy life, and it would suffocate me now to be held captive in a house all the time, even one as fine as yours. Once I didn't know any better, but I do now. I suppose you will call me ungrateful, but I am not. I could still love you very much, dear Mistress, if you would not try to separate me from my young master.

I have lost all taste for bonbons and rich food, and for being treated as a plaything, and if I were back with you, you would not think me so nice as you once did, for I cannot unlearn the lessons of the past two years. You are rich, dear Madame Marboeuf, and can buy as many dogs as you like, while Lucien is poor, and I am all the world to him. He and I live alone. There are no deceitful servants to cuff and abuse me on the sly, and I can't help thinking of this, too. A dog must present the facts of the case as strong as he knows how, mustn't he? This is why I speak of all these things.

I beg of you dear Mistress, that you will let me stay with my young master, and we will both love you always. He says he will pray for you too. I could visit you whenever you wanted me to do so, if you would only let me go home at night.

Anxiously awaiting your reply, Madame Marboeuf, I remain with affectionate respect.

Fox.

Please address: Fox, General Post Office, Paris.

Amid the hilarious shouts of the printers, Fox submitted with a bad grace to having his paw inked, that he might make his mark in true legal fashion below his penned signature.

A few hours after the letter was mailed the following reply was received:

My dear Fox,

As I cannot answer your interesting letter in full in writing, it would give me pleasure to have your friend and you call upon me.

I am much interested to learn more of your new friend.

Your old friend and Mistress, Antoinette Marboeuf.

"What do you think I'd better do," Lucien asked excitedly as the printers gathered about him to hear this letter read aloud. "I'd go if I were you," replied one. "Not I," said another, "I shouldn't go near the old skin flint." "Better leave Fox with us if you do go," said still another. "She is up to something, I'll be bound, and wants to sneak the dog away from you."

Fox, who was seated upon a high stool, grinning and wagging his tail because he felt himself the center of attention, started up with a sharp bark at the sound of his own name. "No, he must come, too," said Lucien, stroking the dog. "You understand, don't you old fellow." Fox jumped up barking joyfully and then sat down to await events. "Madame Marboeuf has the right to take Fox whenever she finds him, so I'd better do as she says," added the boy.

His friends the printers finally agreed with Lucien, and Mr. Germaine gave him permission to absent himself from his work the next morning long enough to make the proposed call.

A Fox In Paris

Chapter 21

Chance Encounter

Where's Lucien?
(Turn the page to see.)
In his hasty flight from the house with Lucien, Gustave ran into two gentlemen coming up the stairs. Lucien's face brightened at the sight of them...

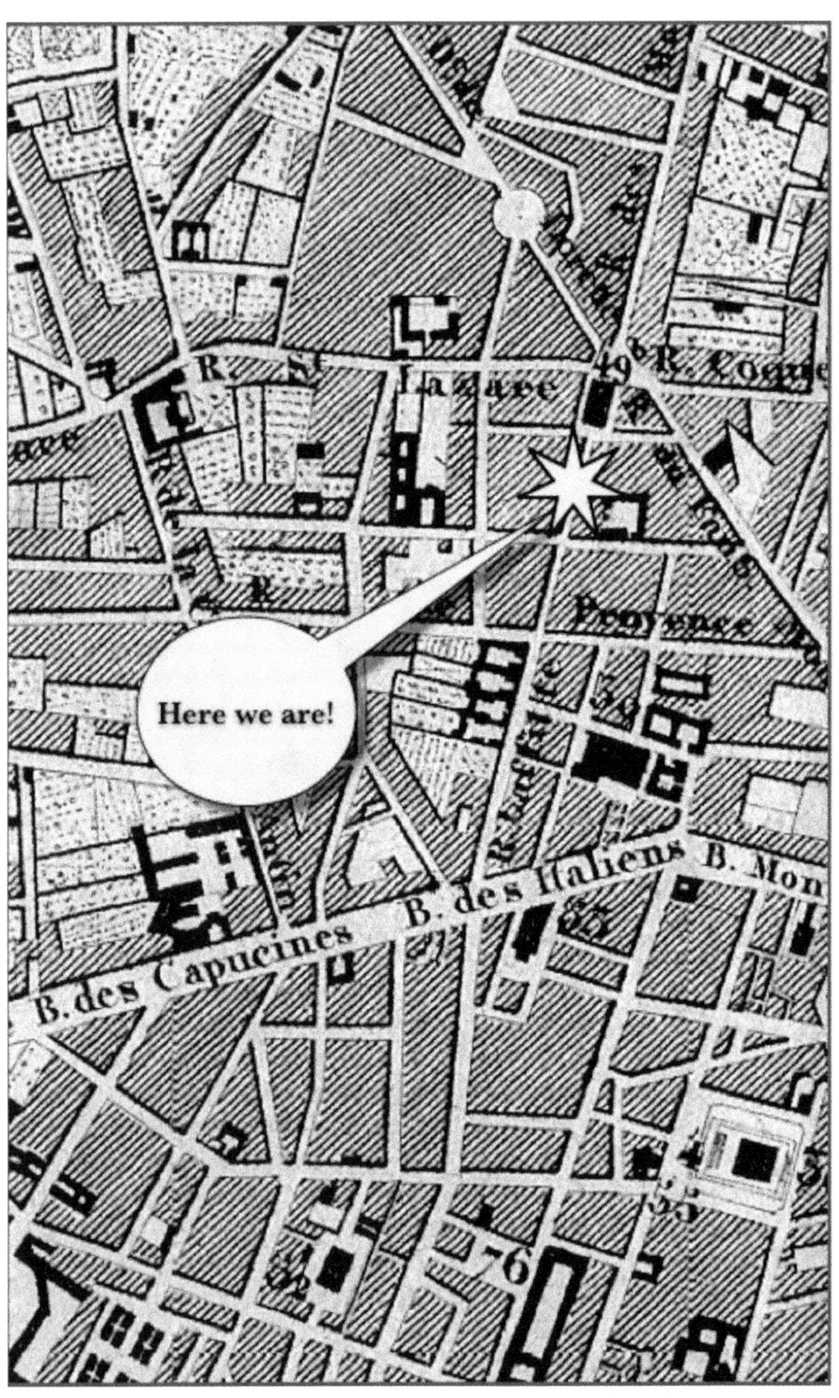
Here we are!
R. St
Lazare
Provence
B. des Capucines
B. des Italiens
B. Mon
76

When the heavy door swung open, the sight of the boy and the dog on the other side brought a smile to old Pierre's face. He studied them for a moment, before bidding Lucien to come in and go right up stairs. "Fox will show you the way," said the old servant, "I am busy."

As they approached the door of Madame Marboeuf's boudoir, the sound of excited voices within made him pause. Fearing to intrude, and wondering why Pierre had not told him of another caller, Lucien waited patiently in the hallway. "Leave my house instantly, Sir, and never set foot in it again!" thundered the excited voice of Madame Marboeuf, from beyond the portico.

"But suppose I find it and return it to you?" a man's voice replied.

"Not one cent should you have. It will be returned, but not by such as you. Now go, or would you prefer to be put out!"

"But, Madame, remember the claim of..."

"I remember nothing!" she snapped, cutting the other short. "You have no claim upon me. Go! If you do not I should call my servants and have them throw you out," stormed the lady's voice angrily.

Fox shivered in Lucien's arms at the sound of it.

The portico was drawn aside, and in the haggard young man retreating from that room Lucien, to his consternation recognized his cousin. Gustave discovered him at the same instant, "What on earth are you doing here?" he hissed in the boy's ear seizing him by the arm.

"Waiting to see Madame Marboeuf," replied Lucien in a low tone.

"She cannot see you now," returned the other in a whisper. "Come with me," he added imperatively, dragging the boy downstairs with him. Lucien was too much taken by surprise to offer any resistance, and strange to say, Fox had not even growled during these summary proceedings. Thinking it over afterward, the boy fancied that the dog was afraid of betraying his own presence, and repeating his recent experiences with this old mistress.

In his hasty flight from the house with Lucien, Gustave ran into two gentlemen coming up the stairs. Lucien's face brightened at the sight of them: "Oh, it's you Mr. Raimond?" he said to the first of the two.

"So it seems," replied Mr. Raimond warmly shaking hands, "and it is you, too, little friend, but how you do grow child! We must put a weight on your head." Lucien laughed lightly. His cousin had dropped his arm, but was chafing with impatience at this parley.

"But, what are you doing here, Lucien, and who is this with you?" Mr. Raimond asked sharply, scrutinizing Gustave's frowning face.

"This is my cousin, Sir," said Lucien, attempting to introduce the latter to Mr. Raimond.

"Come, come," said Gustave, taking the boy by the arm again, "I'm in a hurry, I've got no time to stand fooling here any longer." And he had Lucien down the stairs and out on the sidewalk before the boy knew what was what. They were well away from the house before Lucien had pulled his wits together, then he asked Gustave to explain his strange behavior. "I'll explain later," his cousin replied airily, "I have an engagement now. If you want to keep out of trouble, keep clear of that house, that's all," and he walked quickly away. Lucien hesitated a moment, and then decided to await Gustave's explanation before making his call upon Madame Marboeuf, especially as at present she was occupied with other callers.

From what he had already seen and heard of her, he dreaded to meet her again, and his courage had gone down into his boots at the sound of her stormy voice today, so, he wheeled around and started, with Fox for the office, going at a great pace to work off his excitement. Fox could hardly keep up with him and protested all the way, but, this once Lucien seemed to have forgotten his presence. The fact is the boy was becoming more and more puzzled by his cousin's strange conduct at Madame Marboeuf's, and could think of nothing else. He realized that there was some mystery in the matter, and he had so little confidence in Gustave that he doubted his telling him the truth about it. His face brightened as he remembered that probably Mr. Raimond might be able to enlighten him if his cousin did not. He hoped that the gentleman had seen that his own apparent rudeness on the stairs was due to no fault of his own. At any rate, he expected a visit from Mr. Raimond shortly, and he would apologize and explain. Although they saw little of one another, Mr. Raimond and Lucien were excellent friends.

Not wishing to inculpate his cousin, Lucien offered some rather lame excuses to his friends in the printing office for his failure to call upon Madame Marboeuf. While the men were still plying him with curious questions Mr. Germaine rescued him by summoning him to his side, "I'm glad you are back, my boy, for I want you to attend to some rather pressing errands for me."

"All right, Sir," replied the boy cheerfully, glad to escape further questioning he started off with Fox at his heels.

The two were hardly out of sight when a servant in livery appeared at the print shop and asked to see him.

"He is out," said the foreman Gaspard curtly, eyeing the man with suspicion, suspecting him of intending to kidnap Fox.

"Will you tell the young gentleman, when he returns, that Madam Marboeuf wishes to see him, if you please?" said the man.

"Certainly, no objection to that," said Gaspard, and at that the servant quickly departed.

"I wonder what's up now," muttered the foreman. "How do you suppose that old Tarter found out where he worked," he asked.

"Perhaps she's taken a shine to him and wants to adopt him," said another printer, laughing at the his own joke.

"Well," said Gaspard, "the boy gives us plenty to think about. I don't know what we should do without him and Fox."

"That's so!" was the hearty assent of the other men.

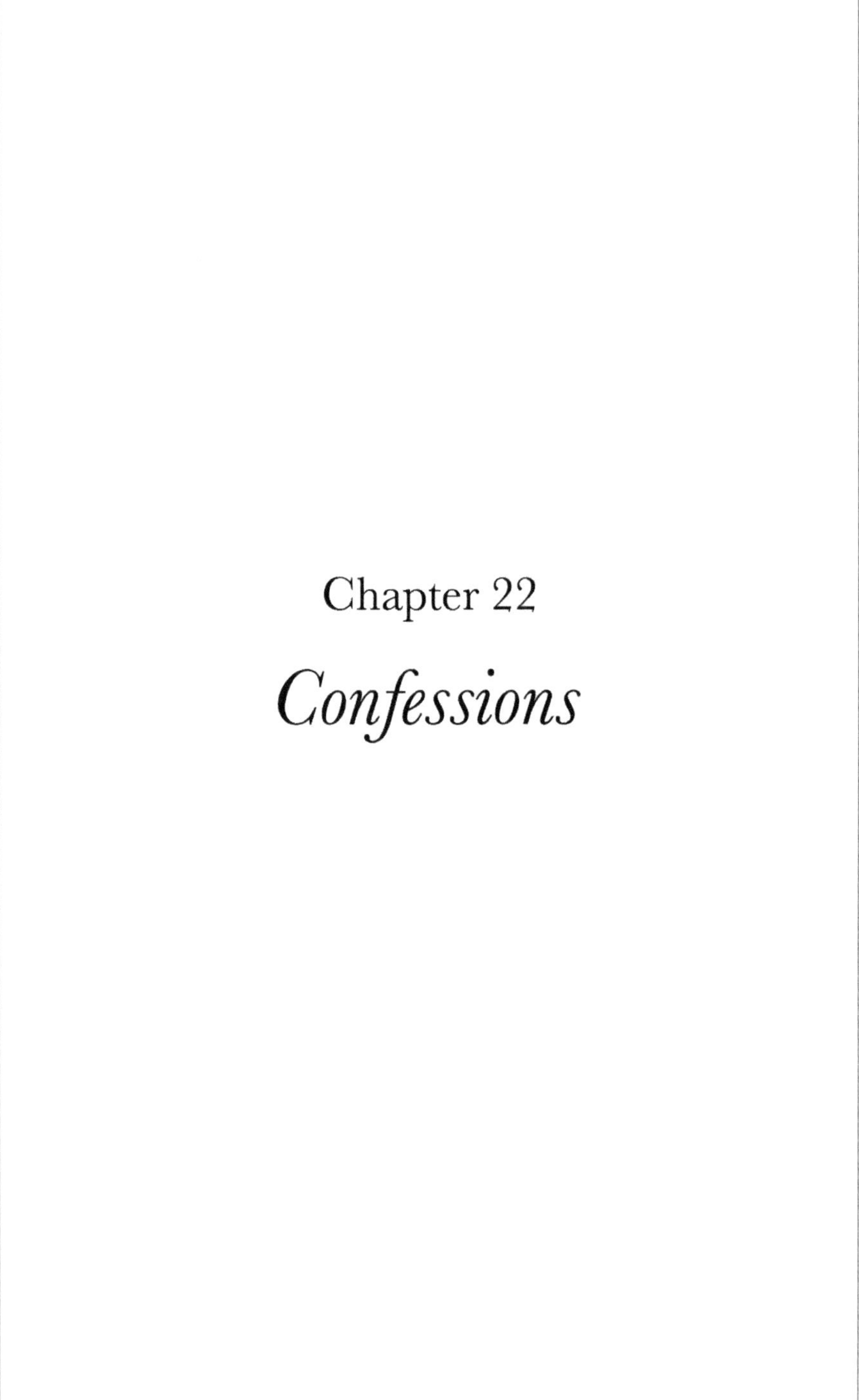

Chapter 22

Confessions

A loud cheer went up in the room from the others who had been waiting in great anticipation for Madame Marboeuf's decision. Gustave raised his head and looked at her gratefully.

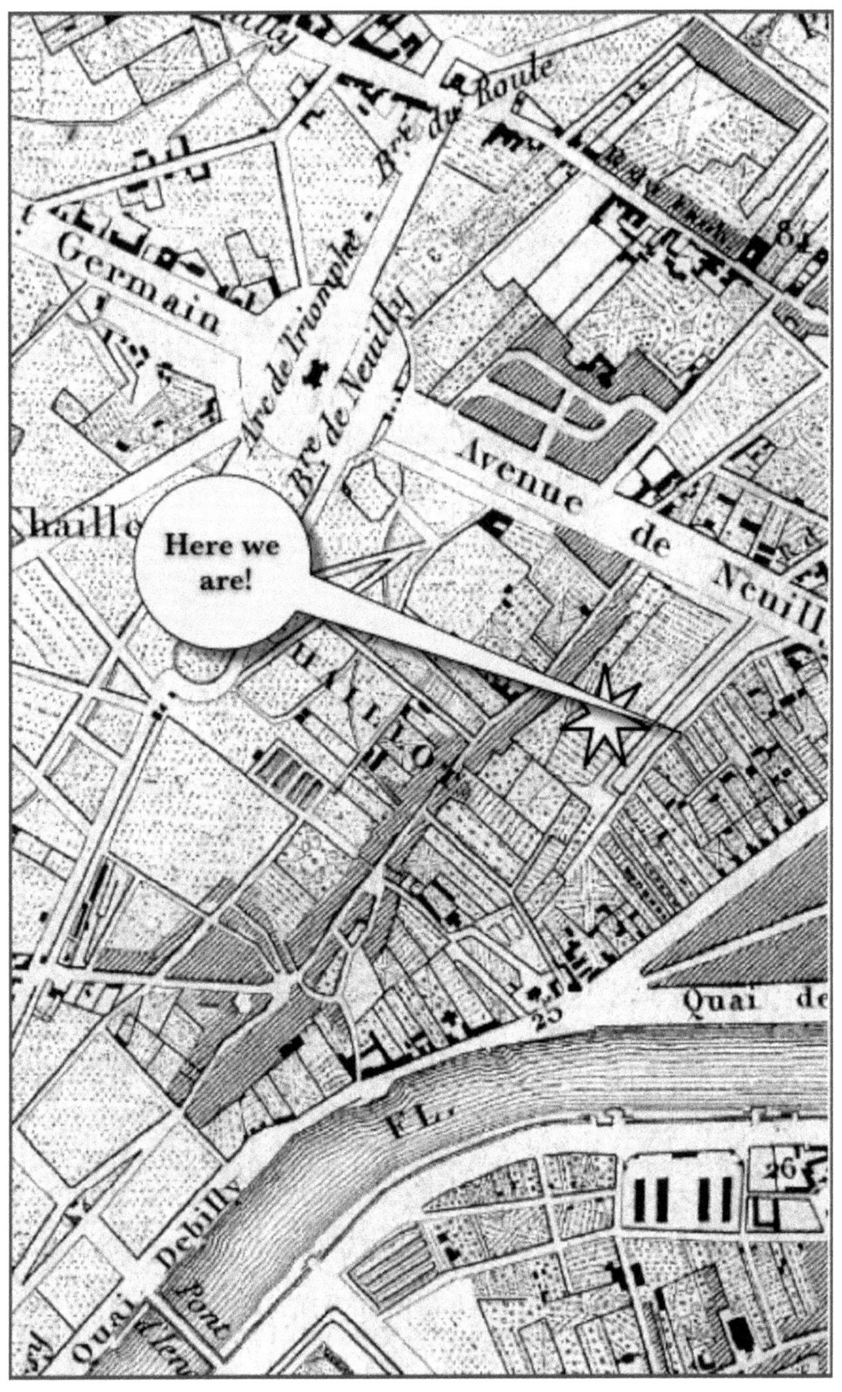
Here we are!
Brê du Roule
Germain
Arc de Triomphe
Brê de Neuilly
Avenue de Neuill
Quai de
FL.
25
26
Debilly
Pont
Quai

Mr. Germaine, seeing how distressed Lucien was by this trouble about Fox, had thought it a good time to set him to several outside matters of business, which would keep him occupied, and out in the air the better part of the day. "It will be late when you get through, my boy," said Mr. Germaine as he was setting out, "I imagine you and Fox will be totally tired when all these errands are done, so you needn't come back to the office today." They were indeed. Lucien thought he had never been more tired in his life, save perhaps those first forlorn days he wandered the streets after his cousin's desertion.

It was almost dark when he and Fox drew near to their "island," and discovered with alarm that the old green gate was standing wide open. Although expecting to find thieves in full possession, he rushed fearlessly into the enclosure, and saw with dismay that the door to the house was wide open as well: since the repair of the great stone wall and the front gate, he had gotten into the habit of not always locking the front door of the house, and he regretted it now. So, with beating heart he held Fox firmly in his arms and crept carefully toward the little stone building, planning to sneak up unnoticed and then make a mad dash through the door to grab the horn hanging just inside, and blow if for all he was worth. Reaching the open door, he stopped to listen for a moment, and heard a low voice, that sounded somehow familiar say, "He will be here soon. It is past time he was home."

With that, he bolted through the door and made a grab for the horn. But, before he could snare it, what he saw made his heart stand still, and froze him to his spot. There, sitting regally in his very own chairs sat Madame Marboeuf with

Mr. Raimond beside her! They were bent close in conversation; Madame Marboeuf fanning herself the entire time.

Once inside and able to see the entire room, Lucien's surprise became bewilderment, and he began to wonder if he was asleep and dreaming! As his eyes adjusted to the light, he could make out, in one corner the blind man, comfortably seated, with both Marie and Paul behind him. Mr. Raimond was nervously tapping the floor with his cane, as Lucien looked from one to another in utter bewilderment.

Madame Marboeuf was the first to speak to him when she said cooly, "Come here, my boy," holding out her hand to Lucien, "and tell me why you failed to call upon me yesterday, as I requested you to do." Out of politeness alone, Lucien put his hand into hers, but he could not rid himself of the unpleasant impression he had formed of Madame Marboeuf. He was dumbfounded then, when she raised his hand to her lips and kissed it, and then clasped it close in both her own.

Before he could reply to her question, a commotion behind him made him turn to the door. There he saw his cousin, Gustave, helping old Father La Tuile into the room. Seeing Lucien, Gustave straightened himself up as he helped the old soldier to a place at the back of the room where he could sit comfortably. Fox immediately spied him and leapt to the floor to run over and give the old man an eager welcome; the old soldier fondly calling him as he always did, his "dear little friend." To Lucien's further surprise, Madam Marboeuf, whom he had supposed to be heartless, was laughing on with tears in her eyes at Fox's carrying on. She did not seem at all jealous that the dog singled out the old soldier, rather than herself to impose his attentions upon.

All eyes were now on Gustave, as he turned to the assembly. Feeling the weight of all the questioning gazes he looked back at Father La Tuile uncertainly.

"Do what your honor demands, show your quality," the soldier admonished him.

With that, Gustave took several steps toward his cousin.

"It seems my game is up, Lucien," he said, "and I'm not sorry. I'm sick of this business." Gustave looked around the room at all the intent faces, "It serves me right to have to make my confession before so many I suppose, for it isn't very pleasant."

Lucien stood looking at him wide-eyed, and still uncertain of the gentle pressure of Madame Marboeuf's hand upon his own.

"You spoke truly Lucien," said Gustave addressing him, "when you said, we were not raised to serve. Your history and mine prove it."

"Yes, I know," responded Lucien softly, "but that's between you and me, Gustave. What is the use of saying anything about what is past and gone?"

"No, it isn't only between you and me, as you'll soon find out. I wish it were," replied the other bitterly. "My first act after the funeral," said Gustave, "was to burn my father's will in which he had provided for you, Lucien."

The boy said nothing, but he was thinking, "so that's what he was doing in my uncle's room that night."

Gustave glanced nervously back at the old soldier again. With a nod of his head and quick wave of his hand, Father La Tuile bade the young man to continue, which he did. "I make no excuse for bringing you to Paris and deserting you so cruelly," he said to Lucien. "I am barely able to speak of it. God knows you are avenged. From that hour to this your image has haunted me. Do what I would, I could never get rid of you. Many's the night I have waked, shaking with a chill, because I had seemed to see or hear you being murdered."

"It is all past and gone now Cousin, why talk about it?" said Lucien fondly.

"Yes, past and gone for you perhaps, but never for me. God knows I am well punished," said Gustave bitterly, hanging his head a moment. "When I got home," he continued, "I found my father's only living relative, whom I'd not seen for years, waiting for me."

"I'll explain to Lucien," interrupted Mr. Raimond. "The reason you have never heard of this relation is because she and her husband had a misunderstanding which left them apart. Her husband finally passed away, just before your uncle was taken ill, my boy. As she had had no children she was left alone in the world, and her heart turned at once toward her only brother, and just as soon as she could do so, she started out for Bordeaux, the rest, you have already learned from your cousin Gustave's tale."

Tears began to well up in Lucien's eyes as he was reminded of his uncle's death, but he did not notice that Madam Marboeuf had also been moved by the tale. "The rest?" groaned Gustave. "No, he doesn't know the rest.

Nobody but I could know this story, since I am it's miserable author." He took a heavy breath and continued, "It sounds simple enough to say I found our aunt waiting there when I got home, but oh, the fright and misery of it. It seems the servants had taken a great liking to you, Lucien, and had told her that you and I had gone to Paris on an overnight trip" said Gustave, "so of course she waited for us to return. First thing she said to me was, 'Yes, you're Gustave; you haven't changed much in looks since I saw you last, but where is Lucien, my sister Amelia's little boy? I want to take him home with me. This big empty house is no place for a child, now that your father is gone. You'd better close it up and go off traveling,' she said to me. Heavens!" cried Gustave wiping his damp forehead, "I little thought how soon I'd have to do that very thing!"

Nobody spoke, and he continued, "There's no question about it; the way of the transgressor is hard. The first thing I did was concoct a story to satisfy my aunt. You see, it was easy enough to pull the wool over the eyes of the servants and the neighbors, but it was very different with her."

Madame Marboeuf moved uneasily, and pulled Lucien down to sit on the arm of her chair, which surprised him as much as the way she had held his hand, but this seemed to be a time of surprises, and all he could do was accept them all.

"I told her," continued Gustave, "that my father made such a pet of you, Lucien, that you were quite spoiled, and your education so much neglected that I had placed you in a good boarding school in Paris. 'Give me the address of that school, I must find him at once,' she said, getting out her notebook. 'Here, you write it down I haven't my glasses.' You may well believe I was frightened," Gustave added. "I pretended to sharpen my pencil to gain time, for I couldn't think of a single address to write in that horrid little notebook. At last I bit one off at random, and she put the dark little book back into her pocket. I've seen it often in my dreams, with it's gilt-lettered cover," said Gustave passing his hand across his eyes.

"She was off for Paris early the next morning," he went on, "and I was in misery for I knew I was found out. Such a letter as she wrote me when she discovered that I had deceived her! I didn't answer it," added Gustave with a grim smile. "I rushed into wild dissipation," he continued, "to try to stifle thought, for if I stopped to think, I seemed to hear my father's voice asking where you were, Lucien. The horror of what might have happened to you grew upon me as time went on. My dreams were terrible," he added with a shudder. "I drank deep to drown my misery," he confessed, "and I suppose that is why I never tried to undo the wrong I had done by trying to find you, or even learn if you were alive or dead, Lucien. I fell in with bad company, too, and before I knew it, my fortune was scattered to the winds. When I realized what had happened to me, I gathered up such things of value that I had left, and came to Paris. By selling or pawning these I lived in comparative ease for awhile, but I came at last to what I was when you found me, Lucien," he said hanging his head. "I had no weapon of any kind, but I had just threatened a man with violence because he refused to give me anything, and it seemed, when I heard your familiar voice, as if swift judgement was upon me. I thought it was your ghost, Lucien, for I felt sure that a delicate child like you must have perished long ago. I know I tried to bluff you off, but no poor wretch could have been more frightened and miserable than I was."

Gustave stopped to moisten his dry lips, and pass his hand over his haggard face, "When I found that it was really you, I had a new fear; I was afraid you'd turn me over to the police. A guilty conscience is a terrible companion to be tied to! May Heaven grant me some peace, now I've made a clean breast of everything?" said Gustave as if praying. "Amen," added Father La Tuile and the blind man in unison.

The sounds of the two voices caught him by surprise and he looked quickly over at the old men. Turning back to Lucien, he catches the boy's imploring gaze. "Don't look at me that way, Lucien. You can't stop me, I'm bound to tell the whole story. If I didn't nobody would believe I was penitent. God knows I am. I have awoken to the realization of my wickedness, and I feel only remorse for what I have done to injure you, Lucien. Don't forget, that I am still my father's son," said Gustave remorsefully.

"I never did forget that," Lucien answered quietly.

"Don't child!" cried his cousin, striking his forehead, "You pierce me to the heart."

"I didn't mean to," replied the boy, "but you know how I loved your father and I forgave you everything for his sake."

Their eyes lock in a deep gaze for a moment before Gustave continues, "I haven't told everything yet," said the elder with a sob. "The notice about Fox, which troubled you so much, pleased me, for I saw in it another vile way to injure you, as well as to get some money for myself. When I went to see Madame Marboeuf about the dog," he added, "I was startled to find you there. I hurried away because I didn't want her to see us together, and you know what happened the last time we met there."

"Have you guessed why your cousin did not want me to see the two of you together, Lucien?" added Madame Marboeuf eagerly.

"No Madame," answered the boy looking back at Gustave for explanation.

"Because he was trying to injure you still more deeply by keeping from me the knowledge that you were cousins. And you can't guess why child? No? Then I will tell you. It is because I am the aunt he has been talking about, your mother's only sister." Lucien was so astonished that he stared dumb, failing utterly to understand Mr. Raimond's hints that he should kiss this newfound kinswoman. She looks at Lucien a moment longer, her face flushed with emotion, waiting for a response, before continuing, "and from this moment on, if you will allow it, you shall be as my own son, for I have no children of my own."

Fox, who seemed to think something was wrong, danced about, offering his paw to Lucien and his old mistress in turn, but neither of them took it. They were looking at one another with shining eyes. It was at this moment that Mr. Germaine appeared at the door of Lucien's little house. Sensing the tension in the room he let himself in quietly, and took a spot beside the door, unnoticed by Lucien.

"Why don't you kiss your old aunt?" asked the lady at last, rattled by Lucien's behavior, "I'm not so hardhearted as you imagined."

"I see that," replied the boy, "but are you sure you are my Aunt?"

"We have your cousin's word for that," said Mr. Raimond with a hearty laugh. "He wouldn't let you answer when I spoke to you on the stairs this morning at Madame Marboeuf's, but after he got rid of you he came back and told us all about you. His explanation must be genuine," continued Mr. Raimond, "for you see, he has told the whole story, not sparing himself in any way. I suppose conscience gave him one more prick than he could stifle. It was he who gave us your employer, Mr. Germaine's address. Your aunt immediately sent a servant in search of you, but you were out," added Mr. Raimond.

"Yes," said Mr. Germaine, stepping up behind Lucien and putting a comforting hand on the boy's shoulder, "I had sent him out. The boy was so unhappy about his dog that I trumped up enough errands to keep him on the go all day to take his mind off his trouble."

Lucien gave him a grateful look, saying, "I did think it queer that you should think some of those errands were so important."

"Mr. Raimond here, filled me in on the details of your story, and it is not from lack of interest that I am so late," added the old gentleman, bowing to Madame Marboeuf, "The truth is, Madame, your nephew makes himself of importance wherever he is, and when he is away from the office as he has been today, I find myself with more to do than I can well get through." A look of genuine distress crossed Lucien's face upon hearing this. "Never mind, my boy," said Mr. Germaine, seeing Lucien's concern, "I couldn't expect to keep you always, and I am just trying to show your aunt what a valuable nephew she has found."

Lucien's face brightened at this, as does Madame Marboeuf's.

"Let's not forget the other nephew," said Mr. Raimond, pained to see the looks of aversion cast in Gustave's direction, by Madame Marboeuf. "It was he who went in search of those other friends of yours, Lucien, for he knew he must make his sad confession before them all. We must give everyone their due, eh, Madame?"

The lady's only reply was a toss of her head and another scornful look at Gustave. "It was I who wanted this 'family gathering' here when you got home, Lucien," she said to the boy. "When I heard what all these kind friends had done for you I wanted to see them and thank them all."

Lucien flung his arms about her and kissed her. "They have all been very kind to me. I would not have survived without them, he said, as he began around the room shaking hands with everyone. He finally came to Gustave, who turned his back upon him, ignoring his outstretched hand.

"Oh Cousin," said the boy, "you must share my happiness; she's your aunt as well as mine."

"Indeed I'm not," replied Madame Marboeuf tartly. "I have but one nephew, and his name is Lucien Lehun."

"But, dear Aunt," cried the boy seizing her hand, "you surely will pardon my poor cousin."

"Poor cousin indeed!" snapped Madame Marboeuf. "No, I don't want anything more to do with him. And he shall never see a cent of my money."

"Perhaps not your money, dear Aunt, but can't you give him your affection, now that you see how sorry he is for what he has done?" pleaded Lucien earnestly.

"It seems to me that you are more ready to share your aunt's affection than her money with your cousin," said Mr. Raimond laughingly.

Lucien, who did not understand the covert sarcasm of this statement replied promptly, "Truly Sir, my aunt says she is going to adopt me as her own son: I shall have plenty of money and anything else I need, and I'll see that my cousin wants for nothing. But, how can I share my aunt's affection with him, unless she herself gives it freely?" Madame Marboeuf and Mr. Raimond exchanged glances of amazement

"Well, well my boy," said the latter, "it seems that everything and everybody gives way before you, and I suppose your aunt will be no exception. Madame Marboeuf," he said to the lady, "you might as well yield this point with a good grace at the outset. These boys are both of your own blood, and the youngster speaks with the wisdom the Lord often seems to put into the mouths of children."

Madame Marboeuf looked displeased. She sat silent, toying with the chatelaine and keys hanging at her side. Lucien, dropping upon one knee, raised her hand and looked pleadingly into her wet face, waiting for her to speak.

Fox was doing his best to establish peace by alternately jumping into her lap, and all over Lucien, but she paid no attention to him.

"Come dear friend," said Mr. Raimond seriously, "in the name of your good husband, and of your brother, the father of this young man, I ask you to forgive him freely. He has had a bitter lesson, and is giving every evidence of true repentance. Come, say you will give him another chance."

Madame Marboeuf remained silent, while Gustave sat near with his head bowed upon his arms. Lucien kissed his aunt's hands, and she abruptly placed one of them upon his head. As she did so, Mr. Raimond, drawing his chair close to her, said softly, and with a new determination in his voice, "And now I ask you, as your oldest, and I hope, your dearest friend, to forgive your nephew, for my sake."

Madame Marboeuf put her hands up to her face and sobbed.

"Yes, yes, dear Aunt," exclaimed Lucien, throwing his arms around her and kissing her over and over. "I couldn't be happy if I thought my cousin was left out in the cold." She leaned her head against him and wept. "It shall be as you wish, Lucien," she said.

A loud cheer went up in the room from the others who had been waiting in great anticipation for Madame Marboeuf's decision. Gustave raised his head and looked at her gratefully. She gave him her hand, which he raised to his lips, saying solemnly, "Aunt, so help me, I will try to live worthily from this hour."

There was not a dry eye in the room, although there were many happy hearts. Poor little Fox couldn't understand it at all, and ran about sniffing and whining, till Lucien, with a sympathetic laugh caught him up, and put him on Madam Marboeuf's lap, laying his own head down beside him. This started his aunt's tears again, "To think I was willing to rob you of Fox, the only comfort you had Lucien. I may well pardon Gustave, for I'm as bad in my way. Can you ever forgive your old aunt?"

"There's nothing to forgive, dear aunt. Fox was your own dog, and anybody would want such a dear little dog back, wouldn't they, Fox?" Madame gave a warm smile at the sound of the dog's, "Yes."

"Besides," said Lucien slyly, "you don't know the whole story, does she Mr. Germaine? If you were trying to get my dog away from me, I was trying just as hard to get yours away from you. I'm just as ashamed of the way I felt and acted, as you are about the way you treated me. So, let's call it square," said Lucien, bestowing upon his aunt a long hug that in her opinion would have atoned for much greater offenses.

Chapter 23
A New Family

Where's Lucien?
(Turn the page to see.)
As a new spring dawned, and the ancient gardens began to bloom again, the old house seemed to reawaken from a sad slumber.

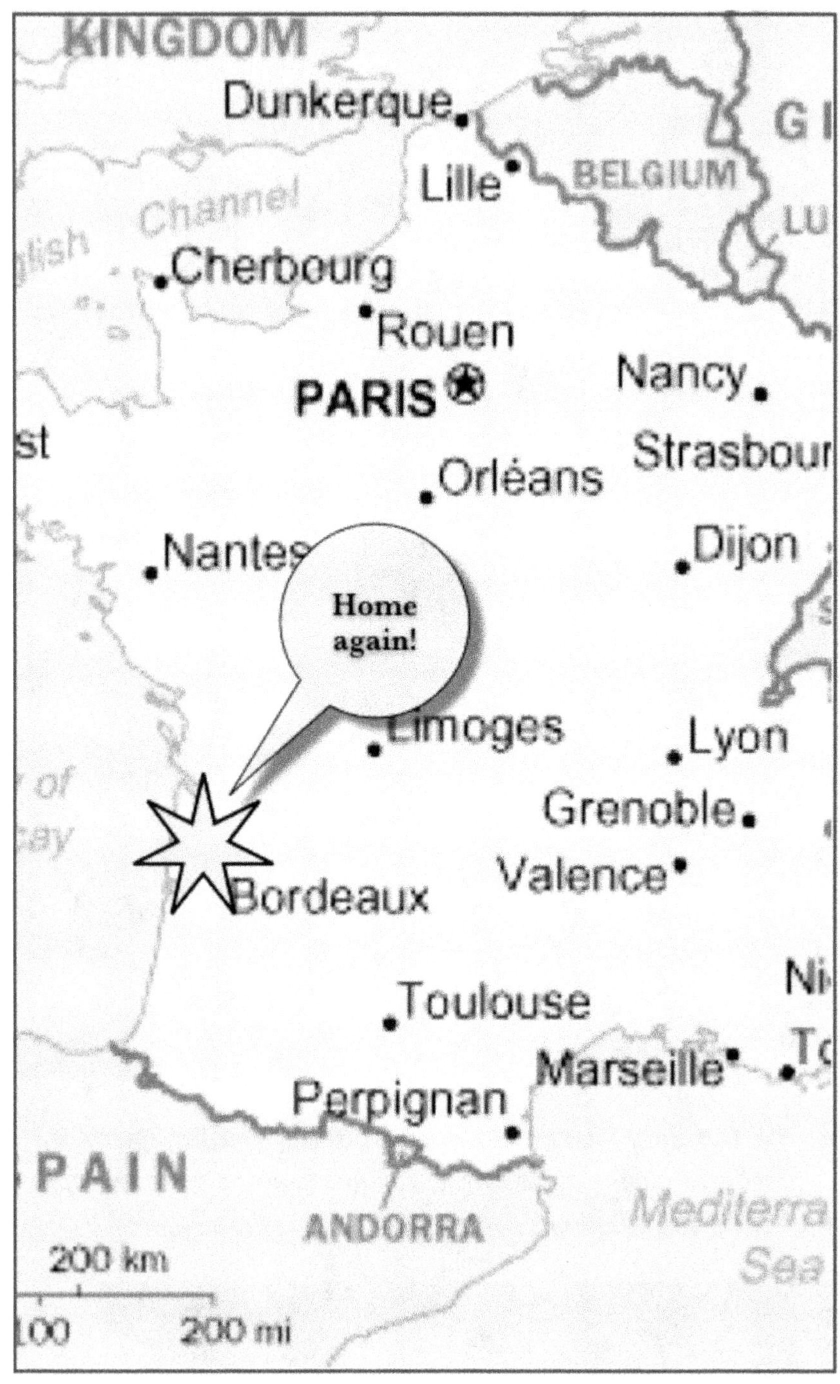
KINGDOM
Dunkerque
Lille
BELGIUM
Channel
Cherbourg
Rouen
PARIS
Nancy
Strasbour
Orléans
Nantes
Dijon
Home again!
Limoges
Lyon
Grenoble
Valence
Bordeaux
Toulouse
Marseille
Perpignan
PAIN
ANDORRA
200 km
200 mi
Mediterra
Sea

The passage of another year brought great changes for them both.

Madame Marbouf, now having a son to raise, had wasted no time in throwing herself into her new role as Lucien's mother. In as much, she had decided to return them both to Bordeaux, feeling that it would be better to have Lucien away from the temptations that abound in any big city like Paris. To that end, she had quickly struck a deal with Gustave, that would not only allow him to pay off his debts, but would also allow Lucien to return to the only real home he had ever known. She purchased her brother's old house in Bordeaux from Gustave for a very good price on the understanding that he would be able to buy it back, once Lucien was grown, and he was ready to assume responsibility for it. Any profits from the sale that were left after Gustave's debts were paid were entrusted to Mr. Raimond, to be invested for him, until he showed himself able to manage the money responsibly. To that end, Gustave had, at the urging of Father La Tuile, entered the Army shortly after Lucien's adoption by his aunt, and was now serving with his regiment in Africa. So far as his relatives could learn, he was faithfully living up to the pledge he had made.

Once in possession of the house in Bordeaux, and with Lucien's happy approval, she had hired back as many of her brother's old serving staff as she could find. They were happy to come back, as they all were very fond of Lucien, and missed the old house, where they had worked happily for so many years. Although Madame Marbouef was nothing like her brother, she was always fair, and with Lucien there to smooth the waters when needed, they all soon became accustomed to her ways. As a new spring dawned, and the ancient gardens began to bloom again, the old house seemed to reawaken from a sad slumber, and was a flurry of activity as Madame Marbouef threw herself wholly into it's resuscitation.

Lucien had been enrolled in a good school nearby, and Fox worked to divide his time between him and his old mistress. He loved Lucien dearly, and was never so happy as when with him, but boys by the dozen were too much for him. He made it very plain to Lucien, whose quick sympathies were always ready interpreters of Fox's meanings, that he couldn't expect a little dog to be very happy in a boarding school. The best of boys will play tricks on other people's dogs sometimes, and Fox resented being used as a ball, or having tin pails tied to his tail. When he sat up begging, turning mournful eyes upon him, Lucien knew immediately that he was trying to say, "Of course you must come to school and get an education, but I'm only a poor little dog, and I can't stand this nonsense." "All right, old fellow," Lucien would reply, "Hide under my bed, and I'll get leave to take you home. I want to see Aunty, anyway it's too long to wait till Saturday."

It was upon one of these occasions, when he and Fox came into the house unexpectedly, that they found Mr. Raimond there. This was nothing curious, for he was now a frequent visitor. His wife had died two years before, and he made the loneliness of his own house his excuse for the many long rides from Paris. He and Lucien's aunt laughed in an embarrassed way as Lucien entered the room this particular day. "Shall we tell him?" said Mr. Raimond.

"You'll have to do it George, I can't," returned the lady blushing like a girl.

Lucien looked from one to the other inquiringly, as Fox set about worrying the cat.

"Has anything happened since I was last home? Has Gustave been..." began Lucien.

"No, no, it has nothing to do with your cousin," interrupted Mr. Raimond, "and the story I am going to tell you is nothing new, it happened a long time ago."

"Oh, George!" murmured Madame Marboeuf putting her fan before her face. "Need you tell the whole story?"

"Certainly Antoinette, Lucien ought to know the whole story."

Whatever the story that was coming, it could hardly surprise the boy more than the easy exchange of Christian names between two people who, out of the arrogance of youth, Lucien thought far too old to have any intimate leanings.

"A long, long time ago," began Mr. Raimond, as Madame Marboeuf gave him a playful swat on the shoulder with her fan.

"Not so long ago, Sir!" she objected.

Mr. Raimond gave her a little wink and continued, "Some years ago a girl and boy were neighbors to one another in Bordeaux. The girl was a beauty," he said, glancing archly at Madame Marboeuf, but the fan hid her face again.

"The boy wasn't too bad looking either," came in a soft voice from behind the fan.

"Oh, he did well enough. Boys are all pretty much alike," said Mr. Raimond with indifference. "To go on with my story, these two grew up together, and fell deeply in love. In truth, neither of them had ever thought of anyone else. It had never entered their heads that their parents would not let them marry when they were old enough, but such was the case."

Mr. Raimond paused, "I was so happy when you came in, Lucien," he said glancing uncomfortably at the floor, "I thought it would be so easy to tell you the...this story, but I admit, I was mistaken."

Madame Marboeuf's lace handkerchief became increasingly busy behind her fan, as Mr. Raimond continued with the tale. "The girl married the ward to whom her parents had promised her," at this, his voice caught in this throat, "and the boy...," he paused.

"What of the boy, Sir?" asked Lucien much interested.

"Oh," said Mr. Raimond lightly, "he did what most boys would have done in such a case; first, he went off to sea, and sowed a lot of wild oats, then he came home and settled down to a humdrum life."

"And did he marry, too?" Lucien asked.

"Of course; they all do," replied Mr. Raimond with a cynical laugh. "What else was there for the poor fellow to do? He married the girl his parents picked out for him, and tried to make her happy, but I'm afraid he didn't succeed very well," added Mr. Raimond. "His mother told him love was not necessary in marriage," he continued, "and that he'd be sure to be happy if he did his duty by his parents and the wife they had chosen for him." Mr. Raimond suddenly looked directly at Lucien, "Don't let anyone make you believe that, my boy; it's a wretched mistake," he said, bringing a clenched fist down upon his knee. A quiet sob from behind Madame Marboeuf's fan punctuated the moment. "No, my boy, marry the girl you love, though the skies fall. That's what I'm going to do," said Mr. Raimond slipping his arm around Madame Marboeuf, and gently drawing aside the fan.

Lucien gasped, "You weren't talking about Auntie and yourself all this time, were you?"

"Yes, Lucien" returned his Aunt, "I was that girl."

"And, I that boy," added Mr. Raimond, looking uneasily at Lucien. "I suppose you think we're too old to marry at this late date."

Lucien could not reply right away, as it took a moment for all this new information to settle into his thoughts. His aunt lowered her fan a bit to be able to gauge his reaction better, and Mr. Raimond looked at him nervously. They didn't have to wait long for their answer. Lucien suddenly gave a joyous, boyish yell, threw his arms around his aunt and kissed her, saying, "I hope I am the first to congratulate you both. I am? That's good, I do from the bottom of my heart, and I ought to be the first, since I am the one who, besides yourselves, is the most concerned."

"And, you don't think we are too old?" asked his aunt.

"I should think not," responded Lucien heartily, "if you've loved one another all your lives."

"We have indeed," said Mr. Raimond with solemnity, taking Madame Marboeuf's hands in his and kissing her.

Lucien threw his arms around them both, crying, "How could I possibly object! It will be like my having both a father and a mother again," and so it proved.

Epilogue

Mr. Raimond had decided to go ahead with the building of his new house on Lucien's "island" He and Madame Marbouef had decided that once it was completed they would sell their former residences and use this new house as their "pied a terre" in Paris. Jean, the handsome young mason who had befriended Lucien was hard at work upon the fine new house.

Father La Tuile, whom Madame Marboeuf had presented with another dog, was living with his new Austerlitz in Lucien's little house as guardian of the "island" property.

Madame Marboeuf had had the blind man's eyes examined by an oculist, through whose skillful treatment his sight had been restored. A place had readily been found for him as concierge, which provided well for his wife and himself. There was no longer any need for them to provide for others, for their son Paul was now doing well, and Jean had not wasted any time convincing Marie that her first duty was no longer at home. "Where then?" she had asked archly when he first broached the subject.

Summoning his courage he had stepped out into the unknown and answered with all the assurance he could, "With me, of course!"

Lucien was best-man at the wedding and Madame Marboeuf made the young couple many fine wedding gifts to start them on their journey.

She had gone in person to thank all the printers for their kindness to Lucien, and had left in Mr. Germaine's hands a generous sum to be divided among them. The boy himself stopped at the office whenever they made one of their frequent trips to Paris, and always found a hearty welcome awaiting him.

Madame Marboeuf had even hunted up the young scullion who had befriended Lucien in his need, and made him happy by the present of a fine suit of clothes. If the young chimney sweep had given the boy any practical aid, she would have checked every flue herself, until she had found and rewarded him, too. She even went so far as to give a pretty necktie anonymously to the girl who had given Lucien the double portion of bread. Remembering what he had said of the woman who scolded her, she thought it better not to betray by an open acknowledgement the girls kindness to a famishing child.

Perhaps the year just past had wrought the greater change in Madame Marboeuf herself, than in anyone else concerned in the story. Her life to that point had been one of disappointment and loneliness, which had made her appear selfish and hard-hearted, although this was not truly her nature. Having plenty of money, it was easier to give that than friendly interest, which would have exposed her sympathies. Gustave's flagrant deceit had made her doubly wary and suspicious of others, and when Lucien returned her dog, she put no faith in his apparent honesty. She was even skeptical about Mr. Raimond's true feelings when he began to call upon her after his wife's death, suspecting him of being out for money, even though it was obvious to all that he had plenty of his own. Thus is the way of a battered heart.

All this was changed however, when Lucien came into her life. His kindly, happy nature made sunshine wherever he was, and filled their new home full of warmth. The sound of his bounding steps upon the stairs would send her rushing to the door to meet him, with Fox at her heels, if he was not already at those of his young master. The dog would never be far from one or the other of these two, whom he loved devotedly.

Even as Madame Marboeuf comes to the door to welcome her boy, so to the boy himself is now standing upon the threshold of manhood, scanning through the open door of opportunity, golden vistas that make his heart beat high with hope and courage.

Here, we must leave him, confident that his feet will not stray from that upward and onward path on which they were so early and carefully set.

The

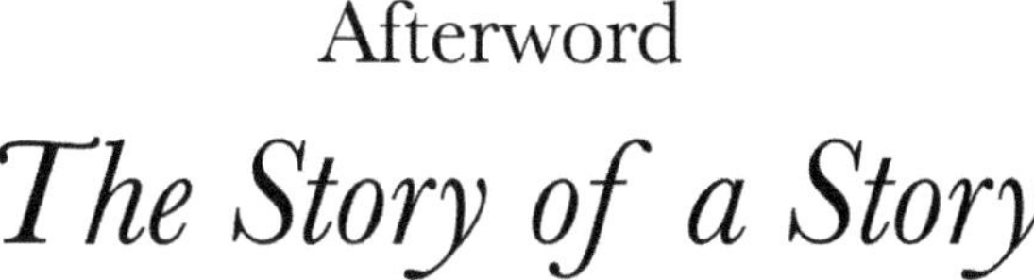

Afterword

The Story of a Story

Every story has its day, but some days take longer to arrive than others.

This story was actually begun by my ancestor, Mary Nelson Carter two centuries ago now. Being that it began as no more than a stack of handwritten, undated notes I can't be sure of the exact date. All I can be certain of is that it is a project she started and never finished. I assume she put it away in order to work on her only other published work: *Phases of Life Where the Galax Grows,* a collection of interviews with the mountain folk populating the hill country in and around Blowing Rock, North Carolina. Mary Carter was very fond of the mountain culture, and she feared that it was on it's way to extinction. "*Phases of Life Where the Galax Grows,*" was her attempt to capture at least some of that authentic culture while she could. That took a bit of time, and it may be that the story of Lucien and Fox suffered for it.

For whatever the reason, it was not until the death of my own mother several years ago that I got my first glimpse of this "story in waiting." While sifting through inherited drawers and boxes I came upon an old, brittle envelope that was filled with several neat little stacks of handwritten pages. Many were virtually illegible, the ink having faded or the pages crumbled, and the rest were not far behind, so I stuck them in plastic "zipper" bags and put them back into the envelope until I had time to figure out what they were. It was not too long after that that I pulled the envelope out again to take another look at the pages. It was then that I deciphered a bit of the first page of the notes, which turned out to be from Mary Nelson Carter, explaining her intentions, and I'm including it in edited form here:

The Story Of a Story

Once upon a time, away back in the long ago, a little girl read a book that touched her heart, and which she never forgot. The story was about a French boy, and a remarkable, little dog.

It was a borrowed book, and the little girl wanted so much to have a copy of her own that she was always wishing for somebody to give her one, but nobody ever did. She even asked the books owner - another little girl - to allow her to buy it. But, having only a few cents in her little piggy-bank to offer for it, she was not surprised when the offer was met with well-merited scorn. She, likewise, rejected an offer to exchange the book for a well-thumbed copy of Robinson Crusoe.

So, after reading the book through twice, and getting solid satisfaction out of the tears she shed over the hero's tribulations, the volume was returned...to it's owner, only to borrow it again and devour it anew.

By and by, she...grew up, married and...had children of her own, and although she told them this "pet" story of hers, she wanted them to have the pleasure of reading it themselves, so she

> searched far and near for the book, but, it was all in vain. The booksellers told her it was a translation from the original French, and out of print long ago... She was unsuccessful in finding either the translation, or the original, and for years gave up the search.
>
> Then, one day, when least expecting it, she came upon an old translation of the story in a dusty secondhand shop. Issued by a church society, Alas!, it was like meeting an old acquaintance miserably changed by the ravages of time...But, acting on a publishers' hint that it only needed some change of raiment to meet the needs of the day, she set about giving it new garb. But the things of the spirit, which give to this story its chief charm, do not change with time or fashion.
>
> - *Mary Nelson Carter*

It was after reading this note that I decided I owed it to my ancestor, and my mother, who had kept the old decaying pages for so long, to transcribe them before they completely fell to dust.

So, with the help of my partner, Tiersa, a couple good magnifying glasses, and plenty of bright lights, we began to decode the pages as best we could, and transfer what was there to a computer file. Once typed and legible, Tiersa and

I both thought that this little kernel of a story was worth resurrecting and completing, feeling, as Mary Carter had that, "the things of the spirit, which give to this story its chief charm, do not change with time or fashion." So, I undertook to finish the work begun so long before me by my ancestor. Without benefit of the original, or a translation to use, I decided to keep my changes and additions as invisible as possible in order to retain the charm and style that was evident in her notes. I wanted it to stay a "period" story, with the flavor that that brought.

At the time, I had also become interested in the promise of digital books, and the enhancements they could provide to readers. This story appeared at the perfect time, and seemed to be the perfect project for me to use to open that door. So, it was decided right from the start that *"A Fox in Paris"* would enjoy it's rebirth, in a new century, as a new technology, interactive digital book, for a new generation of young readers (and their parents).

So, that's the story of THIS story.

PGV

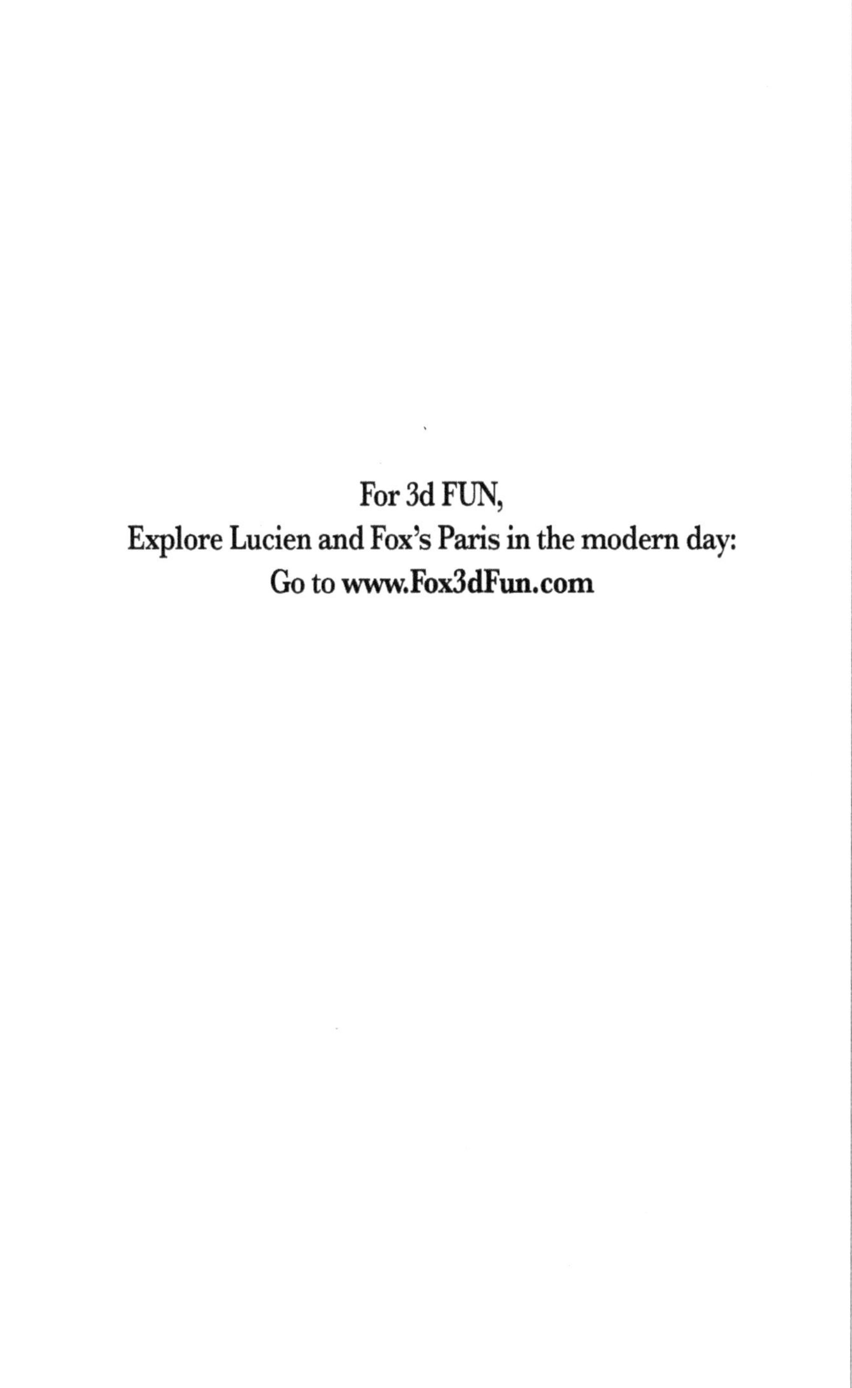

For 3d FUN,
Explore Lucien and Fox's Paris in the modern day:
Go to **www.Fox3dFun.com**

EXPLORE LUCIEN AND FOX'S PARIS

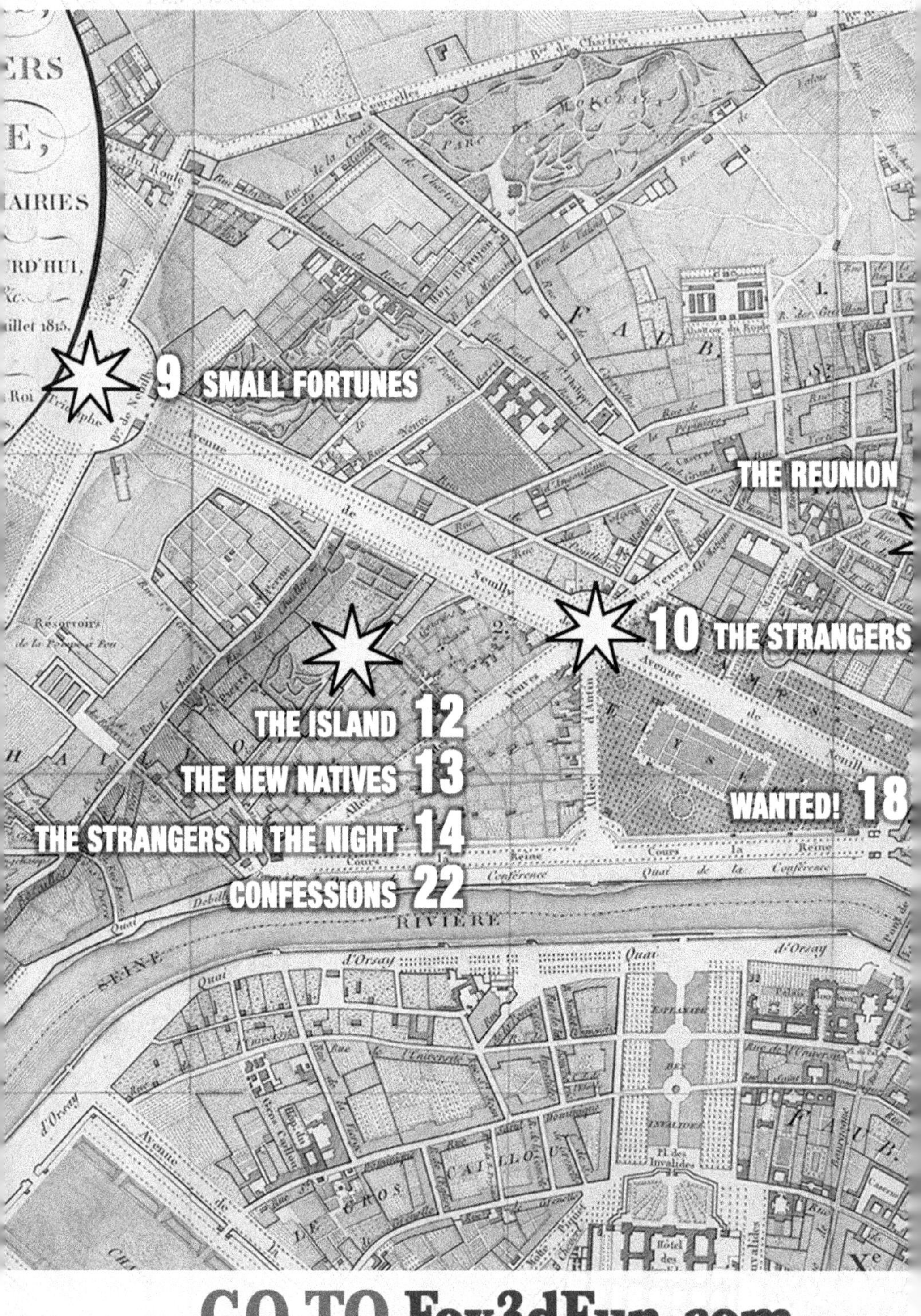

GO TO Fox3dFun.com to Explore Paris in 3D!

Paris c. 1837

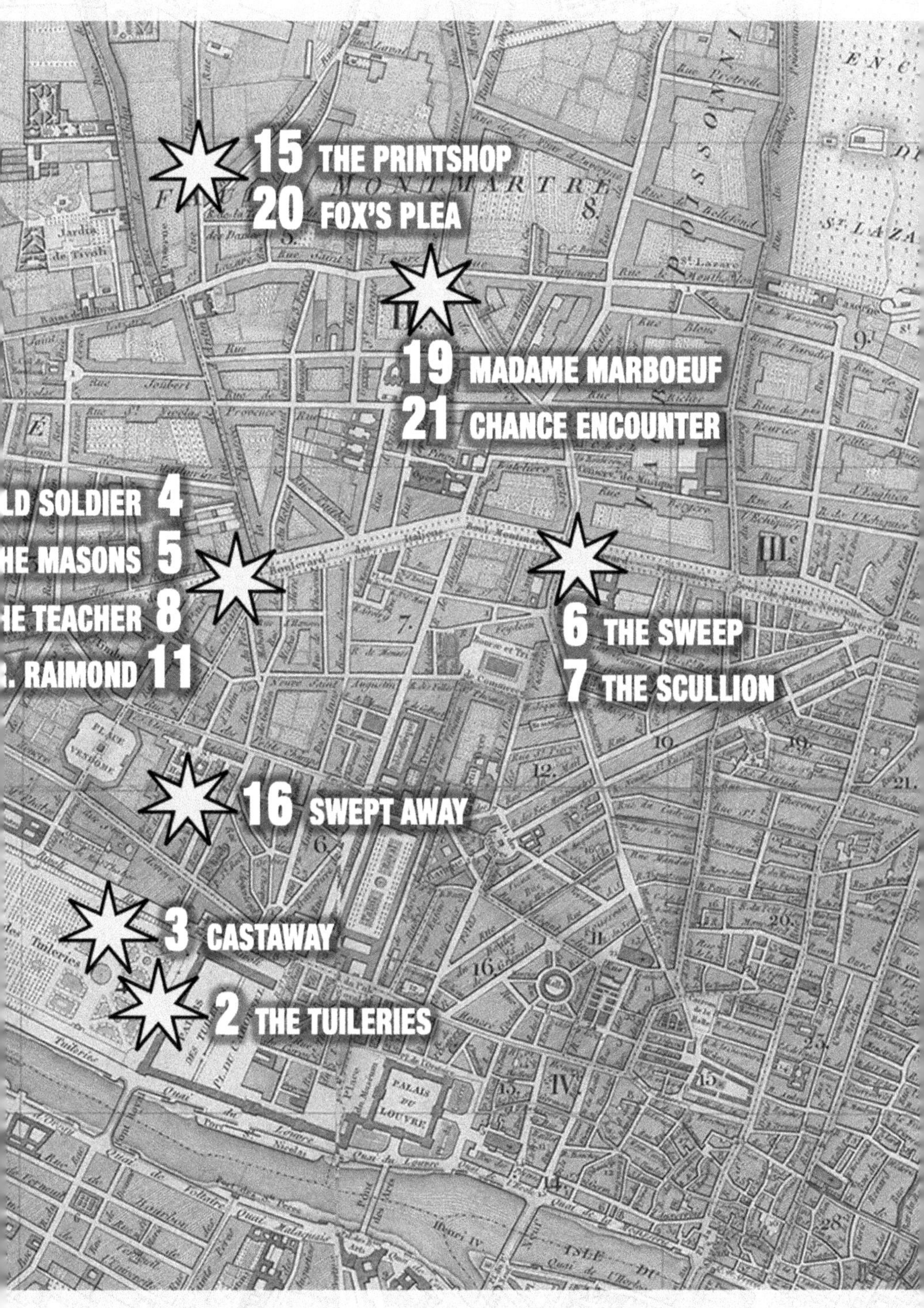

CLICK HERE to see this map as it looks today.
Explore every Chapter at the Street Level in 3D.

CPSIA information can be obtained
at www.ICGtesting.com
Printed in the USA
LVHW080008270522
719896LV00013B/544